BUSTER
UNDERCOVER

BUSTER
UNDERCOVER

Caleb Zane Huett

Scholastic Press / New York

Library of Congress Cataloging-in-Publication Data available

ISBN 978-1-338-54190-8

1 2021

Printed in the U.S.A.   23
First edition, March 2022

Book design by Maeve Norton

For Daz, Herman, Kother, Tabitha, and Ez

⊷ Prololgue ⊷

Tonio had never been in a dog crate before, and if he was being perfectly honest with himself, he didn't love it. Out of habit, he checked to see if his bad feelings were because of anxiety or reality: *I feel trapped.* Well, he was locked in a dog crate, which was really just a nice way to say *cage.* It was a cage designed for a Great Dane, big enough for him to sit down and stretch out. But it was still a cage, so it definitely made sense to feel trapped.

I feel like something bad is going to happen. There was a lot of evidence for that, too. The man who'd just thrown him in this cage certainly hadn't seemed to have Tonio's best interests in mind.

I wish Buster were here. Tonio and his dog, Buster, hadn't been apart this long since they'd met. Missing him made the most sense of all.

"Very cool," Tonio mumbled miserably. "Everything *really is* terrible."

A little whine and the jingle of a collar caught Tonio's attention, and he noticed for the first time he wasn't alone. The room was filled with more than a dozen empty dog crates, but one other was occupied. A few feet from him, a Shiba Inu smirked from behind several

1

layers of metal bars. Tonio jumped in relief and banged his head on the roof of the cage with a clang. He'd been hoping to find her here.

"Jpeg!" he cried, rubbing his head to check for any new bumps.

you think you've had it bad? try going weeks without any internet. The dog bobbed her head and wagged her paws in Underspeak, the physical language of dogs, ending with a gesture Tonio didn't know. Tonio's Underspeak vocabulary had grown a lot in the time since Buster had started teaching him, but every dog's Underspeak was a little bit different. It always took some getting used to. Jpeg did each pose with less enthusiasm than most dogs, giving it a very casual, lowercase vibe.

"I don't know what that word was at the end."

it means lol. i'm spelling it out, see? She repeated the twist of her tail and tap of her paws.

"That's a lot of work to say 'lol.'"

is this what's important right now lol? She huffed air out of her nose. *w/e dude.*

Tonio pressed his forehead against the bars. "I'm sorry. We tried to find you, but instead I got caught, too."

not that I'm keeping score, but that puts you like 0–2 on rescue attempts, my good human.

"Yeah, I know. I'm not cut out for this." Tonio picked at his fingernails. "I never should have talked to him. I knew this would happen. And—" A rhythmic thudding

2

upstairs silenced him. Footsteps. He realized there were no windows here—just cold blue-gray walls and a door without a handle.

you knew you'd be locked up in a dog crate in a basement somewhere, awaiting a shady government organization to finally get serious about interrogating you, lol?

"Nothing about that feels very 'lol' to me, Jpeg."

agree to disagree. Tonio looked around for anything else that might help. He tugged on his crate's padlock, but unfortunately it was doing its job. His backpack was thrown a few feet away, out of reach. He didn't have anything in there that could help him anyway, unless there was a way to pick a lock with fancy markers.

This is why my parents should let me have a phone, he thought. *For when I need a ride home from my job as a secret agent for dogs.* He laughed out loud just a little—Jpeg was pleased—but the joke also made the reality of his situation sink in. He had to squeeze his eyes closed and settle on the rubber floor of the crate when his heart rate spiked.

Now is not a good time for this, some part of him thought, while the rest of him started to feel suffocated. The bars were too close, his clothes were too damp— why was he sweating so much? Why was it so muggy in this room? He didn't know where he was, what he was doing, or what was going to happen to him. He grabbed a bar on either side and pushed out with all his strength but only grew more frustrated and scared when nothing moved. He started to feel dizzy—was he breathing? When was the last time he'd taken a breath?

"ARF!" Jpeg barked. Tonio cracked his eyes open to look at her—her smirk was gone, and she was standing up. *SHUT UP,* she underspoke.

"I didn't—"

SHUT UP. WE'RE GOING TO BE FINE. LOL.

"Nothing—nothing is—what are you *saying*? Everyone thinks I'm at a sleepover. Nobody is coming for us. There's going to—"

LITERALLY WHO CARES. Jpeg's big, exaggerated Underspeak and flippant attitude were surprising enough that Tonio was calming down despite himself.

"How can you say that? How do you know we're—"

EASY. Her right hind leg lifted to scratch around her collar a half dozen loud, jingly times. *i'm gonna break us out of here, lol.*

Buster's Report

— 1 —

On my lawyer's request (hi, Lasagna), I've decided to use my extra time (and nervous energy, since Tonio isn't here) to type up everything that's happened since my Dog Court case over the summer. I'm not *technically* on pawrole, but he thinks having more evidence of our "success" as a human-dog duo will be helpful going forward.

I'm not sure this will be so cut-and-dried, though. Our semester has been complicated, and Tonio and I aren't exactly on great terms right now. So I'm going to be totally honest and let you edit it however you want, Lasagna. Maybe you'll find something useful in here. It'll at least help me gather my thoughts.

My name is Buster Pulaski (formerly Buster Vale, né Buster Stray), and I'm currently licensed as a psychiatric service dog specializing in anxiety and panic disorders. My human is Antonio Pulaski, and he's currently licensed as a sixth grader at Bellville Middle School. Both of us were recently made agents of The Farm, a secret branch of Dog Court operating outside of Dog Law in order to ensure the safety and protection of dogs in a world where humans don't know that we're . . . well, people. (Am I allowed to say that in this report, Lasagna? I hope so. Again, delete whatever you want.) It feels like every dog on earth seems to know about what happened last summer, when Tonio found out the truth about me and, through me, *all* dogs, but the official story is that we're being closely monitored by Dog Court, and no one else is supposed to know about The Farm.

If you saw the court case, you know there was one teeny-tiny (okay, maybe kinda big) thing that I did in front of humans that got me arrested: I played Beamblade, the popular science fantasy trading card game for people of all ages, at a public tournament in front of a couple dozen humans. Whoops!

The rest of our summer was spent covering for that moment. I recruited a bunch of dogs at the shelter in town to pretend that Tonio could train them to play a card game designed for humans, planning to just show it off once or twice and let it fade away, but Mia Lin (the daughter of the shelter's owners and Tonio's best friend) saw potential for a scheme.

That's where this story really needs to start: At the Lin Family Dog Shelter's First Annual Official Beamblade Dog League Tournament and Adoption Day, featuring "genius dog whisperer" Tonio Pulaski.

The shelter was built into what was left of an old farm, from back when this part of town was all farmland. Mia's dad Jeff inherited it from his grandparents, and her other dad Danny is a huge dog lover. When they realized the nearest dog shelter was over an hour away, they repurposed the land, got all the permits and permissions they needed, and started collecting strays around Bellville. Of course, with just the three of them, they realized keeping all those dogs entertained was difficult—so instead of leaving dogs in cages all day, they opened the space as a dog park for everyone in town.

As I'm sure you know, Bellville changed overnight from a nowhere town to a *huge* hub of dog social life. Suddenly, it was easy for strays, pets, and service dogs to connect without being suspicious. The shelter was always packed with hungry dogs, and—for reasons I'm still not clear on—food costs money. The Lins' budget is always tight. Which brings me back to the tournament.

"Ref! We need a ref over here!" a man yelled across the dirt field. He stood up and waved in our direction. I was lying, belly in the sun, beside the kids working the event—Tonio, Mia (who I've mentioned), and Devon, the newest kid to join their grade and Tonio's other best friend. They wore matching sunflower-yellow shirts with the shelter logo, and Tonio had even cut one to wrap around my harness so I matched.

Tonio squinted in the sun and brought a hand up to

7

his forehead to shade his eyes as he looked for Skyler, the older teen who had a Beamblade judge's badge.

Devon nudged Tonio and said, "You should go-nio. You're the expert, and Mia's busy." He grinned before Tonio could raise an argument, red-blue-and-black braces (Spider-Man colors) proudly displayed. "Hurry!" he insisted. Tonio stumbled forward, curls flopping on the side of his head that wasn't shaved down. I rolled over and trotted along behind him.

Cardboard Beamblade battlefields were set up in rows down the field, and dogs were dueling against each other while humans monitored their progress and helped with the parts that required opposable thumbs, like shuffling. The battlefields were a perfected version of what Tonio and I had used for our first game together: low shields on either side so dogs could set down their "hands" without their opponent seeing, and a place in the middle for clashing heroes and fragile Spirit Batteries.

The haircut suits you, I underspoke as we walked toward the waving man. Tonio shrugged, but I could tell he was pleased to hear it. He'd drawn up the style himself and handed it to the hairdresser the day before; it was the first time I'd ever seen him show an interest in his "look," and I suspected it was because Devon was always talking about what he would do if he had Tonio's big curls.

"What's the problem, sir?" Tonio asked the man while I underspoke *What's up?* to the dogs. A small-for-her-age German shepherd named Bella was playing opposite a large-for-his-age tricolor collie named Mozart, who'd had a growth spurt over the last couple months. His face stretched out long to emphasize his permanently cocky expression, and the rest of him grew multiple feet longer. It's always disconcerting when you stop watching a puppy for *one second* and suddenly they're bigger than you! He was just as fluffy, though, and maybe even more irritating.

Don't worry about it, old man, Mozart underspoke. I gave a dismissive tail wag at his answer and looked at Bella.

He's cheating! The shepherd posed emphatically. *And he thinks he can get away with it because humans are watching.*

"They started growling at each other all of a sudden," the man explained to Tonio. He looked nervous behind his reflective sunglasses, and his fingers fidgeted with the camera around his neck. "I don't know if it's because of the game or what, but I thought I should get someone."

Tonio nodded. "I'm sorry if they scared you. Let me, uh, see what I can do." He crouched down lower to the ground and looked at me.

She says Mozart's cheating, I explained.

His hands came together in front of him and did a few quick movements in a way we'd practiced—his hands were ears, front paws, back paws, and tail in that order. It was slower than real Underspeak, but less obvious than imitating a dog in front of everybody.

Mozart, are you cheating? I translated for him.

No, Mozart huffed.

Yes, he is!! Bella gave a little bark of affirmation.

You're not? Tonio smiled. *Then what's the problem?*

The collie shrugged. *She's just mad that she's losing.*

I'm not even losing! With a smooth movement, Tonio held up a card and gave a treat to Bella, to fake like he was doing a training trick. He turned the card and showed it to Mozart.

The Phishing Rod needs energy from four Manabytes, though, and you've still only got three. So how'd this get on the field?

A flash interrupted us, and all four of our heads jerked up to see the man in sunglasses snapping a picture of us talking.

"Sorry!" He dropped the camera back down to his chest and held his hands up when he saw the expression on Tonio's face. "Seeing you training them is just so fascinating—I thought my daughter might want to see! But I can delete it."

Tonio's heart was beating fast, and I could see him thinking through it—what had he been doing? What would his hands look like in the picture? Could we all be in trouble because of this random man? I placed a paw on his foot, and Tonio rested a hand on my head, nodding. "No, it's fine. I was just . . . surprised. Thank you." The man apologized again, and Tonio looked back to the dogs.

Mozart clamped his teeth down around the Phishing Rod card and pulled it away from Tonio, dropping it haphazardly back with the other cards in his hand. *I must have made a mistake.*

Uh-huh, I added. Mozart glared at me, and Bella wagged her tail triumphantly. Tonio scratched Mozart behind the ears and gave him a treat, too.

"It should be fine now." Tonio gave one short nod to the man with the camera and started walking back to the other kids, but he'd barely turned around before the man was in front of him again.

"Actually, I have a question. What's the process if I'd like to adopt one of these dogs?"

Tonio was still avoiding eye contact—he was a lot more comfortable talking to dogs than adults. "You can talk to one of the Lins. But just so you know, Mozart isn't for adoption. He's—"

"Oh, no, I saw on his tag. I'm interested in that dog over there." Tonio followed the man's pointed finger to a Shiba Inu who looked like she was furiously digging a hole at the edge of the field.

"Jpeg?" Tonio blinked, surprised. "Oh no. You don't want Jpeg."

The man was taken aback. "Why not?"

"She's . . ." He looked down at me, and I gave him a sympathetic but unhelpful look in return. There was no way they'd let this guy take Jpeg. "High-energy? And she can't be separated from Leila." Tonio held his hand out to gesture toward the muddy part of the field, where the biggest dog in the whole park was wrestling loudly with a whole group of other dogs and winning.

"Oh, okay." The man looked disappointed but stopped following Tonio and held his hand up in a good-natured wave. "Thank you!"

Tonio dipped his head goodbye again and made a few subtle gestures toward me. *There's something weird about that guy.*

Really? I glanced back at the man, who was snapping a picture of another one of the Beamblade games—which tons of people were doing, including taking videos with their phones. *He seems normal to me.* I figured it was just Tonio's anxiety talking.

After a moment, he shrugged. *Just a feeling*, he told me. I let it drop—probably anxiety, right?

I should have trusted that feeling.

—2—

"SURPRISE!" Devon and Mia had cleared the judge's table of adoption papers and Beamblade cards while Tonio was gone and replaced them with a tray of cupcakes. Tonio froze and looked between their smiling faces like a rabbit watching wolves.

"Is it somebody's birthday?" he asked. "Did I forget to bring a present? I didn't—I'm sorry, I must have—"

Mia shoved a cupcake into his hands, chocolate with vanilla frosting. She'd cut her T-shirt into a loose crop and placed it on top of a tank top for a layered effect—Mia was always like that. Nothing was quite good enough unless she'd had a chance to put her own stamp on it. "They're for you. Devon made them."

"I made the card, too." Devon held out an envelope marked *TO: Tonio Pulaski FROM: Your Best Friends.*

"Yeah," Mia admitted, "but it was my idea."

"My birthday's in February!" Tonio protested, carefully holding both like trophies he hadn't earned.

But Devon shook his head and said, "Read it!"

Tonio had to set the cupcake back down to open the envelope. Mia pulled a big bone off the table—one of

13

those fancy real ones, not the fake chewy kind—with a bow around it and threw it down to me. I snatched it out of the air and chewed gratefully around the wrapping.

Saying he "made it" was generous—Devon had clearly bought a card and scribbled over it. *Originally* the card said *Happy One Year Anniversary,* but thick permanent marker edited it to say *Happy ~~One Year~~ Two Month Anniversary (Of Going To School).* After reading it, Tonio dropped his arm down casually so I could look inside—neither Mia nor Devon knew the truth about dogs, so we had to be careful. Taped to the card was a terribly drawn, fake Beamblade card of Malbrain and Combuster, the Blademaster names for Tonio and me. *Power: 999999; Health: 999999; Special Abilities: Being a Great Friend, Making Things Come to Life by Drawing Them, Eyebrow Expressions, Dog Whispering.*

"We know you almost didn't come back—" Devon started.

"And it's extra hard for you to stay, on account of your brain problems—" Mia continued.

"So it's worth celebrating!" Devon held up a cupcake to make a toast. "Two months!"

"Two months!" Mia cheered, raising her own cupcake to his. I threw in a short bark for good measure. Tonio's whole face and neck had blushed red, and I could tell his eyes were welling up with tears—but he blinked them away and smiled.

"Thanks, y'all." He sniffed. "It hasn't really been *that* hard."

Cupcake crumbles blew in the wind as Mia shook her head. "Maybe *I* should get a card, then, because I wish it was summer already."

"Tonio's right!" Devon argued, mouth full. "It hasn't been bad at all!"

"Oh, really?" Mia wagged a frosting-covered finger in Devon's face. "Is that how your locker feels, too?"

Both Tonio and I tilted our heads at the same time. "Your locker?" Tonio asked.

Devon waved his hand dismissively and grinned. "It's nothing. Don't worry about it." I saw Tonio's jaw set in a way that made it very clear he *would* worry about it, but there wasn't any time to argue—Jeff, Mia's shorter dad, jogged up to interrupt.

"Mia, could you and your friends get another adoption package together? We've got another one. Our tenth adoption today!"

"YES!" Mia cheered, and she high-fived her dad. "Who's getting adopted?"

"Jpeg! She's going home with a nice man visiting all the way from Myrtle Beach."

"YES!" Devon cheered, and raised his hand for a high five. No one gave him one. The rest of us were thinking the same thing: They couldn't take *Jpeg*. I thought of a hundred arguments, and Mia, thankfully, started voicing them.

"Myrtle Beach?" she said. "That's like three hours away!"

"Not even."

"It's practically Colorado," she mumbled. I nudged against her hand to show support. Her best friend, Sloan, had moved to Colorado the year before. Mia still missed her.

Jeff gave her a sympathetic look. "Not nearly as far. And he's really excited—apparently his daughter grew up with a Shiba who died last year. She'll do more good there than here."

Mia's heels dug into the dirt. "We can't just give Jpeg to some random guy who showed up today out of nowhere!"

Jeff lifted his hat to run a hand through his hair. "He didn't just show up today, Mia. He emailed us a few weeks ago, and we've done a video tour of his house. We even talked to his daughter—who I think you'd like. She was a lot like Sloan!" I felt my heart sinking down into my belly. Before I'd met Tonio, Jpeg was one of the only dogs who was willing to be my friend, when everyone else was spitting "Miracle Dog" and accusing me of breaking Dog Law. She was still my best friend, maybe, other than Tonio. And all it took was one video call for the humans to send her away!

I hate being a dog sometimes.

"Jpeg is *ours*. She's been here forever. Why would you—"

Jeff crossed his arms in a parent kind of way, the kind that means you're dangerously close to hearing someone say *And that's final.* "I know. I even asked for a much higher adoption fee, because he was so specific about needing Jpeg, but he didn't bat an eye. There will be more dogs, Mia. This whole event was your idea, and it's *working.* This is good news. Don't let it ruin your day." It had ruined *my* day. Jeff thought better of his crossed arms and opened them, pulling her in for a hug.

Mia glared off to the side and didn't return it. "What color collar?" she mumbled. "For the package."

"Green." Jeff kissed her on the top of her head. "Thank you." Devon caught on to the mood and didn't try to talk over Mia's sour expression. Tonio looked down to me, concerned, because I wasn't following behind.

You can go talk to Jpeg, he underspoke with his hands. *It's okay.*

Thank you, I answered, and left to say goodbye to my friend.

Jpeg mastered the art of secret typing a long time ago. From afar, she looked like a perfectly normal dog digging a hole, but up close she was typing on a tablet buried a few inches under the surface. (It never mattered that she was always digging the same hole, or that she never moved any deeper, because humans' assumptions do a lot of the work for us.) The soft clicking of her nails on the screen was disguised by the noise of the tournament, which was loud enough that she'd foregone Underspeak in favor of actual barking.

"Don't worry about breaking anything—the program's mine and it sets the odds automatically, so they're perfect." She tapped a few more times and gestured for Leila to look over her shoulder. Leila was somewhere between a mastiff, a Saint Bernard, and a bale of hay—and the undisputed wrestling champion of South Carolina. She loved Jpeg more than anything, and Jpeg loved her, too—though she wasn't quite as good at showing it.

"I'm not worried about the program, Jpeg." Leila nudged the Shiba with her nose. "I'm worried about you!"

"Worried about me?" She didn't look up from her tablet. *Click click click click click.* "Why?"

I stepped up closer to get their attention. "Because you're leaving, right?" Leila posed a hello to me, and I posed back. "Today."

"Ugh." Jpeg tilted her head and narrowed her eyes in frustration. "Not you, too. *This isn't a big deal.*"

Leila whined and turned to me. "She knew about this. She saw the video days ago and didn't think to warn me about it. This man lives *hours* away! I just found out she's leaving—basically immediately—and somehow that's 'not a big deal'?"

I felt a prickly, embarrassed feeling in my neck, and that sinking feeling in my stomach got worse. "Why didn't you tell us?" I asked Jpeg.

"Because, like I keep trying to say, it's not a problem. I have a plan!"

That didn't make me feel any better. "What is it?"

"I'm a terrible pet, and if he even has a *flip phone*, dog forbid, or *something* that can connect to the internet, I can ruin his life bad enough he'll be sure I'm cursed in less than a month."

"That's not much of a plan," I argued.

"It doesn't need to be! I'm a genius! I'll turn his smart fridge into a karaoke machine or whatever—I just have to see what the setup is like."

"But what if you like them?" Leila asked, a sad look in her eyes. "What if you meet his family, and you see the beach, and you see how easy it is to play pranks on tourists, and you love all of it?" Her voice dropped low, almost too quiet to hear. "What if you don't come back?"

Jpeg stepped back from the tablet and pushed her face to Leila's, forehead-to-forehead and nose-to-nose. "I wouldn't leave you. Trust me. You'll see me again in no time, you big jock."

I made Jpeg promise to message me on Doghouse chat as soon as she could, then left them alone. I felt

19

helpless in a way that's hard to avoid sometimes when you're a dog. But what could I do? I didn't think Jpeg should have to go anywhere she didn't want to, but it felt like the whole world disagreed with me.

Not the *whole* world, I reminded myself as I walked back through the Beamblade tournament. Lots of dogs agreed with me. Judge Sweetie agreed with me—at least enough to take a chance on me and Tonio. Dog Court might not be ready to tell all humans the truth yet, but we were fighting a future where they would be. I decided right then: I would do anything The Farm asked us to do. My human and I would be the best team we could be, and we'd pave the way for a future where dogs could live however they wanted.

All we needed was a mission.

Monday morning, Devon's parents dropped him off at Bellville Square so he could walk the rest of the way to school with us. Tonio was always up and ready extra early these days to make sure his friend didn't have to wait. But Spencer Pulaski—Tonio's dad and eternal chatterbox—was not quite as concerned with other people's time.

"This place online makes perfect imitations of *Sun Squadron* badges—so I hooked them up with the new lights. Check this out." Mr. Pulaski pressed a button on the badge pinned to his chest and practically yelled, *"Computer: Set lights to 'movie night'!"* Tonio winced, but Devon laughed and clapped as the lamp in the living room switched from yellow light to *slightly dimmer* yellow light.

"Nice, Mr. Pulaski! You sound just like Commander Leftwise." Devon found the matching badge on Tonio's backpack and pushed the button. "Computer: Activate Holochamber!"

"I'm sorry, could you repeat that?"

Mr. Pulaski smacked his forehead in a show of fake

embarrassment. "I knew I was forgetting something! I'll order the Holochamber tonight."

Tonio pushed Devon out the door before a longer conversation about *Sun Squadron* could start. Devon looked a little disappointed. "Your dad's cool."

"I know," Tonio grumbled, "but we're gonna be late."

Devon sang a tune that came—I suspected—from the *Sun Squadron* show. All "bum BUM badadada" and "oo-weeeeee-oooo." Tonio decided to say something that he'd clearly been thinking about all weekend.

"Is your locker okay?" The orange hand turned to walking human, and they crossed the street to the little park at the center of Bellville Square. Tonio turned to follow the paved path, but Devon committed to traveling in a directly straight line across the park.

"Huh?" Devon asked while climbing over the back of a bench.

"Mia said something about your locker. At the dog tournament."

"Oh!" Devon's backpack caught on the bench. Tonio waited for him to unhook and keep walking. "Yeah, my locker's fine."

"Are you?"

"Am I what?"

"Okay?"

"Yeah, I'm good." Devon walked over the low *No Walking on Grass* sign into the grass. "What did you make for Ms. McCauley's homework? I just drew a cool sword."

"A manticore."

"Whoa."

Tonio had to walk double time along the path to catch up with Devon's straight line. "I feel like you're hiding something. But you can tell me if I'm imagining it."

Devon shrugged. "You're not imagining it. But it doesn't matter." He stepped back onto the path and pushed the badge on Tonio's backpack.

"It mattered enough to tell Mia."

"I can't seem to find a setting for 'elephant me up.' Would you like me to search the internet?"

Devon grinned. "Yes." Tonio looked pained.

"Hm. No connection found. Should I try again?"

"That's okay. Thank you. I wonder how long the batteries last on this!"

They crossed the street again and squeezed through the alley past Karaoke Lanes. Bellville Middle School was already visible down the road—a wide single-story building at the bottom of the hill. I watched Tonio try to let the conversation go, but he didn't look like he could think about anything else. He furrowed his brow at the ground silently while they walked.

He's asking you to trust him, I underspoke. I was dying

of curiosity, too, but it was a good chance for Tonio to fight back against the way his anxiety made him obsess over things. *Friends have to do that sometimes.* Like me with Jpeg.

Cars lined the half-loop driveway in front of the school, dropping kids off one or two at a time. The big yellow buses were taking up their own half-circle road—Mia would be on bus 305, so they headed over to meet her. They had to jam all the time together they could before school started, because the only class they all shared was art, after lunch.

Once they found Mia, she said, "I forgot to make anything for Ms. McCauley, so I had to do something on the bus." She held up a colored pencil drawing that had clearly gone through a few potholes on the way here. "What do you think? Not you, Tonio."

Devon grinned. "It looks great!"

Tonio frowned. "Why not me?"

"*You* wouldn't lie to me." She shoved it back into her sequined backpack. "And now I'm satisfied. Let's go!" As she pulled the strap back onto her shoulder, I noticed something weird—a letter, stuck to the bottom of her bag, with an old-fashioned wax seal holding it closed.

I slowed down to stay behind them and inspect it closer. The seal was imprinted with the image of a barn—*The Farm!* I thought. *They must finally have a mission for us.* Careful not to move the backpack too much, I grabbed the edge of the letter in my teeth and pulled. A sticky string of gum stretched as I moved back—Crunchquish™ gum, by the smell of it—and when I yanked hard to break the letter away, the string flopped up and hit me in the eye. *Gross.*

I tugged on my leash gently as the kids walked through the front doors, and Tonio turned to look. His head tilted, and he delicately pulled the gum off my face with the tips of his fingers and took the letter from my jaws. When he saw the seal, he looked back at me with his eyes widened. I posed, *Yeah!!!!* and he smiled. Once he'd tossed the extra gum into a trash can, the letter slipped into his pocket for a more private moment.

We'd both been waiting for a mission; Judge Sweetie wasn't very specific about what she might need us for, but there were so many possibilities! Maybe they wanted us to go undercover and change the formula at a dog food company making something gross. Maybe we were going to break into a secret lab and save dogs from a supervillain trying to get canine superpowers! Or maybe they wanted us to finally teach humans the joys of using the bathroom outside!!!! No matter what, we were going to be helping dogs and moving the world one step closer to dog-human harmony.

I couldn't wait to see what it said.

The school day always started with a short homeroom. Tonio had language arts and social studies with Mia and math with Devon, but neither of them were in the same PE or chorus class. These were already stressful classes for Tonio (who wasn't especially athletic or comfortable with making noise) but were pushed over into "nightmare" territory by Tonio's least favorite people in the school: Miles Roy and Parker Feldman.

I guess you could say those two are responsible for everything—my meeting Tonio, the Dog Court case, and all three kids becoming good friends—but not because of anything they did on purpose. When Devon moved to Bellville last year, those two teased and bullied him to make themselves look cool. Devon took everything in stride, but the new dynamic in the classroom stoked Tonio's anxiety. He didn't know how to stand up for Devon without making himself a target, and the guilt from staying quiet led to a particularly messy incident involving yearbooks and vomit.

Actually, that happened in the same gym they have PE in now. (The elementary and middle schools share a gym.) The floor was polished again to a shine, but it did make me wonder what else had been buffed out of the wood. Kids are gross. (And I didn't like the way the court felt on my paws, or all the loud sneaker squeaking. I don't know how Air Bud could stand it.)

That Monday was dodgeball day, and the class was divided into two teams. I sat in the bleachers while they played. Tonio and Miles were on one team with about a dozen other kids, and Parker was on the other. Immediately, the two bullies were the stars of the show.

"Paaaarkeeeeeeer . . ." Miles dribbled and made his voice sound like a horror movie villain's. *"I'm coming for you!"*

Parker twirled in a perfect spin out of the way. The ball flew past to hit a teammate behind him, knocking him out of the game. Parker immediately picked up the ball and launched it back. Even though he was looking at Miles, he threw his arms out in a different direction and hit a completely surprised Tonio in the face. Miles and Parker both laughed as Tonio rubbed his forehead and walked off the court.

We climbed to the back of the bleachers to open The Farm's letter in secret. Parker used one of his teammates as a human shield to deflect another of Miles's throws; then his jaw dropped open, and he pointed at another of the kids. "Jason! Pull your pants up, dude! That's disgusting!"

Jason's pants were firmly attached to his waist, but in his brief moment of panic and distraction, Parker's team hit him twice. A laugh rippled through both teams, and Jason dropped his ball on the ground, embarrassed.

Tonio had to rip the envelope to get to the letter inside, and when he unfolded it, he looked confused. "It's just smudges." He showed it to me, and I wagged my tail, excited. It was Pawprint—which no one really uses anymore, but I learned it like every other puppy. The "smudges" were carefully placed markings of paws and claws dipped in ink. It took me a second to remember what *left half paw turned ninety degrees and rightmost paw pad stamped three times* meant, but I translated the letter as fast as I could.

It's a meeting place and a time, I explained. *Tonight at the community theater.*

"Why didn't they just tell us in the letter?" Tonio whispered.

"Be advised," I translated, *"we have reason to believe another human in Bellville is actively working to hurt the dog community. Destroy this letter, and ensure you aren't followed." I guess that's why.*

"Sounds ominous." Sneakers squeaked across the gym— the game was down to just a few kids on either side.

Who could it be? I held the letter up in my jaws, and he grabbed the other side. We pulled it apart and ripped it in half; then Tonio ripped it into smaller pieces. He looked nervous, but my tail was wagging. *I bet it's that rude guy who's always at Nice Slice Pizza.*

Tonio shook his head and squished the paper scraps into a ball in his pocket. "I really hope it's nobody we know."

But we know everybody.

"That's what I'm worried about! I don't want to be friends with a bad guy." The other kids in the bleachers gasped as Parker bent backward, limbo-ing under a dodgeball Miles had thrown. Tonio scowled and started petting me—I could feel his heart rate speeding up with worry and frustration. "I hate when they do this."

Do what?

"They're not really playing. Look." Miles tapped one of his teammates on the shoulder to ask her a question, and the second she turned her head, Parker launched a dodgeball at her shoulder, knocking her out. "They're just getting everybody else out."

Both teams were down to just two players each. Miles and Parker kept dodging and ducking until the two teammates were out, then approached each other at the dividing line in the center of the court. Each of them threw a ball high up in the air, then moved to catch each other's throws at the same time.

"A draw!" Miles announced.

Parker shook his head in mock disappointment. "Looks like nobody wins."

"Except them," Tonio grumbled. But a bunch of kids applauded and both boys bowed dramatically. I thought it was kind of funny, but Tonio just looked frustrated. I nudged him and wagged my tail.

Who cares about them? We've got more important things going on.

He nodded. "You're right. Whatever. At least they're leaving Devon alone." Coach Dalton had fallen completely asleep in his chair, and his snores were cutting through the gym and making kids giggle.

Do you think Coach Dalton is the secret bad guy?

Parker threw a dodgeball at the coach's head. It bounced off with a *SPROING*, and the teacher leaped out of his chair, confused, while Miles and Parker engaged in a *very serious* pretend conversation where neither happened to be looking his way. Even Tonio snorted a little bit.

"No, I don't think it's the coach."

4

The manticore was a fearsome beast: Its mane bristled in sharp barbs around its face, vaguely human but with multiple rows of knifelike teeth. Dragon wings unfolded from its back, the ends cut jagged, rough, and smoky, as if singed by flame. The claws on each of its paws were dipped in the red blood of a recent kill, and the tail twisted up and curled over its body, presenting its deadly stinger as the last line of defense for this already-powerful creature. The poisonous tip had gotten a little bent in the box, though.

Ms. McCauley's classroom was colorful and bright—it even had a skylight, unlike the other rooms at BMS. Instead of desks, the room had a set of paint-splattered square tables—Tonio was always first to sit down and claim one for his friends. He smoothed out the wrinkles in the paper and popped open a marker with his mouth, adding red to a few of the claws he'd missed. The whole creature was made from paper he'd had lying around at home—some from his mom's printer, some construction paper, and some of the card stock he used to copy Beamblade cards. Any moment in the last two weeks he hadn't spent preparing for the Dog League had gone into this sculpture, and it showed—especially in comparison to Mia's bus doodle.

"I know I told you to stop holding back," she said as they waited for the bell to ring, "but you didn't have to show me up *this* hard." Her drawing—the assignment was to make something with a "fantasy" theme—was of a goldfish mermaid in a tiny aquarium. "At least Ms. McCauley always gives a good grade on everything."

Tonio nodded and said through the marker between his teeth, "That *is* good."

"Rude!"

He blushed immediately and closed the marker. "I just meant—you only worked on it this morning—"

"Because I was *busy*." Mia shook her head and clicked her teeth. "Mr. Superior over here doesn't have eight hundred thousand dogs to feed every morning . . ."

"I didn't mean—I'm sorry—"

"I'm just joking. I had time." She held out a pack of gum—Tonio turned it down, while Devon's hand reached over to grab one. "But I didn't feel like it!"

"Antonio Pulaski, you have *outdone yourself*!" Devon pulled out his phone and started snapping pictures of the manticore.

Tonio looked nervously around for the teacher, but she was nowhere to be seen yet.

"You're gonna get that taken up," he warned. "And

your gum." Mia blew a bubble. Devon was now filming a video, picking up the manticore by its tail and holding it in front of my face.

"Combuster versus the fearsome manticore! Who will win?!" Devon challenged. I gave a soft huff and crossed one paw over the other, but otherwise looked at him like a dog with a piece of paper being waved in their face. *Put it down*, I wanted to say. *It's delicate.* They didn't know how hard Tonio had worked on it— this was actually the third one, because the other two hadn't turned out the way he wanted. It was two weeks of trial and error, work and attention, to do something different than he'd done before. I was proud of him.

"Mine's a magical talking sword," Devon explained. He set Tonio's sculpture down—*phew*—and pulled out a drawing of a sword.

Mia raised an eyebrow. "That looks like a regular sword."

"There's a whole story that goes with it: The sword has the soul of a hero inside, and so it can talk, but it's wielded by another hero who was cursed to never talk, so the sword talks for him. And they're in love."

"What do they do?" Mia asked.

"Huh?"

"You said there's a whole story. Do they fight dragons or something?

Devon tilted his head. "Maybe I'm not explaining it well. They're in love?"

Sproing. Miles walked into the classroom, Parker close behind. They were bouncing a dodgeball back and forth and laughing at the noise.

"How do they still have that?" Tonio whispered. Mia rolled her eyes.

Sproing! Sproing! The dodgeball's sound was loud and obnoxious in the classroom, but kids were either ignoring Miles and Parker or laughing with them. Finally, Ms. McCauley walked in, all dressed up in a medieval-style tunic and pants, with a foam sword attached to her belt. "It's fantasy day!" she announced. "I can't wait to see what you've made. Miles, Parker, put that away."

"Oh yeah." Parker nodded. "Right away."

Miles smiled. "We were just borrowing it from Devon!" My ears swiveled up to attention, and Tonio looked up, confused. Devon's mouth came together in a thin line. "Catch, Dev!" He threw the ball before he finished speaking, surprising everyone. Without time to catch it, the ball bounced off Devon's head and skewed toward the table.

I sensed what was coming and leaped up from my position next to Tonio's chair. I put both hands on the table and tried to snap at the ball—but my jaws closed right behind it. I missed.

Crunch.

The ball bounced one more time before Mia caught

it. The whole room was dead silent. Tonio's paper man- ticore was squished completely by the ball, careful folds and creases ruined by the addition of a few dozen new ones. Several glued-on details were scattered around the corpse of the creature or stuck to the rub- ber. The magnificent, terrible beast had been bested by a dodgeball.

Some kids in Bellville's sixth-grade class still liked to talk about Tonio's yearbook incident in hushed whis- pers, especially now that he'd shown back up at school with a service dog by his side. Mostly he tried to pretend like nothing was different, but it was undeniable some of the other kids treated him like something delicate. As I nudged into his leg to try and make sure he was okay, I could see them giving each other looks. *Is he going to freak out? Is he going to throw up again?*

I couldn't help shooting a glare at the two bullies— Parker looked nervous, but Miles's eyebrows were up and he was smirking a little.

"What's your problem?" Mia yelled. They didn't answer.

"Oh, Tonio." Ms. McCauley knelt beside the table to inspect the wreckage. "Your poor little monster!"

"It's okay," he mumbled breathlessly, overwhelmed by all the sudden attention. "It's fine."

Devon put on a big smile. "I have pictures on my

phone, Ms. McCauley! For Tonio's presentation."

"That's great, Devon. Thank you." Ms. McCauley stood and adjusted her foam sword. "Class, think about your presentations and talk amongst yourselves. Miles, Parker—let's meet out in the hallway."

Parker sighed. "She's going to stab us." The class tried to hide their giggle.

"Aw, c'mon!" Miles protested. "It was an accident!"

Now." She held the door open for them. I listened for Tonio's heartbeat and watched his breathing—both were more intense than normal, but he didn't seem like he was having a panic attack. He tugged at the body of the manticore, trying to fluff it back out and set it back on its feet, but when he let go, it crumpled again immediately.

"Are you okay?" he asked Devon, who nodded.

"Of course! They were just messing around. Lucky the ball didn't pop on my braces!" He laughed at his own joke, then patted Tonio on the shoulder. "I'm sorry about your manticore."

"It's okay."

"It's *not* okay!" Mia brought her fist down on the table with a *bang*. "I hate those guys. I wish your manticore could eat them . . . But at least with yours gone, I have the best project in the class."

Tonio laughed and nodded, pushing away the

frustration in his face. "I dunno, Lovesword might be the winner."

"LOVESWORD?!" Devon gasped. "That's the *perfect name.*"

Now all three of them were smiling. I hoped the other kids were seeing that, too.

"Is it boring for you, at school?" Tonio asked me, sweeping some leftover scraps of paper into the trash can next to the desk in his bedroom. He'd stayed up late finishing the manticore last night, so there was a mess to clean when we got home. I yawned from my spot on his bed and thumped my tail against the blanket.

Nope, I typed onto my laptop—Jpeg had given me one she'd designed herself; one of her specialties is accessible tech for dogs. This one has four big buttons and a trackball in the middle—typing is like translating through one of those old Simon Says toys, but it's faster with my paws than fighting with a tablet keyboard. I'm typing on it now! *You ask me that all the time!*

"I know. You just seem really excited about the mission from Dog Court, is all."

Aren't you *excited?*

"Not really. I thought the goal was for them to let us live our lives like normal. I didn't realize you *wanted* to be a Farm agent. They didn't really give us a choice."

I paused to think about this. I hadn't really considered it that way, either. But with Tonio's friends looking out for him, and his anxiety calming down, it did mean I had less to do than before. A lot of my days were just following Tonio around until we went to the park, when I could talk to other dogs. But then I thought about who made the keyboard I was typing on.

If we show them we're a good team, Dog Court might take a chance on more humans. This mission could be our way to change the world!

"Yeah, I dunno. That's a lot of pressure." He held up a black T-shirt and shorts. "Should I change into something more . . . sneaky?"

Not sure it matters. What do you mean, pressure?

He changed anyway. "The court is using me as a test case for all humans, right? So if I'm not perfect, if I mess up at all, that means I messed up for *everyone on earth*." He paused with one arm in a sleeve and stared off into the distance. "You've helped me a lot, but it's not just about me. So many dogs want to talk to humans, right? I have to do whatever the Court asks me to do today, or I'm letting all of them down."

He finished pulling on his shirt. I jumped off the bed so he could click on my blue harness and attach the leash. *That's one way to look at it*, I admitted. *But you don't have to be perfect—you just have to be you.*

Tonio pushed the door to his bedroom open and peeked into the hallway. "*I wouldn't be a secret agent*," he whispered as we snuck down the stairs. It was dark out, but his dad was still at the store and music was blasting from his mom's office—so she was going to be working late. They never seemed particularly worried about what he was doing, anyway; a lifetime of never, ever getting in trouble had given him the benefit of the doubt. "So that's already not true."

Judge Sweetie likes us, I underspoke. Bellville Square was covered in streetlights, so it was easy to see my movements. *Whatever they want us to do, we can handle.* After Tonio locked the front door, we headed down the second flight of stairs and turned toward the community theater.

"I guess you're right. Thanks." He smiled a little more confidently. "We're a good team." The theater wasn't far—it was directly across from Bellville's game store Roll the Ice (its neon sign greeted us with *h I*) so we only had to cross one corner to reach that side of the square. No cars were around, but Tonio waited for the glowing walking human anyway.

"And it would be kind of cool to be a hero," he admitted. "Like Voidmask or Sharktective."

Maybe our mission is in space! I agreed.

"Can dogs go to space?" He looked apologetic. "I mean, other than—"

It's okay. We have sent our own crew, more recently than Laika. I raised my snout in the traditional salute to her. *May she watch over us always. But just normal space stuff. No Beamblades.*

"I don't think I would like space very much, anyways." He pushed on the door—it was unlocked, just like the note said it would be. "I'm ready. Are you?"

I nodded. We walked inside.

The theater building wasn't very fancy, but neither was Bellville. The entrance we used was connected to the square, but the building was huge—and the front hallway continued down the street, with an outside wall made entirely of glass. Tonio kept shooting nervous glances at the windows, but I knew Dog Court wouldn't have asked us to come here without a good reason—and a plan. The theater had to be empty tonight.

"Where do we go?" Tonio whispered. I dipped my head, unsure. We were in front of the main entrance to the theater, in a wide lobby lit only with streetlights from outside. A metal cover was pulled down over the box office booth, so that left the main theater entrance and a hallway that led to some offices, I assumed.

I sniffed the air. My nose is pretty farsmelled—I'd be a terrible tracker—but I could make out traces of a few dogs who had been here recently. One familiar scent of wood and old lady—Judge Sweetie, who'd presided over my trial and who brought us into The Farm—and someone else I didn't know. Someone who smelled like . . . nothing. I don't mean they didn't have a smell; it was like smelling smoke without a fire, or a plant that had never been in dirt. This was a dog without anything on them that suggested they'd lived a life. Nothing identifiable.

My hackles rose. Who would smell like that? It was unnatural. Tonio noticed immediately, so I tried to explain.

"That *is* weird," Tonio said when I was done. "Can you tell where it's coming from?"

I lifted my nose and closed my eyes. I couldn't follow a trail or anything, but the highest concentration of old-lady smell was coming from the theater. That could have just been a community theater thing, but it was as good a reason as any to start there. I pointed my nose toward the doors, and Tonio tried them. "It's unlocked."

Lights were on in there—yellow glow aimed up along the walls. Rows of seats with those folding bottoms faced the stage, currently dressed up in a set for something with a lot of vines, fake trees, and . . . a tower? It wasn't finished yet and for now was only a ladder leading up to a cardboard window hanging from above.

"Hello?" Tonio whispered.

"We're here!" I barked. He shot me a look, and I flopped a paw dismissively. *No one's gonna hear me!*

"You won't have to explain why we *broke in* in the middle of the night!"

And then I saw her, standing in the middle of the stage. I hadn't seen her move, but I was certain she hadn't been there before—a greyhound with an all-black coat and eyes so narrow and dark they were invisible except for the reflection of the lights.

"We're here to see Judge Sweetie," I said, much more quietly. Tonio followed my eyes to the stage and yelped, startled by the greyhound's sudden appearance. She didn't respond but after a few seconds turned and walked off stage right.

Tonio and I exchanged a look—*You nervous? I'm nervous*—but decided to follow the dog. I leaped up onto the stage, and Tonio pulled himself up over the edge. He brushed a few paper vines out of the way as we walked between the curtains and passed a table covered in props. The greyhound was waiting for us in a doorway, standing perfectly still until I made eye contact. Once she was sure I saw her, she turned and walked away. Her footfalls were nearly silent—I could barely hear them even when I was focusing.

After a few turns like this, we were heading downstairs into a space below the stage itself—a room filled with big props and set pieces that didn't match the forest above. Storage, maybe?

Judge Sweetie was sitting on a large blue cushion with golden tassels at the corners, right paw stamping prints onto papers her left paw was shuffling around. "Ah!" She gasped when she noticed the greyhound standing less than a foot away from her. "Shadow, you really must warn me when you're approaching."

"My apologies, Judge." Her voice was raspy and quiet—like all the life had been pulled out of a bark and only its ghost was left behind.

"It's fine, it's fine. Are they—" She tilted her head around Shadow to look at us. "Wonderful. Let's get started."

Judge Sweetie is a black-and-white borzoi, which means her fur is long and swooshy. It was always perfectly groomed, so the gentle curls rolled off her ears and body like waves of cookies and cream. Her tail swept side to side as we approached.

How's his Underspeak? she asked me.

Tonio smiled. "A little worse with dogs who aren't Buster," he admitted, "but I can follow along now." Shadow's head tilted just slightly in surprise, which I'll admit was a relief; it was the greyhound's first show of personality.

Perfect, the judge underspoke. *This is Shadow, one of our most talented Farm operatives.* Shadow bowed her head but didn't take her eyes off Tonio. *She's been spying and gathering intelligence for us for years, and it's because of information she's uncovered that I've asked you here today.*

"It's nice to meet you, Shadow." Tonio also bowed his head politely and used his hand to do a tail greeting. The greyhound stepped backward and twisted her lip in disgust.

"It's worse than I thought," she said, speaking out loud to deliberately exclude Tonio. "You handed a human child the keys to all our secrets."

Sweetie sighed. "You'll have to forgive her. She has seen the worst side of humans and does not know the entire situation."

"I know enough to know it's a bad idea."

"And what do you suggest we do instead, hm?" Sweetie growled without growling, in the way dogs with power often can. "You came to me with a problem, and this boy is the solution. Unless you think you have a better one?"

Shadow fell silent and glared at Tonio, whose eyes flitted uncomfortably between the dogs he couldn't understand. He could read tone, though, and posture—I figured I'd better speak up before he got too distressed. *What's the problem?*

Have you heard of the Department of Nonhuman Intelligence? Sweetie asked.

I posed, *Of course,* and Tonio shook his head.

The judge went on. *I understand why you haven't,*

45

Tonio; the humans have treated it much in the same way they've treated Area 51. Sweetie nudged open a folder with her nose and pushed a paper toward us.

Tonio flipped it around and held it up. The page was a typed letter, with a seal on the top featuring a bald eagle with both eyes closed but a third eye open on its forehead. *Spooky.* The eagle was holding open manacles in its claws, and around the rim of the circle were the words *DEPARTMENT OF NONHUMAN INTELLIGENCE*.

The letter itself was labeled *classified*—it appeared to be a message from a central office to an agent named Oscar Sykes, confirming his placement in Bellville and asking for a report on his discoveries. Tonio read through it much faster than I did.

"You think they're studying dogs?" he asked.

Shadow interjected. *We* know *they're studying dogs. They've been trying to gather evidence on us for years. The DNI is part of why we are so serious about teaching puppies to stay quiet.* She shot me a look. *Of course, some listen more than others.*

"I've never heard of this person. Oscar Sykes," Tonio said.

He's new. Sweetie clarified: *Relatively new.*

Shadow bobbed her head in agreement. *I'm not sure how long he's been an operative for the Department, but he moved here a little over a year ago, after he got married.*

Judge Sweetie slipped the letter back into her folder. *We're not sure what Agent Sykes knows, and we're not* sure what he's looking for. *His placement in Bellville is most likely because of the Lin Shelter's popularity*—she stretched on her cushion—*but there could be more to it than that.*

"Is it because of me?" Tonio asked. "Could I have been too obvious?"

I winced—*don't put that idea in their heads*—but even Shadow signaled *no.*

If they knew you could speak our language, I doubt you would be standing here. Sweetie looked apologetic. *They're more of a "kidnap first, ask questions later" sort of organization.*

Tonio looked alarmed, but I couldn't help feeling excited. This was what I had been secretly hoping for, I realized: Something big. Something unusual and important. A real job to prove, once and for all, that humans and dogs could make a great team.

"Hm." Tonio crossed his arms and furrowed his brow. "But . . . you know we believe dogs should tell humans the truth."

Sweetie waved a paw in front of her snout. *The department isn't interested in building a nice community, Tonio. They're trying to assess threats to humans, which means they see us as an enemy first and foremost. We've lost friends— and other Farm agents—to their offices, never to be seen again. They are a danger to you, too, and are part of the reason I've asked you to remain a secret, for now.*

"Shadow already seems like a perfect spy," Tonio pointed out. "I'm just a kid." Shadow looked ready to agree, but the judge cut her off.

You're smart. And you pay close attention to others—that will help us here. Sweetie tilted her head toward Tonio. *Right now, we need a kid. Specifically, a kid at Bellville Middle School.*

That was *not* what I expected to hear.

Sweetie continued. *Oscar Sykes has a son. Stepson. I would like for you to befriend him—at least enough to get inside his house without suspicion. From there, I would like you to try to find Agent Sykes's plan: Why is he here? What is he looking for?* She watched Tonio carefully for his response. *Of course, if I could, I would let Shadow handle this. But Sykes has taken measures to dog-proof his house. Even from someone as experienced as she is.*

Tonio bit on the side of his lip, thinking. "Who is it?"

Before I tell you, I want to be clear that I know your story. I know what you've been through. I wouldn't ask this if I didn't think—

"Just tell me," he interrupted, in the smallest voice. I felt a sinking feeling in my stomach.

The child's name is Parker Feldman.

— 6 —

Sweetie dismissed us with a rolled-up poster advertising auditions for the next community theater show and a stolen script with notes about what would be read at the audition. Apparently, she knew Parker would be auditioning. "It makes sense," Tonio explained. "He's always doing acting stuff. I think his mom is a director."

Of course, the plan making sense didn't mean he was excited about it. Tonio had asked me for some time to think about the situation before we started discussing plans, so I used the rest of that night to start figuring out how it would work. The hard part, of course, was the beginning: How do you make a new friend?

In my experience, making friends with humans was simple: You just wag your tail and bump their hand with your nose, and suddenly everyone's telling you what a good boy you are. I didn't think this strategy would work for Tonio—though I'd never *seen* a human try the nose-bumping trick, so who nose!

Tonio still didn't say anything the next morning, and he was more than happy to let Devon talk all the way to school. I tried to get his attention a few times, but he was avoiding eye contact. I didn't want to rush him. My *whole job* was to be patient, but by the time we made it to gym class, I was *bursting* with ideas! It was running day (my favorite, Tonio's least favorite) so we ran around the border of the very shabby soccer field behind BMS.

I think we should talk to him before the auditions. Tonio, who had the amazing ability to start sweating when he *thought about* exercising, ran slow enough I could under-speak in bursts while trotting beside him. *If you just go there out of nowhere, it'll look suspicious.* I took a few big, extra-long bounds to stretch my legs. *Or maybe it would be better! Throw him off guard. He'll say, "Tonio? Here?! He must be so brave, and strong, and now he's my friend."*

Tonio didn't say anything, but there were other kids around. (Ahead.) I didn't really expect him to. I kept going. *No, I think we should talk to him. Maybe you could sit at his lunch table. Or maybe you could stand up really tall on your hind legs to show that you wanna play.*

Not even a smile. Now I was starting to worry. Exercise can sometimes be something that triggers his panic attacks—the feelings exercise gives you, like a pumping heart rate and heavy breathing, are really similar to what happens with anxiety. Sometimes the feelings are *too* close and kind of blend together.

Are you okay? I posed.

He knew what I meant and gave me a small gesture for *okay.* Then he followed that with the gesture for *skyscraper*, which was very confusing for me at the time. (Now I realize he was wiping sweat off his face.)

The fastest runners of the class were about to lap us. *This is your chance!* I posed. *Say something funny, like "Oh, finally, you caught up!" or "I already did a triathlon this morning, so . . ."* or—oh, there they go. The main clump of kids—led by Miles and Parker trying to trip each other—brushed past without even looking at us.

"You can do it, Tonio!" Jason gave a thumbs-up as he passed. "Only two more laps to go!" Tonio nodded a thank-you, but his jog deteriorated down to a speedy walk as this side of the field was left to us alone.

"I don't want to do it." His voice was breathy as he gulped down air. "I'm not going to do the mission."

My ears lifted in surprise.

"Parker is mean"—he gasped—"and annoying." He tried to jog a few more steps, but it didn't last long. "And he doesn't even get good grades." Even through the panting, I could hear his disgust as he said it.

Bad grades? I was surprised to hear Tonio say something like that. *What does that have to do with anything?*

"I already have friends, and they're better than he is. So why bother?"

I couldn't believe he was serious. *Because it's our job. We signed a contract!*

"So what? We can just tell them we're trying, and it's not working."

But that's a lie!

"And making him my friend would be nonstop lies." He shrugged and pulled the collar of his shirt up to wipe some sweat. I must have looked upset, because his brow furrowed angrily. "I really don't understand why you *care* so much. They don't care about you!"

To be honest, he'd never talked to me like this. I was still not used to having a human's attention on me, really. My tail dipped between my legs, and I struggled to figure out how to respond. *That's not true*, I settled on finally. *She said it herself: She's been trying to protect us.*

"Protect us by putting you in direct contact with the humans who most want to hurt you? Or by making you sign a contract just so you aren't banished forever?"

This is our chance to change all that! I insisted. *I've told you why it matters to me.*

"I know you miss Jpeg, but I don't trust Dog Court."

The group was rounding the corner back behind us, getting ready to lap us again for the last time. I made a gesture to signal that what I was going to say was important. *A while ago, you told me we couldn't be partners if there wasn't something I wanted, too. This is what I want. And you said you'd help me with it.*

"Yeah, but—"

My life can't just be about you, right? I was just parroting his words back to him, but I regretted it right away. He looked hurt, but I saw resignation in his eyes. I'd pulled out a card he couldn't fight back against. Was it fair? No. But it was honest. If we were a team, then what I wanted had to matter sometimes, too.

At least, that's what I thought at the time. Now I'm not sure I should have pushed him.

Okay, he signaled as the group started to pass him. *Fine.* His Underspeak transitioned smoothly into a weak wave toward the crowd.

"Parker!" he wheezed, and pushed himself back into a jog to catch up to the boys in the front. I kept up alongside them, and even I was starting to pant a little in the heat. "Hi."

"Uh, hey?" Parker gave Tonio a pitying look, and Miles raised an eyebrow.

"I can't"—Tonio didn't even have to play up his panting; keeping up with Parker was pushing him to his limits—"do another lap. Could you—"

They slowed down a little to listen to him, and the other kids gradually passed. "You look like you're about to catch fire."

"—help me—"

"Look less like a tomato?"

"—fake it?"

They couldn't have looked more surprised if *I* had asked them. The corner of Parker's mouth tugged up. "Ooh, like—"

But Miles rolled his eyes immediately. "No *way*. We had to run the whole thing!"

"He *is* really short, though," Parker pointed out. "So he's worked harder."

"Definitely *smells* like it." They both laughed. Tonio tucked his head to his shoulder to check his armpit as quickly as he could. (For the record, they all smelled pretty equally like middle school boy.)

Tonio shot me a look, squeezed his eyes shut for a second, then opened them back up with a heavy, sarcastic expression. "Surprised you can smell anything with *that* nose." I almost barked in surprise. *What???* I had never really heard him insult *anybody*, and we were supposed to be befriending these kids, not pushing them away! I thought maybe he was trying to sabotage the whole thing, but—

"BOOM!!!" Parker yelled, and laughed, and after a second of shock, Miles laughed, too. "I *told* you! Your nostrils are *way too small* to be normal."

"Whatever." Miles shrugged. "At least I don't have a unibrow."

Parker shoved him to the side. "It's not a unibrow!"

Miles shoved him back. "Well, not since you plucked it." He faked a camera with his hands. "Time for Parker Feldman's makeup tutorial! Make sure to like and subscribe!"

Parker shushed him and pointed with his chin. We

were coming up to the end of the lap, where the kids who'd gotten ahead were already waiting around the gate out of the field and Coach Dalton was writing down their times.

"Come on, Tonio! You can do it!" Parker turned around and jogged backward, clapping for Tonio. "We're almost there!"

Miles rolled his eyes again but took Parker's lead immediately and clapped in time. "Left! Right! Left! Right!"

When they arrived at the gate, Parker and Miles both high-fived him and made a big show of cheering. He stopped and followed them to the gate, where Coach Dalton turned to check their names.

"See, Tonio, I told you." Parker crossed his arms and lifted his chin like he'd finally won an argument, lying so smoothly I almost believed I'd missed something. "If you just push through the hard part at the beginning, running gets way easier."

"Feldman, Roy, good." The coach paused. "Pulaski— you okay?"

Even skipping the last lap, Tonio was bent over, hands on his knees, gasping. He gave the coach a thumbs-up.

"Good," the coach replied. "That time's your personal best. Keep it up."

Parker bowed as Coach Dalton stepped away. Miles mumbled, "You owe us," and then moved into the crowd. I was stunned! That had gone . . . really well.

I stepped under Tonio's face and looked up. *How did you do that?* I underspoke.

"Like the judge said," he whispered. "I pay attention." But when he straightened back out, I saw him make eye contact with Jason, just now finishing his final lap. He gave Tonio a disappointed look, which Tonio quickly turned away from, face red more from guilt than exercise now.

Nonstop lies, he'd said. I followed him back to the locker room and hoped he was wrong.

Tonio planned exactly how to tell his friends he was betraying them. I say "betray" because that's how he put it—personally, I think that's a bit dramatic. He was auditioning for a play, not going over to the dark side! I gotta hand it to anxious brains, though: When they want to plan something, they can *plan*. The same remarkable ability to imagine every possible version of the future made him great at card games and fueled his habit of overanalyzing conversations that hadn't happened yet.

Tonio scribbled plans in his sketchbook while I spun around and made myself dizzy in his chair. *I have to tell them on a Wednesday after therapy,* he wrote, *so I should probably get it out of the way tomorrow.*

Roll the Ice was totally empty on Wednesdays. Tonio's dad—who paid attention to the ebbs and flows of traffic to Bellville Square because of the grocery store— referred to Wednesday as "Dead-nes-day," and regularly celebrated a boring shift by watching a horror movie with Mrs. Pulaski. (Tonio rarely attended.) Since no one else was using the space, the kids' older friend Skyler let them use the game room for Beamblade Club.

I'll rush over there right away and spend my allowance on ice cream for everyone. He tapped the back of his pen against the front of his teeth. *But tell Skyler to pretend it's surprise free samples.*

Skyler was a college student who had moved back to Bellville when her mother got sick and needed someone to help take care of her. Now she was taking all her classes online, sneaking glances at her textbooks when no one needed her help at Roll.

More clicks of his pen in the dark. *I'll let them win when we play three-player. Mia should probably win— she's happier when she's proud.*

"I was thinking," Mia said while she waited for Devon to take his turn, "that we could make a streaming channel for the Dog League."

"That's a genius idea!" Devon tossed a spell attacking Mia directly. Mia used a counterspell to stop it.

On second thought, maybe Devon should win, he'd written. *That way she doesn't go straight from very happy to very mad, which could be worse.*

Tonio counterspelled her counterspell. Devon laughed, then continued: "I've already got a camera and everything!"

"Now we just have to think branding." Mia rubbed her chin and chewed her gum. She barely noticed Tonio's counter and moved on to her turn. "'Bellville Beamblade Dog League' doesn't really roll off the tongue."

"That's what Tonio's for. If he can come up with 'Lovesword,' he can do anything." Devon nudged Tonio with his elbow and smiled at him supportively.

Tonio clenched at the loop of my leash. *Keep the conversation light and simple until the first game is over.* Not working out so far. "The league is better as kind of a Bellville thing, right?"

"I've just been thinking." Mia kept on going, full steam ahead. "If that guy could come all the way from Myrtle Beach to adopt Jpeg, why couldn't they come from all over?" She shuffled her Beamblade deck. "Our shelter could be the most famous shelter in the country!"

"And Tonio could be famous," Devon pointed out. "Since he's the only one who knows how to train dogs to play. Isn't that right, Buster?" He patted my side, but I didn't tell him he was right. That sounded dangerous! We'd used the Beamblade thing to cover our tracks in Bellville, but it was really pushing the limits of what Good Dogs were supposed to be capable of. Tonio nodded and smiled, shuffling his cards to start another three-player Beamblade battle. "That sounds like a pretty good idea, actually." It honestly made me a little sad to see him getting better at lying. I wished he didn't have to.

"Oh, *now* he's excited." Mia took the first turn. "Ready to be a star, are you?"

Immediate red cheeks. "That's not why!"

"Mm-hmm." She shook her head, smile betraying that she was just teasing.

The game ended in a few more moves. Tonio gracefully played himself into a corner while helping Devon win. Mia, always herself, immediately pretended like the game had never happened. "Can we do a practice stream at your house, Devon?"

"Oh, uh, my house wouldn't be a great studio." He looked apologetic but didn't offer any more details. "Shouldn't we film outside your place? If it's for the shelter anyway."

"But outdoor lighting is *so* finicky," Mia whined in the voice of an imagined fancy director. "We would have to create our masterpiece entirely within the golden hour!"

As planned, Skyler showed up with three cups of ice cream carefully held between her hands and set them on the table. "Surprise! On the house!"

Tonio let out a sigh of relief. Back on track.

"I had a weird session with Dr. Jake today," he said over his cup of cookie dough ice cream. Mia and Devon immediately stopped bickering and looked at him, surprised.

"What happened?" Devon asked, as expected.

"Do you guys remember science fair last year?"

"I remember Mr. Greaves got mad at you." Mia kicked her feet up on the table. "Said you would have placed if you had actually shown up to present your project."

Devon spoke in a quiet voice. "You had a panic attack in the bathroom, right?"

Tonio nodded. "Dr. Jake says I need to work on my public speaking."

Mia said, "If we're gonna make Dogblade famous, he's right! Dr. Jake is a smart man."

"Is that something *you* want to do, though?" Devon asked.

"I think so. Even artists have to tell people about their work, right? I need to be better at talking to people who aren't just you two." He scratched my head. I leaned into it and gave my cutest puppy-dog eyes to paint a full picture of how reasonable and cute the two of us are. "Or dogs."

"That makes sense."

"Yeah!"

"And so . . ." This was the moment. He pulled the poster out of his bag and unrolled it on the table for them to see:

HERACLES, PUT DOWN YOUR PHONE
A Modern Play of Ancient Problems
Auditions open to all kids 9–13. Come join the
Bellville Community Theater's Kids Troupe!

The words launched clip art of cell phones, winged sandals, and the Parthenon out toward the edges of the poster. Between the stacked image of the same snake over and over (the "hydra") and a low-quality image of a character from *The Lion King* (Nemean, I figured) were the dates for auditions. Devon and Mia both stared at it silently for several seconds.

Finally, Mia spoke. "You want to join the *theater kids*?"

Theater kids, of course, was the trio's shorthand for Miles, Parker, and their groupies.

"I know!" Tonio rolled his eyes performatively. "But Dr. Jake said I have to."

"He really said that?" Devon looked confused. "He can't *make* you do anything, right?"

Tonio quickly backpedaled. "Well, uh, no, but if he thinks it's a good idea—"

"I think it makes sense." Mia shrugged. "You don't have to hang out with them or anything. And if you can do a play in front of those guys, you can speak in front of anybody."

"Huh?" Tonio said, startled that Mia's opinion was so different from what he expected.

"I said, it makes sense! Actually . . . what if we auditioned, too?"

"Oh, uh . . ." Tonio's ice cream, barely touched, dripped down his hand onto his shorts. "You guys don't need to do that."

Devon gasped. "I've always wanted to be in a play!

And if we all got cast, we could stick together the whole time."

"But I—"

"It's settled!" Mia finished off her mint chocolate chip with a final scoop of her tiny wooden spoon. "We'll all audition!"

I stood up under the pretense of a big stretch. ("Ooh, big stretch!" Devon mumbled.) This wouldn't work. If the other two joined, Tonio would never get a chance to be alone with Parker. Tonio looked at my pose of uncertainty and frowned. He waggled his hand under the table in a frustrated *I know.*

"What if—uh, I mean, if you guys are there, I—" Tonio swallowed and tried to focus down the buzzing that started when his plan started going awry. "I'm supposed to get good at this on my own. If you guys were there, you'd ruin it."

"We'd *ruin* it?" Devon looked a little hurt.

"I need to do it alone. It would be too easy if you guys came."

"Like two months ago," Mia argued, "you were throwing up any time you looked at his weird face—"

"Hey!"

"—and now we're *too easy* to be around?"

"That's not what I mean." Tonio tried to think of something else he could mean instead of what he meant, which was exactly what she had said. He couldn't find anything new to say. "It's just what Dr. Jake said," he lied, breathless.

Mia narrowed her eyes. "That we're your anxiety *starter pack*?"

Devon tried to shrug casually. "If Tonio thinks that's best for him, then okay. We won't." His voice was dripping with disappointment. Mia glared at him, then back at Tonio, then huffed out a big breath.

"Whatever."

"Do you want to play again?" Tonio asked, holding out his cards.

"I should probably go do the math homework," Devon answered. "I'll see you guys tomorrow."

"Yeah, me too." Mia dumped her stuff in her backpack. "And you should start working on your big solo audition, right?"

Tonio nodded and gathered his things, moving slowly so they'd all leave before him. I nudged up against his hand for his attention, but he ignored me again. He'd spent so long working on exactly what to say, exactly how to say it . . .

"It didn't work," he mumbled, defeated.

I should have tried to talk him out of it. But now it was too late.

Bugs

. . . as soon as I can think of a plan. Jpeg rolled over onto her back, white stomach fur looking yellow in the ugly fluorescent light. It was even flickering—exactly what Tonio expected from a kidnapper's lair, based on scary movies. He never made it far enough into them to see anyone escape, though.

"Buster sent you messages on DogHouse every night after you left." Tonio's voice dripped with guilt, and he ran his hand along the bars of the dog crate. "He was concerned about you, but I—" He stopped. No. Telling Jpeg that would only hurt her feelings.

you were worried about other things, she finished for him, paws kicking and twisting in the air. He nodded, ashamed. *i get it. humans worry about humans, dogs worry about dogs.*

"That's not it," Tonio argued. Jpeg watched him with one eye as he paused, trying to think of what "it" was. "After the summer, when I went back to school, everyone thought I was this brand-new person. Even *I* thought so, at first." He felt everything rushing out at Jpeg, everything he'd been holding in for weeks. "The

65

Court was like, 'Congratulations on fixing yourself. Glad that's over. Now you can finally be *useful.*' And when Sweetie said that so obviously, I realized that's what everyone was saying, really." He counted people off on his fingers. "Mom and Dad stopped checking on me except for chores. Kids at school didn't talk to me. Mia and Devon wanted my help with everything, and even Buster didn't give me a choice. But I couldn't do everything everyone wanted."

did you try turning it off and back on again? Jpeg asked.

"What?"

that's the best i got. She flopped onto her side and rolled her shoulders in a shrug, tail beating gently against the rubber floor of her cage. *idk about feelings, eyebrow boy.*

"It's okay." Tonio kicked weakly against the door of the cage. "I just meant that I'm sorry. And it's my fault you're still here."

Jpeg tapped on an imaginary keyboard with her paws, eyes closed, coding some program in her mind. After a while, she huffed to get Tonio's attention again. *you know about bugs?*

Tonio drew an imaginary looping line with his finger, like a bee traveling from flower to flower, with his other hand twisted into a tail's question pose. Jpeg bared her teeth *no.*

66

the other kind. one time i made a virus that would erase all evidence of the movie shazaam, *featuring the actor* sinbad, *from all websites and databases anywhere on earth.*

"I've never heard of that movie."

exactly. but the code was kind of complicated, and it had a bug where it was deleting everything from computers that referenced shazaam. *so i worked on editing the code, sent out a countervirus to rewrite it, and that was that.*

Tonio was too polite to say what he wanted to say, which was *What are you talking about?!?*

HOWEVER, fixing that bug created a bunch of other bugs. it started messing with references to the berenstein bears books and changed the spelling to berenstain. and that was just the beginning—i'd tried to fix one problem and made a bunch of other weird ones i didn't expect. i got it under control, but not before it erased the hyphen in kit-kat and removed the tail curious george used to have.

Tonio wished he had a tail, so he could do the biggest physical question mark of his life.

life works like that sometimes. fixing one thing means you gotta fix all the other stuff. it doesn't ever really end, but every time you fix something you get a little faster at it.

"In this example," Tonio processed, horrified, "you changed the whole world forever in a bunch of random ways *by mistake?* And that's *good?!*"

bugs, and mistakes, are just the cost of doing business. sometimes "doing business" is living your life, and sometimes it's making sure no one ever has to watch a truly terrible movie again.

"I don't think I agree with you at all."

well, maybe that's why you're so sad all the time.

Tonio winced. Jpeg was already moving on: now, tell me everything that's in your backpack.

8

Parker stared at the cell phone in his hands, hair perfectly swooped across his forehead, eyes hollowed out with exhaustion. "I can't. I can't do it." He let the phone dangle between his fingers as he looked up into the light, voice cracking with grief. "Every time I try to post something beautiful, there are two new posts on the feed from other people, just as beautiful as mine."

He reached his hand out ahead of him, eyes searching the face of someone in the distance. "Hermes, tell me. Please. I'll never get enough Heads on my posts if this keeps up. Every selfie I take is met with two more handsome selfies. Every breakfast photo I take has been taken twice before, by someone with a higher-resolution camera than I could ever hope to—"

Parker burst into a sob. He hid his face behind his arm. "I thought I could do this," he croaked, "but how will I complete all the LABRs if I can't even finish the *second* one?"

A cleared throat. Tonio's voice, muffled behind the script in front of his face. "Are you sure you are doing everything. You could do. Heracles?" He was almost too quiet to hear. *Come on*, I thought. *We rehearsed this!* "Are brunches and hackruts—hasair—haircuts." A deep breath. "Really all you have to offer."

Parker gasped. His eyes widened like Tonio had said the most inspiring thing anyone had ever said. "That's it! I'll never make it to the top of the Hydra feed if I keep doing what everyone else is doing. I need to post something uniquely *me*!" He stood from his chair triumphantly, phone at his side and eyes beaming toward the horizon. "I'm more than my dance moves, or my new pair of shoes."

"You'll never beat mine." Tonio flipped the page of his script. "Anyway. I have the best shoes anywhere. Lifts up feet to show off sandals." An awkward pause before Tonio realized he'd read the stage direction and lifted a foot up like he was showing off wings on the heels.

"Thank you, Hermes. I never could have done this without you. The secret to beating the Hydra . . ." Parker stood up on the seat of his chair and held up his phone with both hands, like a heavy sword. *". . . is being my genuine self online!"*

Parker was a genius. I was sure of it. Watching him perform was totally different from watching movies—and he was leagues above the other kids who were auditioning. I've watched human expression more closely than most dogs because of my jobs alongside them, and as a result, I've seen humans lie all the time. Usually their lies are obvious to me—but when Parker spoke his lines, every little motion connected to his words and even his heartbeat changed with the feeling he was expressing. The smallest *breath* seemed coordinated to convince us he was being honest, and true, as Heracles. It was a fully sensory experience. A person transforming, magically, before my very eyes.

He's so annoying, right? Tonio underspoke when he came back to his seat. We were sitting with thirty or so other kids in a gray rehearsal room with mirrors along one wall and a piano shoved into the corner. The whole room applauded, cueing Parker's proud grin and another one of his bows. Tonio added a few weak claps.

You did great! I answered, ignoring the question. He rolled his eyes.

No, I didn't. He folded over in his chair, head against his knees and hands underspeaking while they dangled by the floor. *All our practice was for nothing! I forgot everything as soon as they were looking at me.*

He kept his eyes buried in his knees, so I couldn't respond. Our problem, based on the information Judge Sweetie gave us, was this: The cast for *Heracles, Put Down Your Phone* was huge, but only a few characters had solo scenes with the lead, Heracles. Parker would absolutely be cast as Heracles (he was a genius, and his mom was the director), so Tonio needed to play one of those characters if he wanted a chance to befriend

Parker one-on-one. He couldn't play Tree #2, or Back Legs of a Mare of Diomedes; the only options were Megara, Hermes, Hippolyta, Eurystheus, Geryon, and Hades. They were only casting girls as Megara and Hippolyta, so that meant four possible roles for Tonio.

Hermes and Eurystheus were the big talkers and required a lot of comedic timing—which Tonio did not quite have, even during practice, and his stage fright made things even worse. *That's okay*, I thought. *There's still two more options.*

Josephine Feldman, the director, called a few more pairs of kids up to repeat the same scene before moving on to the next part of the auditions. "Heracles's tenth task on the LABR app is to steal digital cows from the giant Geryon's server farm," she explained, reading from her notes, "but since he has six arms and three heads, he watches ZeuTube on a dozen tablets at once. Heracles has to distract this *master of multitasking* however he can." She pointed to a pile of foam swords against one of the walls. "Most of this scene is going to be stage fighting, so I need to see how everybody moves. Pairs are . . ." and she started listing names.

"Oh no," Tonio mumbled.

". . . Tonio Pulaski and Miles Roy . . ."

"Oh *no!*" Tonio groaned. He dragged his feet to grab a sword and found his spot next to Miles, already stretching. Miles was tall for his age, just like Parker, and just like Parker he had the hair of a TV show star—though where Parker's was swooshy, his was sculpted upward into a wave of hair above his forehead. In fact, I realized that even his *outfit* looked just like one of Parker's—always exercise-style clothes, always of the same two brands. He didn't look at Tonio at all while Mrs. Feldman and her assistant described stage-fighting safety rules and showed the simple combination they would be practicing.

When they were finally given time to practice on their own, Miles turned to Tonio and held his sword up with a glare. "What are you doing here?"

Tonio wiped sweaty hands on his shorts and lifted his sword with both hands. He noticed the glare late, because he was staring down at his feet, trying to figure out where "shoulder width" was. "I'm . . . auditioning."

The foam blade of Miles's sword swiped horizontally as he barked out a laugh. "No, I'm being serious." Tonio ducked under just in time and jabbed his sword forward for Miles to jump back.

Their foam swords came together with three squeaky slashes in a row. Tonio looked baffled. "So am I." He pushed forward as Miles pushed in response, and they both stepped forward—I'm sure it would have looked like a dramatic standoff if the swords weren't bending goofily back over their shoulders.

Miles leaned over their blades and sniffed at Tonio's

face, nose wrinkling in disgust. "What's that smell?" he whispered. "Did you already throw up?"

He hadn't. But his eyebrows bunched together, hurt, and he forgot the next step in the fight; Miles hit him on both sides with two loud *thwaps*. My ears flattened in anger, and I had to hold on to a growl. Tonio had to defend himself.

"You did, didn't you?! Wow. I was joking." Miles lifted his chin proudly as he pushed the fight even faster, taking every opportunity he could find to hit Tonio for falling behind. "Makes sense, though. No offense." He grinned as he slid around Tonio's gentle jab. "But if you can't even sign a yearbook, you can't be in a play. And you have to be able to talk." I patted the ground helplessly with my paws. Miles and Parker had left Tonio alone at school so far—why was he being mean *now*?

"You're right," Tonio mumbled, letting his sword fall to his side. "I don't want to be here, either."

"What? I can't hear you." Miles was still smiling, but I could feel something else in his expression. His heartbeat slowed slightly, and his whole body relaxed a little. Was he . . . relieved? What had he been worried about before? Was he scared of Tonio being here for some reason?

"Never mind," Tonio replied. I was curious but needed to set it aside for now. That blank expression never meant anything good for Tonio, and I had to find a way to snap him out of it. *Don't fall for it*, I underspoke. We needed to win these guys over as friends, which meant trying to understand the meaning behind their behavior. *Be like Devon*, I suggested. *Stay positive!*

Tonio watched me say this and shook his head, just a little. Miles went to get a drink from the water fountain before it was their turn to do the fight in front of the director. *Won't work*, he underspoke. *They don't care about "positive."*

You made friends with Mia and Devon by being genuine. I tapped my back paw and wiggled my ears, trying to underspeak in an extra-cute and comforting way. *If you stick to being nice and find a way to be true to yourself even if they're difficult, you'll win them over.*

The look Tonio gave me sent my hackles up—a stare down his nose like I'd said the stupidest thing he'd ever heard. *If I were being true to myself*, he underspoke slowly and deliberately, *I. Wouldn't. Be. Here.*

Yeah, I snapped with quick, harsh Underspeak, tail pointed in frustration. *You'd be in the city, alone, without me or any of your friends.*

He knelt and pretended to be adjusting my harness. "Maybe I should have gone," he whispered. "If I'm throwing away all my real friends anyway."

I wanted to bark *You're being selfish!* But I followed one of Dr. Jake's pieces of advice for dealing with strong emotions: I waited, and thought, before I answered in anger. What did I *actually* think?

Mia and Devon will forgive you, I underspoke. *And I stand by what I said. But you know them better than I do, and if you don't think you can be yourself, then who* can *you be?* I watched his face carefully for signs of what he thought, but he was working hard to keep his face flat. *Do you have a better idea?*

He chewed on his lip. *Devon is always nice to them, and they walk all over him. Mia fights back, so they avoid her.* He tucked his sword under his arm. *They only care about people who play the same game as them.*

I did not like the sound of that, but I thought back to how he'd acted in PE. *Surprised you can smell anything with* that *nose,* he'd said. And magically they'd turned their teasing on each other and decided to help him. It went against everything I knew about making real friends—

But these weren't real friends. That's what Tonio was trying to tell me. No matter how much I thought they *could* be, he didn't believe it. That's why he was frustrated with me and why he'd been ignoring the plans I'd tried to develop all week.

Arguing with Tonio felt awful. I wanted it to be over. *Okay,* I said finally. *How can I help?*

"They poke at the things other people are self-conscious about." He scratched behind my ears, a thoughtful look in his eyes. "I need to know what those things are, for them."

There was one thing I noticed, I realized, *while you were fighting . . .*

"What are you scared of?" Tonio asked in a small, pleasant voice. He posed with his sword confidently as Miles's eyes narrowed over his own blade.

"Huh?" The same motions again, but this time Tonio was focused. He ducked down as Miles's swipe began, and his jab caught a bit of the other boy's shirt before he hopped back. "Nothing. What?"

Three squeaky slashes where their swords met in the center—Tonio slid his feet forward just a little with each one, forcing Miles back. "You seem really worried I'm gonna get cast." Tonio shrugged, casual, but underneath, his heart was thumping so loud I looked around to see if other humans could hear it. "Scared I'll take your role?"

"No way. Mrs. Feldman loves me." Their swords hit in a fourth slash, and they stepped forward face-to-face again.

"Hurk—glchh—" Tonio's cheeks bulged out.

Miles flinched away. "Whoa! Hey! Don't—"

The air blew gently out of Tonio's mouth, rippling his lips in a raspberry sound. "Just kidding." The other boy's face went from disgust, to shock, to—was that a glimmer of *awe* I saw? Was Miles *impressed*?

Thwack, thwack. Tonio hit him once on either side of his body, even though that was technically part of

Miles's choreography. "Let's start over. We look better if we both look good."

I watched Miles search his face, looking for what had changed since the last time they'd fought, but he wasn't going to find anything. Tonio had one big eyebrow up and a small, fake smile underneath it. Inside, his heart was still pounding. *Now you just have to act like this in front of an audience,* I thought, *and you'll get in the show for sure.*

"Yeah, okay." Miles nodded, then waved his sword at Tonio's legs. "Your feet are too far apart."

When they finally performed their fight for Mrs. Feldman, Miles still came out looking a lot better. Tonio was winded from running it four times in a row, but Miles didn't break a sweat. Compared to the others, he seemed exceptional at the rhythm of stage combat—plus, as Parker's best friend, he was a shoo-in for Geryon. Still, my human looked a lot better than he would have without the other boy's fighting tips.

Only one option was really left among the main characters: Hades. The god of the underworld was written as powerful, confident, and intimidating—three things Tonio was not really known for—but he had the fewest actual lines of the lead characters, so we hoped we had a chance.

"Like the other gods featured in the show, Hades will

be onstage often even while he isn't speaking," Mrs. Feldman explained. "This means Hades must be very expressive, even while he's silent. He'll have to do a lot of what I like to call 'eyebrow acting.'" My ears swiveled forward and lifted as high as they could go. Tonio gasped, his eyebrows shooting up into the stratosphere. We shared a glance: *More than a chance! This was our moment!*

"Everyone, please look over the sides for this scene—I'll call on pairs to speak in a moment. Tonio Pulaski, will you come here for a moment, please? Bring Buster." We walked to the back of the room, where Mrs. Feldman's desk was covered in scripts and notes she'd taken during auditions. She looked a lot like Parker—the same thick brown hair with lighter blond bits sprinkled throughout, the same big eyes and perfect teeth. Didn't seem as mean, though, at least.

"You know Heracles's last labor is to take Cerberus, Hades's dog, for a walk. I was planning on using a puppet, but . . ." She smiled down at me. "I've heard Buster is really remarkably trained. How do you think he'd perform onstage?"

Tonio looked extremely relieved to have the attention directed toward me instead. "Perfectly!" he said. "Buster can do pretty much anything. We, uh . . ." He searched around for a lie. "We practice different expressions and things all the time. He'd be a great actor."

"Does he need verbal commands?"

"No, I mostly talk to him with hand gestures." Which was true. "I can show you, if you want. He can growl." Tonio did a quick fake hand gesture, and I flattened my ears and rumbled. "Or cry." I lay on the ground and covered my eyes while whining. "Or even sing!" I howled, drawing the attention of the whole room—some of the kids laughed.

Mrs. Feldman grinned and clapped her hands together. "*Much* better than a puppet. All right, let's try it! Parker, come up here. Tonio, see if you can read as Hades and guide Buster to react as well. Let's go back a few pages to where Heracles first approaches Cerberus at the gates of the Underworld."

Parker stepped up, but he looked uncomfortable. "Mom, are you sure—"

"Of course I'm sure. Hush." She stood and marked the lines of the stage with her feet. "This is the River Styx here, so don't step in this area. The gate to the Underworld is here, and Cerberus stands in front of it. Hades, when you enter, it will be from that side. Got it?" Tonio and Parker nodded. Parker gave me a weird look I didn't understand, but it was gone in a flash when he put his Heracles face on.

The room fell silent as Parker walked toward me onstage. Tonio watched the script and underspoke stage directions to me from offstage. I tried to imagine I had three heads and a snake for a tail as I bowed my head forward and bared my teeth, growling at him.

Parker leaped back, fear in his face and hands up in surrender. "Whoa, whoa. Sorry, boy. I'm not here to hurt you. I just want to take you for a walk." He held his hand up for me to sniff—I leaned forward and smelled it, then opened my mouth wide, snapping at him slow enough he could jerk his hand away. "Oops. I probably still smell like Geryon's cows, huh? Tasty?"

I sat back and eyed him suspiciously but kept a low rumble in my throat. *I need to really sell this,* I thought. *I'm our best chance at getting cast.* I filled my eyes with all the suspicion I could muster and tried to move my brow in a way more like how humans express anger.

"I'm going to clip these three leashes to your collars, okay? And then we're going to go for a nice walk." Heracles slid forward one slow step at a time. I reared back on my hind legs to look more intimidating. "Get you some sun—bet it's been a while since you've seen the sun, huh? Maybe we can catch something from the surface to eat?"

That sounded good to me. I licked all three sets of lips and lowered myself back down. "Yeah, that's right! Just a few quick clicks—"

Tonio stepped forward from the side, face buried in his script. "What is the meaning of this?" he mumbled.

"Oh, uh—" Parker tried to step in front of me to

81

hide the leashes, but I bounded through his legs to get to Hades, barking happily and tripping Parker in the process. Tonio grabbed at the imaginary leash Parker had clipped to my first head and lifted it up to inspect it.

"You were taking my dog?" Tonio, for all his nerves, was still just Tonio. He glanced up at Parker occasionally, nervous, and sometimes accidentally looked at the audience but mostly kept his face buried in the script. I tried to nudge him supportively.

"The LABR app says I'm supposed to take him for a walk!" Heracles smiled and shrugged, managing to seem scared even though Tonio wasn't being intimidating at all. "Totally free, don't worry about it."

"My dog? The guardian of the gates to the Underworld?" Tonio paused to turn the page. "The last line of defense keeping the spirit world from overrunning the land of the living?" He spoke slowly, deliberately, no more energy in one word than the next. *Come on, Tonio! I* thought. *You did so much better than this in practice!* But he was still so nervous with all these people staring at him.

Heracles winced. "I see now why that's a problem."

"What miserable creature put you up to—" Tonio was interrupted by the door to the rehearsal room opening. I saw the man entering through the big mirror along the opposite wall first, and he looked right at me through the mirror, too, his face falling suddenly into a scowl and then lifting back into the smile he wore when he'd stepped inside.

Oscar Sykes! The man from the picture! The agent of the Department of Nonhuman Intelligence!

Tonio saw him, too, and we shared a glance.

"Sorry for interrupting!" Agent Sykes smiled pleasantly and held up a bag—the logo on the side said *SizzlePop: Fried Chicken on a Stick*. He was a tall adult, a little older than Tonio's dad—but his hair was cut short and simple, and his clothes were crisp and ironed with an effort far beyond anything the Pulaskis had time for. "Just wanted to bring some food by for your *incredible* director."

He slipped his way across the back of the room to Mrs. Feldman's desk and placed the bag down for her. Parker glared across the audience of kids. "We were in the middle of a scene."

Agent Sykes ignored his words and kept smiling. "There's some for you, too."

They watched each other in silence for a few seconds before Parker said, "Thank you, sir."

His stepdad nodded, and his smile fell a little as he glanced at me again. I pretended to be interested in an itch on my neck and lifted my back leg up to slap at my collar and jangle it loudly. Like a Good Dog does.

"Jo, can I speak with you outside?"

"We're already going to run long, so I—"

"It'll only take a second."

Mrs. Feldman smiled and nodded. "Sure. We'll start the scene over when we get back. Keep practicing, everyone." She stood and followed her husband through the door he held open for her, and they went out into the hallway to talk.

Did you see the way he looked at me? I underspoke to Tonio.

He nodded. *They said he knows about dogs. Or . . . thinks he knows.*

Parker stared at the door as the volume of the room grew around him, kids practicing lines or talking about what roles they wanted. He moved with purpose toward the door, and I decided to tag along behind him.

I'm going to go listen, I told Tonio. *You focus on the audition.*

Tonio nodded. I left him mumbling Hades's words again and made my way along the wall, lying down in a pile of backpacks near enough to the door that I could hear through it.

Instead of going through the door, Parker grabbed a script and leaned against the wall next to it while pretending to read his lines. I swiveled my ears to try and do the same thing he was doing—listen in on his parents' conversation outside.

"—so you can understand," Agent Sykes was saying with the voice of someone who was trying to show how patient they were, "why I'd be surprised to see Parker so close to that thing after we've talked about this so many times."

Mrs. Feldman sounded defensive, like she was in trouble for breaking the rules. "There's a dog in the play, Oscar. And it's a service dog, so I obviously couldn't turn him away—"

"My allergy is *deadly*, Josephine."

"I understand that, and we'll make sure we change clothes when we get home—"

"To be honest," the man said with a sigh, "I'm surprised you're comfortable treating my life so casually."

Her voice came out quick, aggravated. "Now you're being dramatic."

A pause. "I see. Well, of course, it's up to you. But I'd appreciate it if you considered whether it is *worth it* to cast this boy in your show."

She was about to respond, but I got distracted by Parker throwing his script to the ground and charging back through the crowd, straight toward Tonio. I left the door and bounded over behind him, arriving right as he yanked the script out of Tonio's hands and threw it several feet away, to his yelping objection.

"I see now why that's a problem," Parker said, as Parker, without a Heracles voice. Tonio stared at him in total confusion. "What's the next line?" he prompted.

"Oh, uh . . ." Tonio swallowed and stared into

Parker's face, searching for an explanation for this sudden aggression. "What miserable creature put you up to this?"

"It's just an app. If you complete twelve tasks you get a prize and, ah, my phone."

Tonio looked down and reached a hand out for the script. Parker lightly smacked his hand down. "There," Tonio said, staring at the ground. "Your master is defeated."

"Do you have any rice?"

"Nothing grows in the land of the dead."

Parker grinned. "Yes. See? You already know the scene. Why are you staring at your paper?"

Tonio swallowed, still uncomfortable with this much direct attention from Parker—especially with the weird, rushed energy to Parker's words. "In case I forget, I guess."

"You won't. And stop acting like you're scared of me." Parker, glancing at the door to make sure it was still closed, pushed Tonio's shoulder back and chin up, making him stand up straight. I wanted to step in to stop him, but Parker wasn't hurting him—just guiding his posture.

"You're not actually that much shorter than me. Huh." Parker took a step back and looked him up and down. "Hades isn't scared of *anything*, right? He's the guy in charge of everything that everyone else is afraid of. *I'm* scared of *you*. You're terrifying."

Tonio looked down his nose, chin frozen where Parker left it. "Why are you doing this?"

"I want you to get cast."

"Why?"

Parker didn't answer. "You don't have to change the way you're speaking much. If anything, sound *more* bored. *Less* emotion, just louder. And your eyebrows look pretty scary naturally when you're making a face like that!"

"Face like what?!" Tonio near whispered, brows furrowed in a scowl of confusion. Parker was right: With his chin up and his suspicious face, he looked like someone who might lock you in Tartarus for a couple centuries if you said the wrong thing.

Parker flicked him on the forehead.

"Hey!" Tonio threw his hands up—Parker made a big show of flinching backward at the gesture, then looked at him seriously, raising his own voice and picking up the scene.

"If I do all the tasks, I'm supposed to get a special prize!"

"Oh, really?" Tonio gasped, voice louder than I'd heard in months. "And what is this *prize*?"

"I don't know!"

"So you—" Tonio laughed, anxious breathing giving it a raspy quality. "Mindlessly follow the commands of a being that promises an *undefined reward*."

The door to the rehearsal room opened, but nobody else noticed. Both of them—and the entire room of kids—were too focused on the performance. Mrs. Feldman quietly shut it behind her and watched them carefully. No sign of Agent Sykes.

"YOU ARE A FOOL!" Tonio yelled, as sincerely as anything he'd ever said. "I have seen many driven to my realm by such thinking."

"Everyone is using LABR," Parker argued. "Hera told me so! But I was doing the best of all of them until *you*"—he stepped forward toward Tonio, jabbing his finger into the other boy's chest—"threw my phone into the River Styx! That'll wipe *all* of its memory."

"Maybe you should talk to Zeus, then," Tonio spat, voice booming with anger, chest heaving with stress on the edge of a panic attack. "See if the god of thunder saved it to his *CLOUD*!"

The audition scene ended there. Tonio and Parker stood staring each other down as the rest of the room applauded.

"All right, that's plenty," Mrs. Feldman called from the back. "Next pair is Lawrence and Nelson, same scene."

Tonio left the room in a rush, yelling "Bathroom!" and hiding himself down the hall, head between his knees on a toilet until his breathing finally calmed down. *It's okay.* I licked at his forehead, and tried to underspeak as supportively as I could. *You're gonna be okay.*

Two days later, the cast list was announced: Tonio was Hades, and I was Cerberus.

We'd done it.

— 9 —

Dr. Jake's sessions with Tonio had continued unbroken since the summer. Typically, seeing Dr. Jake was really helpful for Tonio—even though we couldn't tell him the truth about how smart I was, Tonio was finally comfortable speaking honestly about everything else, which meant he was making good progress.

Now, though, we were back in a situation where Tonio couldn't speak honestly about any of the most stressful thoughts he was having. Instead of looking forward to Dr. Jake's conversations, he was dreading them.

"You auditioned for a play." Dr. Jake was tall, but he folded up onto a short stool so he'd be closer to eye level with Tonio, who always sat in a blue beanbag chair. "That's exciting!"

"It's scary," Tonio corrected. "But I got in."

"Are you proud? I'm proud of you."

"No."

"No?"

"I don't feel like it's because of anything about me." He picked something out from under his fingernail. "I only got in because I didn't act like myself at all."

"That's interesting." Dr. Jake pushed his rolled-up sleeves back above his elbow, then set his hands in his lap. He seemed to take notes less frequently now, but his pen and notebook were ready just in case. "What does it mean to act like 'Tonio'?"

Tonio gave him a suspicious look. "You want me to realize I said something wrong."

But Dr. Jake smiled. "I don't think you said anything wrong. I want to make sure I understand what you mean."

"I'm shy. I'm embarrassing when I speak in front of people. I'm not someone who performs in plays."

"Then why did you audition?"

Tonio shrugged. "I thought it would be a good idea," he lied.

Dr. Jake carefully considered his next words. "Something seems different in your mood today, Tonio. It sounds like you might be talking around what you're feeling." From Dr. Jake, it didn't sound like an accusation; I understood, now, that he was often trying to help Tonio feel noticed and observed. Usually this was helpful, but Tonio's face was all scrunched up in pain.

I made little motions for him from my red beanbag. *You can tell him more about the situation without giving it away*, I suggested. *Maybe he can help!*

Tonio nodded slowly. "There's someone in the show who I want to be friends with. The show seems like the best way to get to know him." He squished farther down in his beanbag. "But he's a theater kid, and he's funny and popular. He's not going to pay attention to someone like me."

Dr. Jake's hand tightened around his pen just a little when he heard something they could dig further into. "You know that for sure?"

Tonio's lips flattened together, caught in an anxiety trap they'd talked about before. "I know I can't tell the future, but it's pretty likely he won't."

"So *you think* he won't."

"Yeah, I guess I think he won't."

"Is there any evidence one way or the other?"

Tonio bit the inside of his cheek, probably remembering how auditions had gone. "He's already talked to me more this week than any other time in my life," Tonio admitted.

"Sounds like you're on the right track, to me," Dr. Jake pointed out. "So maybe instead of what you think, how do you feel?"

"I feel scared. I feel a lot of pressure, and I'm really just guessing about how to make friends with someone like him."

This got a nod from Dr. Jake. "I don't think we've spoken directly about labeling yet, but it's another one of those anxious thoughts—cognitive distortions—we've talked about before. Deciding on a label for yourself based on just one part of you, or just a few things you've done, is really a way of limiting yourself. When you say 'I'm embarrassing,' or 'I'm shy,' you're cutting out all the other parts of you, and the times you've acted differently."

"There's *tons* of evidence for it, though!" Tonio argued, and counted on his fingers: "I am scared to talk to new people, I don't like speaking in front of crowds, and I stumble all over my words when I have to do either of those things. All the time! People laughed when I was auditioning. Even Buster—uh, probably—thought my audition as awkward. That's *shy*, and that's *embarrassing*."

"We've talked a lot about how people can change—that's why you're here, in therapy: because you know you can change parts of your thinking that are getting in your way. But people can change *all the time*. Sometimes, being around certain people can bring out totally different parts of us. Placing labels can keep you—or others—from feeling comfortable with those changes. It can stop us from growing."

Something clicked for Tonio, and he suddenly looked a lot more awake. "That's what bullies do," he realized. "They take labels people are already afraid of and make them seem obvious and real. Like they're 'popular' but other people are 'weird.'"

Or "Good Dog" and "Bad Dog," I thought.

Tonio did not sound, to me, like he was having a positive revelation. He looked distracted, like the subject had changed completely, but Dr. Jake didn't seem to notice. "That's one way to think about it," he agreed. "So when you can, try not to be your own bully. 'Tonio' can be whoever you want him to be, at any moment. We are our *actions*, not our labels. And auditioning for a play, in my opinion, is neither shy nor embarrassing."

"Thank you, Dr. Jake," Tonio said. "I think you did help."

⊢ 10 ⊣

Coach Dalton never ran out of dodgeball variants, but the next one was truly the worst so far. It was called "Dog Catcher," and the kids were sorted into "puppies" and "dog catchers." The puppies tried to run between corners of the gym (called "cages") while the dog catchers threw balls at them to try to get them out. Honestly, I don't think the theme made a lot of sense. In what situation were puppies trying to get from cage to cage while humans were trying to . . . hit them?

Plus, if you were struck with the ball, you traded places with the dog catcher—so dog catcher became puppy, and puppy became dog catcher. The whole thing is gruesome, and apparently this is a perfectly normal thing kids do in gym classes across the country. I spent the whole game having a very *what even is the* deal *with humans????* moment.

"I never really thought about it before." Tonio looked a little queasy. "I'm sorry you have to see this."

Coach Dalton blew his whistle for the game to start. The goal was to stay a puppy for as long as possible; Tonio got stuck as a dog catcher pretty quickly. Miles and Parker clearly expected to take this one easy and rack up points as puppies, but a couple of kids made it their mission to frustrate them: Roel, who only stood out to me before then because his shirts were all the same shade of green, and Kimberlyn, who played tennis with Mia.

Neither were theater kids, and they weren't notable targets, either. Something had inspired them to fight back against the duo's repeated showboating during gym, though, and they came into Dog Catcher with an amazing focus.

When each round began, they'd jump in front of two of the dog catchers' balls and target Miles and Parker, forcing them to become catchers—and then dodge and stall until the boys, frustrated, targeted someone else and became puppies. Then Kimberlyn and Roel would become dog catchers on purpose again to target them.

After weeks of uncontested supremacy for Miles and Parker, they were getting shut down for the first time—and it was riveting. The whole class was paying attention to the mini game happening inside the real game, even as they dodged balls on their own. After several rounds of this, the eternally sleepy Coach Dalton even stepped in.

"Lozada, Summers, Feldman, Roy! What's going on?"

"They're not playing fair!" Miles crossed his arms. "They're just trying to get us out."

Kimberlyn, whose blue-dyed hair was messy and flat

from wearing a beanie whenever the teachers weren't looking, dropped her lower lip and held up a hand in mock surprise. "Oh no, did it really feel that way? I'm so sorry."

Parker gave her a flat look but didn't say anything. He seemed nervous confronting the coach directly.

Roel stood up straight to try to look as adult as possible. "They never play games right! Why don't you ever stop them?" *Wow, Roel!* I wanted to bark a cheer—it was nice to see someone stand up against Miles and Parker.

Coach Dalton shook his head. "Targeting specific students is against the spirit of the game and not allowed in my class. Don't do it again."

Kimberlyn didn't like that. "So when they ruin the game for *everyone*, that's okay, but if the Drama Kings aren't having fun, we have to stop the whole class?" A few kids snickered at her name for them. (I thought it was perfect.)

"Watch the attitude before I write you up, Summers." Coach Dalton was the only teacher who used kids' last names, I think to be intimidating. Comes off stuffy and boring to me, though. He blew his whistle and yelled, "Five-minute break and then a new round. No funny business." The class walked back to their roles of "puppy" and "dog catcher" again, this time with no funny business allowed.

The Drama Kings looked furious, which was confusing

to me. They hadn't even gotten into trouble, but— "They don't have anything to say back to Kimberlyn," Tonio whispered. "Both of them are usually quiet, so Parker doesn't know enough to make fun of them."

She's got blue hair? I suggested. *And Roel's thing with the shirts.*

"It doesn't work like that," he explained. "She dyed her hair on purpose, and he likes those shirts. You can't just make fun of someone for something everyone can see unless you have a reason why it's something to be ashamed of." I nodded, but I only sort of understood. Sometimes, I feel like this is the best example of what his anxiety does: He is forced to constantly be considering all the layers to how things could go wrong, and so he notices things I don't. "It's my chance."

We moved toward the Drama Kings, who were leaning against a wall. "So annoying," Miles was grumbling. "And trying to tattle on us? Sorry you don't know how to have fun, *Kim.* I should show her how hard I can *really* throw these."

Parker flicked his head, tossing his hair across his forehead smoothly. "They don't have any respect for us," he said. "That's the problem." The words came out so seriously, but I wanted to laugh. *That sounds like something a movie villain would say,* I thought. *Is that really what he thinks?* "And we can fix that without—"

"Congratulations on getting cast!" Tonio said from

behind Miles, who whirled around to glare at him for interrupting. "Heracles and Geryon, right? That's perfect."

Parker nodded coolly. "You too." Whatever energy he'd had for Tonio had disappeared since auditions—Parker hadn't even acknowledged him since then.

"I wouldn't say it's perfect for you, though," Miles spat.

Tonio nearly took a step back in surprise, but I stood behind his legs so he couldn't wobble backward. "Uh, yeah. Maybe not." He pulled his fingers through the long side of his hair, but they got caught in his curls, and he kept his hand there extra long and pretended it was a natural place for his hand to rest. "You're almost right about Kimberlyn."

Their eyes narrowed together with the casual sameness best friends develop. "What?"

"It's not that she can't have fun—she had fun messing with you today. It's that she's so angry." I had to look like a regular Good Dog, so I couldn't cover my face and ears and burrow down into the ground a million feet so I didn't have to hear this. (Based on Tonio's heartbeat, he would have burrowed right down with me. But he was doing his best secret-agent-delivering-classified-intel impression.)

Tonio was diving straight into his plan: Consider the years of knowledge he'd accumulated about everyone from being quiet, observant, and working with his dad at a grocery store frequented by everyone in town—and turn it into a label for the Drama Kings to use. His father got everyone talking—and they always forgot Tonio was listening.

So he knew everything. But that didn't make saying it any easier. "Kimberlyn's mom made her go to an anger management thing after she punched her sister last year."

"She *is* yelling all the time." Miles smirked. "I totally believe that." He clapped a dodgeball between his palms. "I can give her something to really get mad about."

"Coach is already paying attention," Parker warned. "Be cool." He looked back at Tonio. "What do you know about Roel?"

"Roel?" Tonio hesitated. "He's—"

The whistle blew, and it was time for the game to start. Tonio sighed with relief as their attention turned away from him. Miles scouted for the puppy cage Kimberlyn was in, and Parker followed—stopping at the last moment to put his hand on Tonio's shoulder.

"Tell me at lunch," he murmured, then walked away.

A lunch table invitation already?! I felt sick to my stomach but had resolved to be supportive. This was the plan, and there was no use arguing about it with him anymore. *I can't believe it!*

"Yeah." Tonio raised his hand and volunteered to start

as a dog catcher this time so he could see everything easily. Someone threw him a dodgeball. "It . . . worked?"

As Tonio walked away, I saw someone else watching him just as intently as I was—Jason, the boy whose "pants fell off" in that first dodgeball game. Had he been listening?

It doesn't matter, I told myself. Tonio wasn't doing anything *actually* wrong. He wasn't the one bullying anyone. Besides, I was probably just being paranoid.

Miles and Parker put on an amazing performance in the next round, but not in the way I expected. Instead of targeting Kimberlyn directly, they pretended she didn't exist—and because she was invisible to them, they were always getting in her way. Without ever looking directly at her, and while keeping clear focus on the game, they repeatedly trapped her in situations where she was stuck between them or had to go closer to the dog catchers to get around them.

The rhythm of it was honestly impressive, especially since I hadn't seen them discuss anything. Miles picked up Parker's signals so quickly and clearly they might as well have been using Underspeak. Finally, after Kimberlyn had rotated back and forth from dog catcher to puppy a few times, she started to get frustrated.

"Would you *stop*?"

Parker swerved out of the way of the ball and looked

around. "Huh? Oh, are you talking to me?" He looked at Miles, who shrugged performatively. "Stop what?"

Kimberlyn made a frustrated noise in the back of her throat and went back to playing. The Drama Kings stayed out of her way for almost a minute; then they were standing right at the edge of a cage, blocking her way into the safety zone so she got hit in the head with a dodgeball.

"What the *heck*, guys?"

Parker turned to look at her, patting Miles on the back. "Oh, sorry. He just needed a break from running."

"This *isn't funny*."

"Kimberlyn, please. Coach asked us to *calm down*."

"No, he didn't!" Her voice was rising. "He said to *stop targeting specific people*, which you're doing!"

"We're not doing anything. You're just being sensitive."

"Yeah!" Miles said, turning around and jogging back out into the court. "Why are you so angry all the time?"

Kimberlyn's chin lifted, and she took a heavy breath through her nose.

"Maybe you should go to a class for that or something," Parker suggested with a kind, helpful tone. "I hear they can really help people who get mad at nothing, like you're doing."

"Shut. Up."

Parker laughed and moved to follow Miles back into the game, but not before he pulled the beanie out of

Kimberlyn's back pocket and waggled it in front of her. "Toro! Toro!"

A loud *SMACK* reverberated through the gym, followed by a sliding squeak. Parker was on the ground, stunned, blood on his face and the floor where his nose struck it. "I said *SHUT UP!*" Kimberlyn yelled over him as he brought a hand to his face and lifted the blood up to look at it.

Parker might have been too surprised to speak, but Miles wasn't. "COACH DALTON!" he yelled. "KIMBERLYN PUSHED PARKER! HE'S BLEEDING!"

The game ended immediately, of course, and students crowded around as Coach Dalton yelled in all directions and immediately sent Kimberlyn to the principal's office. Tonio walked the opposite direction, against the crowd, and directly to me in the stands.

I wasn't sure what to say—I was overwhelmed by all the crowd noise, and my farsmelled nose made the blood seem like it was everywhere. Tonio sat beside me until the bell finally rang.

That was my fault, he posed with his hands. *All of it.*

If this were normal anxiety, I would have plenty of things to say—everyone made their own choices, Miles and Parker didn't have to act on the information you gave them, you were only a part of it because Dog Court asked you to be . . . Because I asked you to be.

Not just your fault, I finally said. He shrugged.

I already didn't want to do this anymore.

— 11 —

Lunchtime came too fast. Classes were busy, and Tonio was "buzzing"—the feeling he got when his anxiety was crawling around his whole body and it was impossible to feel like any action was the correct one. He described it to Skyler once as a thunderstorm in his mind, but on the outside he came across as antsy and distractible.

You don't have to talk to him right now, I underspoke while we waited in line for chicken nuggets. *We can wait and tell him later, if that's easier.*

I shouldn't stall. But . . . His hands dropped to his sides, trailing off.

Mia and Devon might find out you sat with them. They had a different lunch period, but it could happen.

He nodded. *No sign of Kimberlyn. I wonder if Parker is okay.*

I turned and focused, swiveling my ears to try to cut through the crowd noise as much as possible. The kids at the Drama Kings' table were laughing, and Parker's hands were up and moving as he told a story. "She *literally* did one of those nose breaths like—" His nose still had a bandage on it, so he looked at Miles. Miles drew in a deep breath through a scowl and expelled it out his nose with loud force. "It was like a cartoon! I could see the steam curling around her face."

"*We* were just joking," Miles cut in, "but she really *was* like a bull!"

Well, I underspoke flatly, *he seems fine.*

I'm already this far, I guess. He tugged at the built-in belt on his shorts. *I want to get this over with as fast as possible.*

Tonio had to hold his tray with both hands and couldn't underspeak anymore: The time had come to choose a table. Usually he sat at what I would affectionately call "the quiet table," made up entirely of kids whose friends were mainly in other lunch periods. They were nice to each other but didn't talk much, and Tonio drew or read after eating most days. Roel was at that table.

There was an empty seat next to Parker, though, and really the decision had already been made as soon as Parker willed it; Tonio had to sit there.

"Everyone," Parker said as Tonio forced his feet to walk up closer, "have you met Tonio? He's Hades."

Miles did not look happy at this intrusion and opened his mouth to say something—

"Yeah! Malbrain!" Weston, on the other side of the empty seat, smiled from under his mustache. He was in eighth grade, bigger than anyone else at the table.

He often wore anime T-shirts, played Beamblade, and was Eurystheus in the play. He pulled the chair out for Tonio and scratched behind my ears. "And Combuster, of course." Tonio was horrified to have his Blademaster name brought up right away—Beamblade was not "cool" by Tonio's telling—but I saw Miles close his mouth when Weston spoke. Parker, too, let the names pass without comment.

Interesting, I thought.

"I'm sorry Kim got all violent on you," a sixth grader named Piper, who was Megara in the play, said to Parker, resuming their previous conversation. "But what you said about her going to anger management totally makes sense. I took photos of the tennis tournament last weekend for the yearbook, and look at this." She held up the back of her camera for everyone to see the image on it. Kimberlyn's mouth was open wide as she hit a ball with the racket—it looked like she was roaring. "She yelled every time she hit the ball. I thought it was so weird."

That sounded like a perfectly normal sports thing to me. Also, who *didn't* lose composure at the sight of a bouncing tennis ball? But the other kids bought in immediately and laughed.

"Can you send that to me?" Miles asked.

"I'll put it in the cast text. Oh, Tonio—" Piper looked at him. "What's your number?"

"I don't have a phone," Tonio said. "But I use my dad's phone sometimes, if that—"

"What?" Parker laughed. "Do you think we want to text your dad?"

"No, of course not." Tonio turned red. "Sorry." And immediately dropped into *guess I'll die* mode and shrank down in his chair.

You got this, I posed. (Normally I would lay down next to his chair, but the cafeteria floors were awful during lunch.) *Remember the attitude that got you through auditions. Can I have a chicken nugget?*

"What are you signaling to your dog?" another eighth grader named Autumn asked.

"Oh!" Tonio refocused on the table. "Just . . . normal stuff."

Parker grinned. "Is he worried about the tests next week?"

Tonio latched onto the joke gratefully. "Yes," he answered, "but he's studied enough that I know there's nothing to worry about."

I wagged my tail as Weston patted my head again. "I wouldn't be surprised! Did you guys know Tonio taught his dog to play Beamblade?"

"A card game?" Miles rolled his eyes. "That's impossible."

"Spoken like an arrogant human," Autumn sighed, and Miles looked alarmed that she'd sided against him—just for a moment. I think I was the only one who noticed. "To think animals need your permission to be smart. My cat watches *Jeopardy!*"

Tonio gave me a look. I tilted my head. *It's possible.*

"He's really good at it!" Tonio admitted. "Sometimes it feels like he's teaching me."

Autumn nodded. "I'm always saying that."

"Okay, but what about dance-pad games, like DDR?" Piper said. "We should try it!"

"Maybe!" Tonio smiled. "We could have a cast party or something. And we could have it at your house." He gestured to Parker. "So the director could be there, too!" *Nice,* I thought.

"No dogs allowed at my house," Parker grumbled, sounding aggravated. "Oscar's allergic."

"Oscar's his new dad," Autumn explained, "and he's the devil."

"He's not my dad." Parker glared at Autumn, who smiled back innocently. Piper laughed.

The conversation switched to other drama things, leaving Tonio to sit quietly with his nuggets. It was only when the older kids had left that Parker looked at Tonio and asked, "What were you going to tell me earlier? Something about Roel?"

"Oh, just . . ." Tonio's heart rate spiked immediately. Did he really want to do this again? After what happened to Kimberlyn? I wanted to say he didn't have to, but I'd already tried that. And here we were, a whole lunch period later, still sitting at the table. We knew it was coming. "Have you played *Land of Yggdrasil: Untimely Fates*?"

They stared at him blankly. "What?"

He blushed under their stares. "It's an app game."

"I've got it pulled up." Piper held up her phone to the store page of a game with lots of smiling cartoon men and women with swords and staves. "It's one of those anime games."

"Why?"

"Roel plays it. Well . . ." Tonio gave a pained look. "*Played* it. He had to stop . . . when he accidentally spent two thousand dollars of his parents' money on in-app purchases."

"WHAT?!" Parker said, at the same time Miles said, "No way."

"It's true!" Tonio continued, glad in the moment to get the response he was looking for. "I know because my dad—" And he froze. He hadn't wanted to say this, I don't think, but now he was already halfway there. ". . . had to give their mom groceries on credit for a while. Until they got it figured out."

"How do you spend *two thousand dollars* on *accident*?" Parker asked.

"I don't know," Tonio answered honestly.

"If I'd done that," Piper said, "I'd have met an *Untimely Fate*, that's for sure."

"Will you send me a link to that game?" Parker asked.

"Me too!" Miles added. Piper nodded and tapped on her phone. I didn't want to think about what they were planning to do with *that*.

The bell rang, and everyone got up. Parker touched Tonio's shoulder to get his attention and asked, "Do you know something like that for *everyone*?"

"Yeah." Tonio stared right into Parker's eyes and smiled, just a little bit. The fur on my back rose with a chill. "Everybody."

"C'mon, Parker!" Miles called. "Let's go!"

Parker held Tonio's gaze for another moment, clearly surprised at his response. Eventually, he lifted his hand in a little wave. "See ya."

"See you." Tonio let out a little breath as Parker left. When we were completely in the clear, he whispered to me, "We have to figure out the allergy thing with his stepdad. But we're almost there. I can feel it."

Tonio was right. We *were* close to our goal. But he didn't know yet what it would cost to get there.

— 12 —

Mia rallied everyone to her place to try her streaming plan for Beamblade Dog League, and the three of them rushed to the Lin shelter to maximize their time while the light was good.

"I only ever get one or two viewers at a time, but those are good practice numbers." Devon attached a webcam to a tripod he'd brought, and Mia gave him a stool to put his laptop on. Extension cords connected everything to the side of Mia's house. Shelter dogs crowded around to watch, but carefully kept themselves busy so it would seem like a coincidence. Only Mozart, who was always at Mia's side, was up close. He patted his Beamblade deck on his side of the cardboard playmat we'd use for the video.

Mia stood back with Tonio while Devon fiddled with the computer. "Did you hear Kim got in-school suspension? They're saying she might not get to play tennis anymore, because she got in trouble. Parker and Miles are such jerks."

"Yeah," Tonio said.

Mia looked at him curiously. "Then why'd you sit with them at lunch?"

"I— It's just that—"

"What's going on, Tonio?"

"Nothing! I'm just—"

"Lying to me."

"What?!"

"Okay, whatever." Mia crossed her arms and took a step away.

"Wait!" Tonio yelled. Devon looked over at them, but Mia waved a hand to say it wasn't a big deal. "Have you ever . . . had a secret?" *Careful, Tonio.* "A big one. That you had to keep for . . . someone else." He glanced at me, but Mia didn't notice. I pushed against his leg. "And really, you think that if you *said something,* things would be better, but they asked you not to—and it's important, so—"

Mia's face pressed into an expression I couldn't quite understand. "Yeah," she said flatly, with a glance back to make sure Devon was okay on the laptop. "I have."

"Please don't say anything to him," Tonio whispered. "I don't want him to worry about me, and maybe if they like us, they'll—"

"I don't want those guys to like me," Mia interrupted. "And fine, I won't say anything. But *you* should." She sounded just like Tonio talking to the judge. I couldn't help but think she was just as right—but we couldn't.

"I'm sorry," Tonio mumbled.

"Camera's working!" Devon cheered. "Test, test, test—mic's working! Who's playing?"

"Mozart and Buster," Mia answered, and walked over to the playmat. Tonio breathed hard, fists clenched at his sides, but he wasn't running away—and he wasn't having a panic attack. *At least there's that,* I thought. He could rest while Mozart and I played Beamblade.

Whoa, Mozart underspoke over the board. *She usually only talks like that when I steal burgers off the counter.*

You really shouldn't steal human food, I warned. He flopped some cards off the deck and nudged them over while Devon stepped in front of the camera, explained what Beamblade was, and sang the praises of Antonio Pulaski, genius dog trainer. *They'll kick you out of the house.*

Me? Never! Mozart gave me some sweet puppy-dog eyes over his long nose, fluff framing his face perfectly. He really had gone straight from adorable puppy to beautiful dog—it wasn't fair. I would say he looked noble and elegant if he wasn't such a brat. Collies could get away with anything. *They love me too much.* He reached over the playmat to push his paw on my nose. *You better do a good job, old man! Mia's counting on us!*

When Devon finished his intro, I realized we probably shouldn't underspeak on camera. Tonio stood in the frame and pretended to "train" us by passing treats our way every once in a while. Occasionally, Mia would chime in with the shelter's website and information on how to adopt a dog from Bellville—all certified "Beamblade Ready!"

By the end of the game (which I won) I was feeling better. The trio transitioned into a much sillier hangout, and once they shut down the stream (which got a whopping one view), they helped Mia with chores around The Farm and had a normal, fun hangout. Like old times.

Still, I could see a strain between Mia and Tonio. I kept it to myself—rehearsals were about to start, so it would be a while before things went back to normal. We could make it, though. I believed that.

And then the next day, the Drama Kings pushed it too far.

"Thank you *so much* for your time, everyone." Parker smiled sincerely and warmly from the front of the chorus room, just two minutes before the bell rang. His voice was dripping with *so much* compassion. Too much. "I want to make sure everyone knows about our new fundraising project today. As you know, Bellville is a small town and *nobody* here is rich. But some of us need a little more help than others."

He held out a hand to Miles, who spun around a coffee can with a picture of Roel's face on it. Every muscle in Tonio's body tensed up—I placed a paw on his lap, ears flattened back nervously.

"Families *in your community*, like Roel Lozada's, don't have enough money for five-star warriors in games like *Land of Yggdrasil: Untimely Fates*." Parker bowed his head sadly and held up an image of a cartoon girl with cat ears and a pirate costume dual-wielding daggers. "Heroes like Calico Jill don't come cheap, especially in today's world, where it can sometimes take hundreds of summons before you find exactly the one you want."

Kids were already giggling, confused—where was Mrs. Campbell, the chorus teacher? Why wasn't she stopping this? Tonio and I looked, simultaneously, up at Roel, who was frozen at the top of the risers with sheet music clenched in both hands.

"Poor Roel Lozada . . . last time, and this is true, he spent *two thousand dollars* and the best hero he summoned was . . ." Parker flipped the picture he was holding for another one, a very buff robot with a question mark for a face. "Allen Luminum. Still five stars, but you can see"—he held Calico Jill up next to the robot—"he simply doesn't compare."

The bell rang, signaling the start of class. *Where is Mrs. Campbell???* Tonio and I underspoke simultaneously.

Parker kept going. "So this time, we're hoping to raise *ten thousand dollars* for Roel and his family, to *make sure* he rolls Calico Jill and can compete in the high-level raids and endgame content." Parker waved to Miles, who began walking down the risers and holding the can out for donations. A few kids plunked in some quarters between giggles. "Every little bit helps. Thank you, folks."

Roel finally stood when Miles started to make his way up the risers. "Please, you have to—"

"Sorry for the wait, class!" Mrs. Campbell flowed into the room, all folded cloth and long jewelry. She made a pushing motion with both hands for Miles and Parker to get to their seats and found her spot beside the piano. "I trust you already grabbed your sheets from the table. I'm seeing lots of sheets, good. Last chance if you haven't— Mr. Garrison will be here in a moment to begin. There he is. Warm-ups first, can I get a C?"

I didn't have to sing, so I was able to look around. Roel was staring directly at Miles and Parker, who were pretending to be focused on warming up—mischievous smiles kept creeping onto their faces between the notes, though, so I knew they were gloating in their heads. How many times had they done that bit today? How many people had they told? I'm sure Roel was thinking all that and more.

Tonio wasn't singing. I nudged him, and he snapped back into the moment and jumped in before Mrs. Campbell noticed. (She was *very* serious about participation and didn't allow any downtime in her class. The Drama Kings were smart to give Roel no chance to respond.)

I heard a small hiccup in someone's voice—tiny, barely audible even to my ears—so I looked back up at Roel. He was back in the top row, standing behind everyone, and he was singing—but he was crying, and trying to get a sleeve up to wipe his eyes before anyone noticed.

By the time their warm-ups ended, his face was damp but his expression was set—back to the strength I saw in the boy who'd pushed back against Miles and Parker during the Dog Catcher game. "Mrs. Campbell." He raised his hand. "Can I say something?"

"If you must."

"I *did* get Calico Jill," he croaked, and tears misted up in his eyes again immediately. "So you—I don't—" And then he was crying too hard to finish the sentence. "I—"

The class was dead silent and staring at him. Mrs. Campbell cut in immediately. "Well, I don't know what that means, but you look like you need to use the restroom. Is that true?"

He nodded.

"Well then, the pass is hanging by the door. The rest of you, 'Afternoon on a Hill.' Five, six, seven, eight—" Mr. Garrison started playing a sweet, quiet song, and the class sang while Roel fled the room, barely stopping to grab the hall pass. From the front row, Parker looked back at Tonio just for a second—the tiniest *we did it* smile on his face. He winked, and Tonio just stared down his nose, singing, trying to keep his breath under control enough to hold the notes.

And I saw it there, in Tonio's eyes—the emptiness. The scary expression that looked like he wasn't feeling anything. *I did this*, he was thinking. Or maybe I was thinking that and just projecting it onto him. Because wasn't *I* doing this? Wasn't I hurting all of these kids? But this was for dogs, right? This was all to prove dogs could speak up and—

—and make the world better for everyone. Especially their humans. I had a hard time seeing how this mission was doing that, but ... what was I going to do at this point? We were already in. If we gave up now, Kimberlyn would have gotten in trouble for nothing. Roel's secret would have been revealed for nothing. We had to make it worth it, and we were *so close*! And besides, it was our job. It was the condition we accepted to get to be real friends. We had no choice.

Unless Dog Court let us off the hook. *Might as well try*, I thought.

That night, I used an early version of this document to send my report, alongside a request for a meeting. I pointed out all my fears about the long-term impacts on

Tonio's life and emphasized how much was still standing in our way. Oscar Sykes's "dog allergy" meant he would *never* let Parker invite both of us over, and if he didn't even want Tonio at rehearsal, he couldn't possibly want him at his house. Every step closer to our goal seemed to push Tonio further away from the happiness he'd been finding since I told him the truth. There had to be an easier way.

I sent all that to Judge Sweetie's email and shut my laptop. I had gone alone to Tonio's room while his family ate dinner, and I realized it was the first time I'd been by myself in weeks. It was a weird feeling. I opened my laptop back up and tried to message Jpeg for the hundredth time.

WELCOME TO THE DOGHOUSE V.4.1:
THE FUTURE IS WRITTEN IN PAWPRINT
CREATING PRIVATE ROOM ... INVITING
SELECTED FRIENDS ... DONE! ROOM
CREATED. USERS IN ROOM: FireBuster
INVITATIONS WAITING: dotpng

FireBuster: Jpeg, are you there?

FireBuster: Somewhere?

FireBuster: ...

FireBuster: This isn't funny if it's a joke, you know.

FireBuster: Everybody misses you.

FireBuster: I know you're probably just working on hacking their fridge.

FireBuster: Like you said.

FireBuster has gone idle.

FireBuster has returned.

FireBuster: Okay.

FireBuster: Maybe next time.

ROOM CLOSED
YOU'RE OUT OF THE DOGHOUSE!

— 13 —

I awoke in the middle of the night to a strange and familiar smell: nothing. The smell of a ghost—a dog without a history. I couldn't say why I woke up—there was no noise or movement, but when I lifted my head, there she was. *Shadow.* She was perched impossibly on the second-floor windowsill, balancing on a single inch of space without the slightest suggestion of stress or discomfort in her posture.

Tonio rolled over when I stepped off the foot of the bed and made my way to the window. Up on my hind legs, I could nudge the bottom up a few inches, and she flattened to slide herself beneath it and slink through, her body opening the window only just as much as she needed to fold inside.

She watched me, motionless, for several seconds. I decided she was waiting for me to say something. So I started with, *Are you—*

We have a mission. Shadow underspoke like a dog without an opinion—no specified emotion with her tail or ears. Information only. I nodded and turned to nudge

Tonio awake, but she was in front of me in a flash, teeth bared. *Not the human*, she posed. *Only you.*

I don't know if you've met her yet, Lasagna, but Shadow is not someone who gives the impression she's interested in being argued with. And while I wasn't clear on our relative positions in The Farm, it seemed like she was probably in charge of me? So I listened and left Tonio in bed to follow Shadow.

She launched herself out the window and descended the building like a mountain goat, silently jumping from sill to sill. I *absolutely* could not do that, so I made my way out of Tonio's house the normal way: by using the front door, which had an easy pull-down knob.

On the street, a few minutes later, Shadow tilted her nose up in disgust. *You are too dependent on them.*

Because I use doors and stairs?

These are things the humans created to slow themselves down and to trap us. They do not deserve our respect. She began walking out of Bellville Square, so I followed. *Your collar is too loud.*

The jingle of my name tag was something I'd tuned out ages ago, but before I could argue, Shadow had clamped it in her jaws and unhooked the clasp in a quick jerk. The collar landed in a flower planter outside of Tomorrow Grocery. I glared at Shadow, startled, but she kept moving ahead like nothing had happened.

We have a long way to go. Her muscles tensed under

her fur, shining black like a phone screen in the street-lights. *Prepare yourself.*

Of course I was going to ask, *Prepare myself for what?* but she leaped forward in a burst, legs hitting the pavement rapidly as she ran away. I was only a second behind her, but it felt like I'd lost a mile in that time. Shadow shot from street to street, taking tight corners no problem and nearly losing me at every turn.

Bellville isn't huge, and I realized as we left the relatively tight neighborhoods for the wider, wilder outskirts that we were headed straight for the highway.

"Where are you taking me?!" I barked ahead, into the wind. "What's the mission?"

She didn't answer, and she was running farther and farther away. My heart thumped in my chest and I was running out of breath—I could feel myself tilting side to side as my legs barely missed tripping over each other. Shadow's posture was no different from when we'd started, and her speed was just as good. I fell farther behind. I felt a thrill when I realized this was the first time I had run—really run, like a true dog—in months. Maybe in years. No leash slowing me down, no human to worry about, nothing. Just the thrill of the chase. It felt good.

The highway came into view, and she dove into the trees alongside it. I lost sight of her immediately but kept running in the direction she'd entered—my feet crunched on fallen branches, and I tried to jump over bushes to avoid getting scratched as much as possible. *Where did she go? Where am I going?*

For the first time, I wondered if this was some kind of trap. Shadow didn't like me—that was obvious—and I'm sure she wasn't the only one connected to Dog Court who was upset with my sentence. And I'd jumped into it without even considering—what was I thinking? Tonio would be so worried if I—

Shadow appeared, suddenly, in front of me. "You're slow."

"You're," I panted, "fast!" I would never make fun of Tonio's running again. *Am I slow for a dog?* I wondered. It had been so long since I'd spent an extended time with any other dogs—and I wasn't in a racing league.

She considered this and nodded. "This way." And she took off in another direction, slower, but with a posture that felt like she was showing off how easy it was. I don't know how long we ran for—longer than I'd ever run before, that's for sure—but eventually she led me out of the trees and dropped to the ground, nose pointed toward a small house hidden off a dirt road.

Have you been here before? she asked.

I posed, *No*, and she seemed to consider what to say.

Be on your toes, she said finally. *They can smell weakness from a mile away.* And then she was moving again, keeping to the darkness at the edge of the trees and circling closer to the building. The single-story old house had a big van out front, and no lights in the windows I could see. A pile of junk was off to one side, mostly bent metal and broken plastic. The back door had a small flap built into the bottom for dogs, but no fence in the yard.

I raised my nose to the air and sniffed—I didn't sense any humans. Not recently, anyway. Lots of different dog smells, though.

Stay quiet. She posed as she crawled forward in the tall grass, unkept around the home. *I don't want them to know we're here.*

At this point, I was tired of almost-asking questions, and if this was a trap, I was probably already in it, so I stayed quiet and moved forward with her, trying not to pant too loud as my body recovered from the run. When we reached the doggy door, Shadow tilted her paw to show she was going to count down in swipes and waited for my nod.

Three, two, one—GO!

She dove inside, and I followed after her, ready for whatever was coming with all these dog smells around. Were we getting into a fight? Was I about to get put in a cage? Whatever it was I was leaning on my hind legs, growling and ready to pounce—

A hanging light bulb flickered on in the darkness, and several dozen giant eyes blinked at me in confusion.

"SHADOW'S BACK!!!" a voice squeaked from behind me. I turned around and saw a puppy standing on a washing machine, paw pressed against the light switch. Immediately, the room full of eyes burst to life, and a wave of little furry children was crashing into me in their rush to get to Shadow, who was very smoothly dodging their leaps.

"Who's he?" a puppy with one eye asked. "He smells bad."

"Like *humans*!" another puppy, who was missing clumps of fur along her flank, giggled. "A lot of them."

"Yes. The smell goes deeper than you know." *What's that supposed to mean?* I thought. Shadow continued dodging their leaps until the puppies eventually calmed down. Without words, Shadow began a bedtime ritual, and I followed: We portioned out dry food, I negotiated scuffles over who slept in which dog bed, and finally they started to fall asleep. On each puppy I saw a different injury: hurt legs, snotty noses, a wobbly walk.

"Who are these puppies?" I whispered. "Why am I here?"

Shadow had already disappeared. Confident the puppies were asleep, I went out the back door to look for her. Up closer, I saw what all the junk there was— smashed dog crates, ripped carriers, and torn leashes. Bars, plastic, and cloth all mixed together in an intimidating mess.

"We saved them from a man who was keeping them

captive." Shadow had climbed to the top of the roof, looking down at me. Then she leaped off the roof— for just a moment, she stretched perfectly in front of the full moon. I stepped aside quickly, and she landed exactly where I'd been standing, feet perfectly filling my paw grooves in the dirt. "We've almost completely eliminated such places, but some new human always thinks selling our children by the crateful is an easy way to make money."

She tilted her head to watch me with one eye. "Humans don't truly care for us, even when they think we are helpless." Shadow wove through the pile of garbage, and her quiet voice forced me to follow her. "And that's when we *aren't* something they think they can 'war' against."

"If we were honest about who we were— Ow!" I almost stepped on the sharp, broken bar of a dog crate. "We could *make* them stop."

"I already make them stop. And then I show the puppies how to destroy the boxes that trapped them." Shadow, in a sudden motion, kicked the door of a kennel. It slammed shut and cued a small avalanche of garbage. "You were a stray, too, but we found you first. Your parents made sure of that."

"My parents?!" I barked, startled. I'd never met them—barely even thought about them, honestly. Why was she bringing them up? "You knew them?"

"Yes." She turned back to me as the last pieces of the junk avalanche clanked and crunched around us. "And they would be ashamed of your request tonight."

My . . . request? Oh. "The report I sent Judge Sweetie?"

"You are concerned these human children are having a few bad days, and so you would give up entirely on your own kind."

"That's not fair!" I argued. "We don't even know what the DNI is planning. Oscar Sykes has been here for almost *two years* and hasn't made a move against us. Why the—"

"You are wrong." She bit down on a manila folder from the pile of junk, and threw it at my feet. *Had that always been there? How much of our conversation had she planned?* "And worse, you aren't paying attention."

In the folder were two big printed-out pictures of human men. On one side was Agent Oscar Sykes, the target of our mission. On the other was—

The man who adopted Jpeg? With the sunglasses, and the camera, and the fidgety fingers. Why was he—

Oh.

Oh.

The same haircut, the same hands, the same skin tone. These were the same person, hiding behind a different style and a pair of sunglasses. I'd only seen this man the once, and I'd only met Oscar Sykes once as well, so I hadn't noticed. But if that was true, then . . .

"They have Jpeg," I realized. "The Department of Nonhuman Intelligence. They caught her."

"Apparently, she was careless hacking government databases. They figured her out."

"That's impossible. She's the best!"

"I wish we had realized before she was adopted, but I was out of town on a mission when he made his move. Because of this, I believe there's a chance I've been compromised as well." *Which is why they need us.* Shadow shut the folder and watched my expression carefully.

"Why didn't you tell us about this?!" I asked. "We have to save her! We have to find her! The Lins have paperwork—the place in Myrtle Beach she was adopted to—"

"Doesn't exist. That entire family doesn't exist."

"Have you been there, though? Have you searched it? We need to *go*—"

"Agents are still there, looking. They have been since before you were brought onto the mission. No sign of her."

"Then we need to break into that house now! Why did we waste time here when we could have—"

Shadow growled to snap me into focus. "We cannot solve this problem by creating a bigger one. You and Tonio are still our best chance to save Jpeg without causing an incident. I don't like it, either, but that's the situation."

I let out a whine and couldn't stand still. My paws padded the dirt under my feet. "Why didn't you tell us? We should—we would have—"

Shadow continued. "That human of yours is fragile. Even in your report, you admit the stress of this situation is pushing him to his limits. The Judge and I are confident he will jeopardize the mission if pushed too far—and this would push him too far."

She has a point, I thought. Tonio's anxiety was bad enough without added pressure. He already believed the fate of dogkind depends on him, but if he knew Jpeg's *life* did, too, there was no telling how he'd take it.

"I am telling you this to show you the urgency," Shadow said, "with the understanding you *will not jeopardize the mission.*"

"I understand." I looked up at the stars rather than looking Shadow in the face. She wasn't moving to express anything, but I could tell she felt satisfied.

"We'll finish the mission," I promised. "We'll bring her home."

— 14 —

Director Feldman welcomed everybody to the first rehearsal in the same room we did auditions in—long mirrors on two walls, slightly squishy floors, foldable chairs lining one wall and a piano in the corner with a wireless speaker set on top of it.

A quick look around confirmed that every kid who'd auditioned was still here. They didn't all have leads like Tonio, but the show had a lot of crowd scenes and minor parts for everyone else. Lines had already been drawn, though—the leads identified each other and made a celebratory group on one side of the room.

"I worried it would be *dreadfully* boring for some of you if our first rehearsal was a line readthrough," Mrs. Feldman began, "so I decided to start with the scene of the show everyone participates in: the musical number 'Five, Six, Seven, Eight'—a montage of Heracles's labors with the Augean stables, Stymphalian birds, Cretan bull, and mares of Diomedes. If your role says 'lead' cattle, bird, or mare you're up front—and Charlotte, of course you're the bull—but everyone other than Heracles will play an animal in the group." She turned to the speaker and set her phone next to it on the piano. "Think of this scene as more of a dance—but a comedy! A funny story told through choreography." She clicked a button on the wireless speaker.

"Pairing complete!" Tonio's backpack said as the speaker chirped. He dove for it immediately.

"Sorry! My fault!" His voice was doubled through the speaker—the *Sun Squadron* badge was acting like a microphone, sending the audio straight to it. He flicked a switch on the back to turn it off. "My dad got these from a weird knockoff website. It's an aggressive pairer."

Mrs. Feldman waved it off, *not a problem*, and connected it with her phone this time. She played a long, peppy song and talked over it, explaining roughly how the choreography would go: Heracles would stay primarily in the same place while the entire cast moved chaotically around him, showing Heracles's struggle and success through different labors. First, with the stables, was a cowboy line dance. Next was kind of a disco thing, where the metal Stymphalian birds were reflecting lights around and giving the stage a dance hall atmosphere. The Cretan bull labor was a tango, and the mares of Diomedes brought the cowboy theme back while combining all the styles into a big jumble of dancing animals.

Tonio was a bird, along with Miles. Parker stood

beside them while Mrs. Feldman taught the other animals their steps. "In the real story, the horses eat people," Parker said, smirking at Tonio and patting his shoulder with one hand. "So do the birds."

"Oh," Tonio said, as if he didn't know that already. Then he added, "There's also a lot more poop in the stable story."

Parker laughed and shook his head in mock sadness. "Censorship! They'd never tell us that in a story for kids." He was about to say something else when the door to the rehearsal room swung open.

"Parker!" a man's voice barked. "Get away from there!" Country line dance music continued to play in the background as Agent Sykes threw a bag of SizzlePop fried chicken down on the floor and flipped his hand up in a beckoning motion. "Outside. *Now.*"

The entire room knew the sound of a kid in trouble, and the energy changed immediately. Parker looked at his mother, who looked back but didn't say anything to contradict his stepdad. Parker was bristling—his teeth would be bared, if he were a dog—and when he saw Sykes had already turned around to walk outside, he suddenly knelt down and petted me all over, pressing his forehead into mine. "Good boy!" he said loudly. "Good boy, Buster!"

I barely registered it. I felt an anger—and a fear— unlike anything I'd felt before. This was the man who'd kidnapped my friend. He was siding with the humans who were everything Dog Court feared—everything *dogs* had to fear.

"Parker—"

"I'm *going*," he snapped, interrupting his mother. He dropped his hands and stomped out the door. She immediately tried to get the room back on task by playing the song and yelling directions.

I didn't even have to say anything. *Be careful*, Tonio underspoke. He quietly unhooked my leash. *Don't let him see you.* I bobbed my head in agreement and dashed behind the dancing crowd to the door—slipping through just before it closed.

They were headed through the hallways, past the large wall of windows and out the door Tonio and I had entered for our meeting with Judge Sweetie.

Sykes didn't wait for his stepson to catch up, and Parker wasn't rushing to his side, so there was a long distance between the three of us as we moved down the hallway. "We can just talk in here!" Parker suggested. The agent ignored him and swung open the door to the square. Parker grumbled and followed, stomps louder with every step.

There was no way to follow them outside completely without being seen, but they looped around the building in front of the windows. I hid behind a potted plant on this side of the wall and watched them face each other down on the sidewalk.

Oscar was almost two feet taller than Parker and stood up straight to take full advantage of that. "Do you know why I asked you out here?"

"You should step back," Parker answered. "I'm covered in dog fur."

"So you do."

"Head to toe. You'll never believe the places it gets."

The man sighed. "You're being obnoxious."

"I've tried to keep it off of me, but even being in the same *room* as a dog apparently means you get completely coated in—"

"Parker," Agent Sykes interrupted, shaking his head. "Does talking this much make you feel charming, or do you just believe it fools other people into thinking so?"

Parker didn't answer. I was stunned—I had never heard an adult talk to a kid this way.

"Your mother told me all about the tantrum you threatened to throw if she didn't cast that boy—*this morning*. After she'd announced it to everyone else." Oscar crossed his arms and stared his stepson down. "I don't appreciate how the two of you are treating me. It's clear you don't care about my safety."

"You're right. I'm sorry." Parker held his arms out wide. "Hug it out?"

It took a moment for that to process. Agent Sykes's face hardened. "I see. You're grounded."

"What?!"

"For two weeks. Not only are you disrespecting me, but you have made a threat against my life." Oscar made the pained face of a man who was deeply hurt. He mumbled as if he was talking to himself, but it was definitely loud enough for Parker to hear. "I knew it would be a struggle to get along with you—your mother warned me—but I didn't think you would be *this* committed to being horrible."

Parker stared down at the sidewalk. "I'm sorry. I was just jok—"

"Be quiet. I don't have time for fake apologies." Oscar's voice rose for just a moment; then he brought it back down to the same chilly tone. "I came here to bring you dinner. To try to be *nice*! I should have known better."

Agent Sykes *sounded* sincere, but . . . I didn't believe it. Mrs. Feldman told him about Tonio being cast this morning, and then he came to rehearsal and got mad when he saw Parker next to Tonio. Parker had rubbed all over me *after* that. I think he came to rehearsal *so that* he could get mad at Parker.

"Clearly," he continued, "we need to work on your attitude. Two weeks. And if you speak to me without being spoken to, I will add a week." I could tell Oscar was working hard to stay quiet—trying not to make a scene on the public street. Parker's face was bright red—it was the most like Tonio I'd ever seen him look. "And that *boy* is not your friend. Stay away from him and that dog."

Agent Sykes walked away. Parker couldn't hold his tongue. "So no hug?"

Silently, Oscar held up three fingers. *Three weeks.* I wanted to whine, frustrated. The longer Parker was grounded, the longer we'd have to wait before we could get into his house—and the longer until we could save Jpeg.

Parker watched his stepfather climb in his car and drive away. He yelled a word Tonio was not allowed to say and turned to kick at a bush in front of the mirrors, snapping a twig. I flattened myself completely below the plant until I heard him stomp back around the edge of the building, then ran to the rehearsal room. Tonio, watching from the little window in the door, gently pushed it open and let me inside.

A minute later, Parker followed behind. He pulled open the paper bag Agent Sykes left and gasped in fake surprise. "SizzlePop! My *favorite!*" He walked over while the Mares clomped around and set a box down for his mom. Tonio and the other leads were hovering near the front, too, sitting and looking at their scripts. Parker made straight for them and sat down in the middle, holding out the bag.

"Who's hungry? Tonio, you like fried chicken?"

He didn't say a word about being grounded. I guess he'd already decided how he felt about his stepfather's words.

— 15 —

Parker didn't listen to his stepdad at all. From that point forward, I would even say befriending Parker was *fun*. I was worried about Jpeg, but it felt good to throw myself into a project that I knew was going to help us find her instead of wallowing in fear. And Parker made it so *easy* to like him, now that he'd decided to like Tonio; separated from school and in his natural environment—play rehearsal—I started to see why he was able to hold the attention of older kids, and keep control of the sixth-grade class.

He moved like someone who always knew he was in the right place—not fast, not slow, not worried. Parker seemed to believe everything he did *mattered*, and it made his opinion contagious. When he turned his attention toward someone, it made them feel special—because *he* mattered, if he was listening to you, *you* must matter, too.

"What does your dad do?" Tonio asked once, at lunch. Parker laughed.

"Imagine a cop, but *way* more boring. And—"

"He's not my dad," Piper said.

"He's not my dad," Coop said.

"He's not my dad," Autumn said.

"He's not my dad," Weston said.

"He's not my dad," Miles said.

"He's not my dad," Tonio said, all simultaneously.

Parker grinned. "Right, exactly." He took a bite of some Salisbury steak. "I don't really care what he actually does. He used to be in the military, but now he works for the IRS. Like, with taxes."

Tonio nodded agreeably. "That *is* boring."

"Right! But he acts like the most important guy on earth. *'My work is critical to the fate of our country.'* It's like, it's taxes. You know?"

Miles asked, "Are you going to be grounded for the Fall Festival?"

Parker looked confident when he answered, "I don't expect this to last more than a few days. I'll get out on good behavior."

"Maybe we could come see you?" Tonio offered. "When he's not around?"

"He set up his paranoia cams all over the house. He'd know right away I had friends over."

Ugh. I covered my eyes with my paws. *This* was the most frustrating part of our job. Now that Parker was grounded, we were making no progress at all.

What are we supposed to do? I complained later as Tonio got dressed for rehearsal in his room. *He's only hanging*

out with us to make his dad mad, but his dad being mad means we can't go to his house!

"Just talking about us got him in trouble," Tonio agreed, adjusting things on his desk. "Inviting us over seems impossible."

Inviting us over! I realized. *But what about just you? He thinks you're just a regular kid.*

Agent Sykes *did* take a picture of Tonio during Dog League, but Tonio didn't know about that, and it didn't necessarily mean anything—Oscar had given me strange looks, but not Tonio.

He nodded, but didn't look very enthusiastic. "That's definitely more possible."

But . . . he's grounded.

"I'm stuck in the play until then, anyway." He rolled pens on his desk with the palm of his hand, head pressed down a few inches away. "There's not really a rush."

There *was* a rush: saving Jpeg. But I couldn't tell him about it. I watched him push at his pens and realized he hadn't been drawing for a while. Had he made anything at all since his manticore got crushed? Not that I remembered. As I watched him stare down into the wood of his desk, I realized there was a question I hadn't asked in a while: *Are you okay, Tonio? How are you feeling?*

He sat there for a long moment like he was deciding whether to respond. I didn't want to rush him, and it wasn't like I had anywhere to be. We sat in silence.

When the first minute dragged into two, I walked over and nudged his hand with my nose. He patted the top of my head lightly and finally said:

"Do you think Kimberlyn and Roel would understand? If they knew what was really going on?"

I hadn't really thought about it. But I could tell Tonio had—the words came out hard and clear, like he'd said them over and over in his mind. And I knew his anxiety pretty well by now—he'd probably stayed at the question, never digging much deeper. Letting his mind keep asking the question, over and over, so he didn't have to think about the answer. Doing that . . . well, it let him believe the *best* might be true, but it also let him keep believing the *worst*, too.

Yes, I underspoke. *I think so.*

His eyes snapped to mine suddenly. "Then can I tell them?" He was serious—there was a desperate, tired look in his face. "If they knew about the mission, they would know that I didn't *want* to tell their secrets. None of this is their fault! But Kimberlyn got suspended. Roel got humiliated. If they knew *why*, maybe that would make it okay. They would know I wasn't trying to hurt anybody, and then—" He paused. "And then, uh . . ."

Dog Court would step in. I tried to look apologetic. *Even if they believed you, they'd be monitored for the rest of their lives. They'd be forced to keep the secret, and scared of DNI, and none of that would be their fault, either.*

"Not if everyone knew."

I bobbed my head in agreement. *We're working on it, right? But we can't change the world in a big way like that without help, and especially not with Dog Court trying to stop us. We need to convince them.*

Tonio's eyes returned, defeated, to his desk. "And until then, we keep hurting people."

I winced. Of course, I understood where Tonio was coming from. I basically thought he was right! But he didn't know Jpeg was captured. And he already looked so stressed—I couldn't add more to his plate.

Dr. Jake would probably keep asking questions. Try to help him get to the root of his concern or pick a new course of action he was comfortable with. If he knew the whole story, he'd probably agree with Tonio about being honest with Kimberlyn and Roel. It was the right thing to do if the situation was easy. But it *wasn't* easy, and being a secret agent wasn't ever going to be.

I couldn't fix everything right now. I just needed Tonio to feel better long enough to get the job done. We could worry about the rest later.

You feel guilty. I get that. I typed on the tablet so he wouldn't have to worry about translating. *But you're doing this for Dogs—which already makes you a hero to my whole species!*

"I don't feel like a hero." Tonio shrugged. "I feel like a bad guy."

You're not! I insisted. *But you're focusing on the hard stuff, and not thinking about the* possibilities.

He gave me a dubious look. "Like what?"

When you were talking to Mia, you said befriending them could protect your group. Maybe that's still true.

I scooped all *my* guilt into a little baggy and threw it into a trash can on the side of the park trail of my mind. There was no use worrying about whether my advice was *good*, only that it did the job. *That's my responsibility now*, I thought.

Tonio tilted his head thoughtfully. "You're saying I should stand up to them?"

Not exactly. But . . . Maybe a little? You're part of the show, and part of their group. As long as you're careful to stay friends, they might be nicer around you.

"I'm no good at talking when I'm nervous." He picked up a pen and tapped it against his fingernails—but I saw some light come back to his eyes. He was considering it. "And I get so scared every time Parker's in the same room as my friends."

Think of it as rehearsal! I suggested. *Hades wouldn't let anything hurt his friends.*

"He would send an army of the dead to destroy his enemies."

We should really get one of those!!! I typed. *But until we do, you can at least try to use our situation to your advantage.*

Tonio stood up and nodded. "You're right. I've only been thinking about the bad stuff. You, and Dr. Jake, and everybody, have worked so hard to make sure I don't do that anymore." He scratched the top of my head. "I won't let you down."

I should have told him that wasn't possible. He *couldn't* let me down. He was a good friend and a caring person. He was responding to a bad situation with worry, which was a normal thing to do. But it wasn't convenient to me—it wasn't convenient to Dog Court—that he felt bad. So instead, I just said: *Thank you.*

In that moment, I was *so proud* of him. He was fighting back, and I felt he was proving Shadow wrong about one thing: Humans *could* be trusted. Tonio was absolutely one of the good ones.

But as I finish this report . . . I realize I'd already changed. I was sorting humans into the same categories I said dogs shouldn't be sorted into. Good and bad. Tonio shouldn't have had to prove he was one over the other, especially not to me.

I'm so sorry, Tonio. I hope you're okay.

Super Fart

thank you for going over every color of marker you brought, Jpeg underspoke to Tonio, *but I don't think that's going to help.*

"But that's all there is!" Tonio insisted. "Other than books."

shouldn't a kid your age have a phone by now?

"I keep saying that, but my parents say *they* managed just fine."

i've seen movies from before cell phones. Jpeg turned up her snout in disapproval. *so many problems would have been fixed if they could have just called each other.*

Tonio nodded. "I keep saying that!!!" His neck was starting to hurt, sitting all folded up in the dog crate. He tried to stretch. "But Agent Sykes looked in my backpack before. I think he would have taken it anyway. And I didn't bring a computer."

Footsteps above them, again. Tonio dropped to a whisper. "I wonder if—"

"Pairing complete!" his backpack chirped. Jpeg yelped in surprise, but Tonio put a finger to his mouth and switched to Underspeak.

The badge! he gestured. He didn't know the word for Squadron. *Sun . . . army. My dad got it for our new lights. It's probably transmitting to something. We should be quiet.*

Jpeg understood immediately. *a knockoff, right? keeps pairing with things it's not supposed to?* Tonio nodded. *did he get it from SmarterTheWorld™?* She spelled the letters very tiny with her paw.

Tonio nodded again. *It says that on the back.*

Jpeg pushed back onto her hind legs and waved her paws up and down in silent celebration. *why didn't you say anything sooner? those things are a MESS!*

That's a good thing?

in my line of work, bad code is the best code! that thing is our way out of here.

The footsteps moved away, quieter. A door closed. "Device disconnected."

Jpeg barked with excitement. *OKAY, CAN YOU TALK TO IT FOR ME?*

"You have to hit the button first." Tonio pushed his hand through the bars and tried to reach out to his backpack in the middle of the room. There were at least two more feet beyond his farthest reach. "I can't get it."

He tried again to push on the bars, but nothing happened. From a crouch, he hopped forward against the wall—but it was no good. Something was holding the cage in place. *Ugh.* No one knew where Tonio was, not even

Buster. But he had talked so much about how good of a hacker Jpeg was—and if that was true, the *Sun Squadron* badge *was* their only way out. Other than however Agent Sykes was planning on getting rid of them—

Breathe, Tonio. He stopped himself and focused on his breath. *I don't know what they want to do. But I know Jpeg is right here, and she has a plan.*

His clothes wouldn't be much help—he wasn't wearing anything with heavy buttons or a belt. He could throw his shoes, but that meant only two tries. No way to break the bars, but—the bottom of the cage was a rubber mat. A thick, heavy rubber. The whole thing was glued down, but if he could rip off pieces . . .

His fingernails weren't very long (he'd chewed off what was left of them), and he didn't have claws like Jpeg. Pulling at the corner of the mat hurt his fingers, but after a minute of prying, he had a small chunk of rubber.

Jpeg watched him weigh it in his hands. *i'll tell you what to say.* Tonio nodded. The badge was facing straight up in the air, so all he had to do was land the chunk on top. He reached his arm through the bars, tested the arc a few times, and threw!

It sailed far beyond the backpack, hitting a cage on the opposite side of the room. "Oops." His face turned red.

first try, that's okay. stay focused.

Tonio nodded and peeled off another chunk of rubber. He set up his arm, focused on throwing lighter—

And dropped it far short of the backpack. At least it was still at the edge of his reach and he could grab it again.

you're just calibrating. Jpeg waved her paw like it was nothing. *you'll get it!*

Another deep breath. *She's right,* Tonio thought. *I can't give up. I'm the only one with arms.* He thought about his first throw—and then his second—and tried to find a spot in the middle. His arm bent, threw—

Click. The tiniest click of the button as the chunk of rubber landed on the badge.

nice! third try!

"Thanks." Tonio sighed in relief. "I've played *so much* dodgeball this year."

"I'm sorry, could you repeat that?"

Oops, oh no oh no—Jpeg was quickly underspeaking so Tonio could correct his message before the microphone shut back off.

Tonio translated her words, struggling with the more complex ones: "Activate . . . passive listening . . . mode. Use . . . activation . . . phrase . . ." He thought for sure he was interpreting her wrong, so he made the signal for *repeat*. She did it again, and he didn't want to run out of time, so— "Super fart?"

"Passive listening activated. Just say 'super fart' when you need assistance!"

okay. the batteries will die faster, but now you don't have to hit it again.

"Is 'super fart' some kind of special hacker code?"

"I'm sorry, could you repeat that?"

i just thought it would be funny to make you say it a bunch. and it is! repeat after me:

"Super fart. Search for nearby Wi-Fi networks."

"Wi-Fi network located: L-G29H51. Network locked. Please state username when ready."

oh, gross. that's a government router, so the modem will be, too. it's not connected to the internet *internet.*

Which means?

it's on . . . Jpeg tried to find the Underspeak word for *intranet. a network that is closed off from the rest of the internet. it piggybacks off the internet, sort of, but it's only connected to itself. so we can only use it to connect to devices* also *on the private network.*

Tonio sighed. *And we don't know the username and password.*

actually, that part is hilarious. watch this. repeat:

"Username: mega fart. Password—" He glared at Jpeg. "Ultra fart."

"I'm sorry, that username and password is not correct. Cannot connect to network L-G29H51."

He looked confused, but Jpeg's little smirk came back. *it's about to say some numbers—try to remember them. repeat:*

"Super fart. List IP address of most recent connected Wi-Fi network?" The badge repeated back a long string of numbers separated by periods. Tonio repeated the command a few more times before he really had it memorized. "Super fart. Connect to previously connected network with the following IP address . . ." And he repeated the numbers.

"One moment. Connected to network L-G29H51!"

Tonio stared at Jpeg. "Why did that work??"

there's a long version, she said, *but the short version is that these smart devices are the dumbest things on earth.*

"Shouldn't it need the actual password?"

my absolute best friends ever over at SmarterTheWorld™ made these things with, well, basically a virus that lets them connect to whatever. that thing on your backpack has connected to every device and network you've even walked past—but instead of fixing that, they just made it so the badge lies to you and says *it's not connecting.* Tonio had never seen a dog underspeak the way Jpeg underspoke— extremely fast but without looking tired at all. The tiniest, most precise movements. *if you skip around the login dialogue with the ip address, it just does it.*

"So . . ." Tonio stared at Jpeg, wide-eyed, deciding

it was fine that he didn't really get it. "What do we do now?"

NOW the hard part starts. Jpeg tossed her head side to side and stretched her paws as far out in front as she could to get out the stiffness. *let's get to work.*

— 16 —

Art class became an anxiety minefield as soon as the mission started. Mia and Devon were just a few feet from Miles and Parker at all times, and any moment something could force Tonio to combine his two worlds—revealing the truth of his friendship with the bullies, or accidentally drawing too much attention to Devon, their old favorite target.

He wasn't alone in avoiding a clash, though—Parker rarely spoke directly to Tonio after lunch, and our friends disliked the Drama Kings as much as the Drama Kings disliked them.

"I. Love. Clay!" Devon cheered. He raised up a squishy bowl he'd made by pinching clay into a curved lip. "We have created something from nothing. Like pioneers!"

Tonio was carefully molding the antenna on a robot he was building instead of the bowls Ms. McCauley had suggested they make. "Beep, boop," he agreed. "My robot is *just* like the pioneers' robots."

Mia was also making a bowl, but she'd shaped hers into a star. "Are we still on to stream at the shelter today?" she asked. The boys nodded.

Ms. McCauley interrupted the conversation to pass out folded and stapled little booklets to the class. "Seeing as we're about halfway through the semester, I want to celebrate everyone's work!" Tonio got his packet early on and flipped through pictures of a few art pieces. "I've created a little zine of my favorites of each of your assignments. Take a moment to appreciate yourselves and the beautiful things you've made. *And* to notice how I folded and stapled the pages, because you'll be making your own zines for our next assignment."

Tonio found his page: She'd decided to use a photo Devon had taken of his manticore. I was halfway through yawning, so it seemed like I really was about to eat it. The manticore looked great, though. "We've got sculptures, drawings . . . even a story that was submitted with one project!" Another teacher knocked at the window and waved her outside. "Be right back."

Mia proudly presented a bracelet she had made—but Devon looked a little sick. "Oh!" he said. He flipped through the rest of the zine and found his page. "That's . . . interesting." (Which was about as close as he ever got to saying something negative.) Tonio tilted his copy down so I could see: *LOVESWORD BY DEVON WILCREST.*

What's the problem? I asked. Tonio underspoke back that he wasn't sure.

"It's nothing," Devon assured Tonio's face. "Didn't know she was going to show everyone, is all."

Snickering started at the next table over almost immediately. "Wow, Devon!" Miles called. "This is"—he snorted—"*really good.*"

Devon gave him a thumbs-up and a smile. "Thanks! I worked hard on it."

Miles cleared his throat. "'But do you really love me . . . or do you love your reflection, shining in my blade? Do you love that I speak, or only that I speak *for you*?'"

Of course, Parker jumped in immediately to play the other role. "'The curse kept the silent hero from speaking or writing his feelings, and he had always been a man of words. But his true love needed him to say *something*. But he could not. Or *could he*?!'"

The Drama Kings couldn't stop giggling as they spoke. And the voices they used were clearly demeaning— voices pitched dramatically high and low to play up the romance, batting their eyelashes and cackling at Devon's writing. Still, he kept an awkward smile on and watched them like everything was fine. I listened to his heart and sniffed at the air. Devon was nervous, and he was sweating. They were reading something he had written for fun, and for his teacher's eyes only—not for the whole class to hear. I looked at Tonio, but I could tell he didn't need dog senses to see what was happening. His eyes were trained intensely on the Drama Kings with a glare—

But then I saw him change. Tonio leaned back in his chair and let his brow relax. He flattened his face and expression to a look we'd seen on Parker's face a hundred times—a look like he wasn't emotional. Like he didn't care at all about what was happening, because he was, of course, *way* too cool.

"'The sword wished he had eyes, so he could look at—' Wait." Miles stopped, awful grin on his face. "They're *both boys*?"

Mia's chair flew backward as she stood up and stepped toward their table. "Got a problem?"

"Whoa, whoa, no need to send your giant girlfriend after—"

"Shut up, Miles." Surprised, I looked at Parker first—but Parker wasn't talking. The voice had come from closer to me—Tonio? I looked up, and there he was making that face. It must have taken him a minute to work up the confidence, but now he was shutting Miles down in the same way Parker did when he was getting too worked up for Parker's "cool" energy. "This is embarrassing."

It was a good trap, and one Parker used a lot, I'd noticed, when he wanted to regain control of a situation. "Embarrassing" didn't really mean anything specific—it just meant something other people didn't like. One person could label ANYTHING another person did "embarrassing," and it became true simply because they said it. And it was a nearly universally embarrassing behavior to say something *wasn't* embarrassing, so fighting back would just make it worse. The only time this trap didn't work was if you didn't care about the opinion of the person who said it, but they had to care about Tonio now because he was part of their group. And the Drama Kings, for all their pretending, really did care about other people's opinions. Their status in the class was their only power.

(I had a lot of time to think about this because Miles sat, stuck in the trap, trying to decide what to say. And it's a lot like anxiety, when you think about it, just weaponized. Forcing someone else into a bad circle where the only good move was not to play.)

"What?" Miles finally spat out, face red and scowling.

"You're trying to get everyone to look at Devon's page, because you're mad about what Ms. McCauley picked for you." Tonio held up his zine—a page with Miles's name and pictures of an old truck. "You didn't even do this, right? You asked Piper Hensley to borrow these pictures at lunch last week. Kind of awkward she thought that was your 'best work.' Seems like you should leave Devon alone."

The whole class was listening now. Mia was grinning,

and Devon was staring at Tonio, mouth open and braces twinkling. Parker was keeping control over his face, watching Miles to see how he reacted. (Not sticking up for him, I noticed.) Miles scrunched up his face and pushed it toward Tonio.

"So what?" he spat. "I don't care."

And then, the final blow: Tonio brought his eyebrows together with a disappointed look and sighed, folding the zine back down on his table. "Sure *sounds* like you do. But, uh, okay. Keep on yelling about how not mad you are."

As laughs rippled through the other kids, Miles could tell immediately that he'd lost. Parker stepped in finally and patted him on the back. "It's okay, buddy," he said, like a coach at the end of a game. "You can take your own car pictures next time. I'll teach you how to use a smartphone."

The class, given permission by Parker's involvement, laughed even more. Miles took this cue, too, and laughed along—it was his main chance to save face, at that point. Conversations shifted to other things, and Ms. McCauley came back into the classroom. The whole exchange had been less than a minute long, but it felt like an important shift—Tonio had protected his friends, using the same tricks the Drama Kings used to try to hurt them. I could tell he was proud, even as his friends looked concerned.

"You didn't have to do that," Devon whispered. "I'm really fine."

"No." Tonio shook his head seriously. "I am not letting them start on you again. Not after all this time."

Mia shrugged. "I loved it."

"But . . ." I could tell Devon didn't want to bring the mood down. "They always swing back, right? I heard about what happened with Roel and Kim, and that was over a *dodgeball* game."

Tonio started packing his things away for the next class. "They talk like that to each other all the time. I'll be fine."

"If you say so."

"Hey!" Tonio reached out and poked Devon on the shoulder. "I'm the one with anxiety, right? And I'm saying it's fine." Still channeling some of that "so cool" Parker energy, he smiled. "And your story sounds really good. I'm excited to read the rest."

Devon beamed and leaned in. "It's not even done yet!! I took your title and thought about how—it also says 'love's word,' right? And since it's a story about talking, I decided—"

Parker was standing over us suddenly. Devon clammed up. "Hey, Tonio." Parker reached out a fist to bump, and Tonio did. "Are you off book yet?"

Tonio stared at him. It was nonsense to me. Off the book? Was that some kind of code?

"Have you learned all your lines."

"OH! Uh, almost. We have to by next week, right?"

"Yeah. Let me know if you want to practice." He gave a little wave to Mia and Devon. Mia pretended she didn't see, but Devon quickly waved back with a grin. "See you tomorrow."

"Sure?" Tonio nodded, all of his cool energy erased by Parker's sudden appearance for apparently no reason. "But aren't you grounded?"

"AGH! I keep forgetting!" Parker smacked himself in the forehead with both hands in a big cartoon motion. Devon laughed in surprise, and even Mia smiled a little bit. "You're right, never mind. I don't exist. I am a ghost who haunts only my house."

I had no idea what this was about, but he seemed . . . normal? He continued making casual conversation with Mia and Devon in a way he never had before. Out of instinct, I looked around for Miles—and found him staring back at us from his table, alone. He hadn't been invited, I guess. His glare could have made me nervous, but instead I was kind of proud. *You deserve this*, I thought. *Maybe you'll learn something about picking on my friends.* For this moment, Tonio had proven he was worth Parker's attention—even more than Miles.

It felt good.

— 17 —

On our way to the Lins' shelter that evening, I remembered there was someone I needed to talk to: Leila. She was closer to Jpeg than anybody and deserved to know what was going on. The kids started streaming Beamblade with border collie Charmander and a new Chihuahua named Paperclip (who had actually won the Dog League tournament—her yellow-blue deck was amazing), so I had time to go off into the park on my own.

The Farm was busy! Bellville nearly skipped fall completely—it was always too hot and then too cold in South Carolina—but we were in the middle of the few weeks it actually existed, and people were celebrating. Mia's dads had already put up some decorations for the festival, and colorful leaves were piling up around the forested area. I took a few extra minutes to hop on them with a satisfying *crunch*, both because who wouldn't??? but also because I was stalling. Leila would *not* be happy to hear that Jpeg was captured by an anti-dog government organization, and she would be even less happy that there wasn't anything she could do about it. I wasn't sure how to tell her.

I checked in the fields, where she'd normally be wrestling with visiting challengers—but the dogs there said she hadn't been playing much lately. That made sense. I didn't see her over by the stable or the Lins' house, so I followed the creek into the forested area and sniffed her out eventually, lying by a tree where Jpeg had hidden one of her many laptops.

"Still no messages?" I asked. She lifted her giant head and shook it, fluff blowing in the gentle breeze. She looked like Tonio had looked—worn out and sad. I thought about changing the subject, but . . . figured it was kinder to get right to it. "She's not avoiding you. I found out where she is."

Her ears lifted up, but her expression was unsure. "Oh?"

I bobbed my head yes. "The man that adopted her was from the Department of Nonhuman Intelligence. They caught her hacking and faked the whole adoption so they could capture her."

Leila stayed much calmer than I did when I learned this information. Instead of hopping up and running around, she laid her chin down on the dirt. "I was afraid of that."

"You were?"

"She was acting so strange that day. You know, once,

Jpeg used her computer to call a man that was going to adopt me and fake an emergency, so he would leave? Every week she deletes our listings off the shelter website and makes it look like a bug. She's protected me—both of us—for so long. But she gave up so easily."

"She knew?"

"I wouldn't be surprised."

I would. The idea made me kind of mad. "Why wouldn't she warn us, then? Let us try to help her?"

Leila pushed herself up and started walking deeper into the woods. I followed. Walking beside her always made me feel so little—you could fit three of me inside of one Leila. "Jpeg's not that kind of dog. She always has to be the one doing the saving. I'm sure she doesn't think they can hold her."

"But it's been *weeks*!"

We came to the fence at the edge of the property. Leila sniffed along the edge and then pushed her paw on a loose board that flipped out smoothly, creating a hole out into the world.

"Wait, no!" I stepped in front of the hole. "You can't go after her!"

"Why not?"

"It's not safe. You don't know where she's gone—or what they're planning. You could end up caught, too."

She turned one eye on me with a squint. "You've got a better idea?"

"Yes. Tonio and I are working on it."

"How?"

"It's a long story, but we know who took her, and his son goes to Bellville Middle School. Tonio is going to get into his house and look for clues!"

Leila shook her head. "That's not a better idea." She batted me aside again and began squeezing through the hole.

"WAIT! Wait." I patted the ground. I couldn't lose Leila, too. But—if I were in her position, I would do the same thing. I *already* wanted to do the same thing. Maybe I could at least keep her from making any big mistakes. "Let me tell Tonio. I want to come with you."

A grunt told me she had heard. I ran to tell Tonio I'd meet him back at the house.

Parker lived in a gated community called Chime Hollow, which was a few miles away, across Bellville's busiest neighborhoods. Leila moved through town like she had every right to be there, and it made me nervous! I didn't even remember being a stray—all my life had been about carefully moving through spaces a dog was *supposed* to be in, and most of the time I was chaperoned by humans. I didn't want to end up caught by anyone, so I was trying to keep eyes in all directions. Leila wasn't worried.

"Worst thing that happens here is you get dropped off back at the shelter. We leave all the time."

"I don't think that's true anymore." We stepped to the side of a house while a pack of moms and strollers rolled by. "Not with the DNI snooping around."

"I'd like to see them try to hold me." She rocked back and forth, stomping into her wrestling stance. I got the message. *No one can move her.* Of course, any adult human could throw *me* around no problem. I'd be in one of DNI's cages in less than a minute if they really tried.

"Leila—" I started, then stopped.

She looked at me without turning her head. "Yeah?"

"Do I care too much about humans?"

"You care too much about everything."

"I mean, do you think it's true that humans don't really care about *us*?" Shadow's words had been rolling around in my head for a while now, and . . . I kept thinking myself in circles. I needed some outside input. "I know Tonio does, and Mia does, but they . . . a human took Jpeg. And I used to think Dog Court was being dramatic when they talked about how humans act, but I've seen a lot of how they hurt each other lately. Even kids. Is there any chance for something more between us and them?"

Leila huffed a little laugh. "That's too big of a question

for me. But you're always sticking your nose in every-thing, so why *not* the way the world has always worked?"

My ears dropped. "You're making fun of me."

"No, I mean it." She stopped and batted my face with a paw until I looked up at her. "You helped all of us this summer, and you did it by being nosy. But your nose isn't anything without your brain." She tucked her left paw behind her right one, Underspeak for *truth*. "I can't answer that question for you. You have to decide for yourself what you want. If you don't, you'll follow your nose around in circles—or, worse, into a trap someone else made for you."

"It doesn't matter what I want," I argued. "We have to save Jpeg!"

"Even so," she agreed, "we're always making little choices. Make sure those choices have a purpose, too." She kept walking.

I huffed, frustrated at all her nonanswers. But then, I had just told her her favorite person on Earth was in danger. She didn't owe me anything. "You're a lot calmer than I expected."

"I'm furious." She shook her head. "At her, and at those humans. But being mad isn't going to save her."

Chime Hollow is basically a fancy cul-de-sac carved into the side of a hill and surrounded by a stone wall on three sides. The fourth side was the only entrance, and to open the gate, you had to interact with a panel on a pillar beside the road. We stayed far away from the gate—the panel had an obvious camera above it—and climbed up the hill to look down at the houses.

They were all big, two-story homes that were three or four times the size of the Pulaskis' house above Tomorrow. All were nearly identical other than the coloring—blue, red, pink, yellow, and white walls in an alternating pattern. Any of them could be Agent Sykes's . . . and any of them could have Jpeg trapped inside. We crouched at the edge of the wall.

Shadow said the house was "dog-proof," I reported. *The Dog Court agent I'm working with. She . . . seems like someone who would know. And is definitely sneakier than either of us.*

Leila's claws dug into the earth beneath her. She didn't answer me, just glared down over the cul-de-sac.

I'm guessing that means cameras, motion detectors . . . She made it sound like we shouldn't even get close.

Her eyes darted around the neighborhood below, searching for movement. A few cars rolled in and out of the gate.

Do you have a plan, or—

Which house is it? she posed abruptly.

Maybe we should think more about this before you—

WHICH ONE? she punctuated with a growl.

415! It's number 415! And then she was moving again. We stayed low to the ground, crawling through the bushes down the other side of the hill. Leila spotted a roof close to the wall. I leaped over easily, but she landed hard and scrambled to keep from sliding down the slope, scraping shingles off in the process.

The houses across the street are 406 and 408, I pointed out. *So Sykes's house should be a few down that way.* Leila followed my nose and jumped onto the first level of the house with a rattling thud. I jumped behind but froze when I heard a window opening.

"Sorry, I heard something." An adult human's voice. "Hello? Is someone up there?" They sounded scared. Leila kept moving, unbothered, but I had to do *something.* I opened my jaws and made little raspy barks in the back of my throat. I threw in a little squeaky chitter sound, too, just for good measure.

". . . Huh. Big squirrels."

I waited until they'd walked away from the window and followed Leila down to the ground. She moved through the backyards, keeping as close to the houses as she could. In the shadow of the yellow house that I suspected was 413, I growled a warning.

"Look." I pointed my nose to the next home. Stuck to a corner of the roof was a camera pointing out over the backyard. We crept closer to the edge of the yellow house and looked toward the front yard—same thing there. *I can't be seen on those,* I posed. *Sykes already suspects me.*

With a huff, Leila turned around. We crossed the street a few houses down and made our way around to the other side of 415. But it was the same there, too: cameras at every angle. His whole yard was monitored. I could feel Leila's frustration building, but when she finally spoke, her words were a surprise.

I can't smell her.

I sniffed the air—I didn't smell her, either. I mostly smelled outside smells, with a layer of laundry, air-conditioning, and . . . food. Fried chicken, I guess. If I *really* focused I thought I could smell Parker, but I might have been imagining that because I expected it. *Me neither. But . . . would you? It's been a while, and—*

I thought I would at least smell her. There was a defeated energy to her poses. I understood now. Leila didn't have a plan, and she didn't really think she could save Jpeg on her own. She just wanted something to hold on to. Something to help her trust that Jpeg would be okay.

Leila, I—

The front door of 415 opened. Both of our ears perked up, and we flattened against the wall—I wiggled under her belly so we could both squeeze into the shadows as much as possible. Oscar Sykes stepped out in another perfectly crisp suit. He turned three different keys in three different locks and then input a code on a keypad next to the door. *A security system.*

His car was in the driveway, but the agent didn't head for it. He walked across his front yard to the sidewalk and then the curb, where he checked his watch. His phone must have buzzed, because he held it up to his ear and answered.

"I can't hear him," I whined as quietly as possible. Leila bobbed her head in agreement.

His conversation was over quickly. He pushed a button on his phone and then put it back in his pocket. A few seconds later, a car drove up beside him on the curb. The car was silver with a blue stripe down the side and long lights attached to the top. *A police car.* The police officer opened the passenger-side door for Agent Sykes, who sat down inside and shut the door behind him.

The car didn't move, but there was no way we could hear anything from here. We needed to get closer. I crawled out from under Leila and started around the other side of 417—there were two trucks parked in their driveway. Leila was too big to fit underneath them, but we could crawl to the end of the driveway past them and probably get close enough to hear something.

I looked back at her. She nudged me forward, and I nodded. As I crouched down and slunk beside the trucks, I felt my heartbeat rising. This was *fun*, like running with Shadow had been fun. It reminded me of chasing fires and all the reasons I wanted to be a service dog in the first place—the excitement of doing something to help someone else, even if it was dangerous.

Leila dipped her head low and spread her legs in a stable stance—I followed her lead and jumped onto her back and then into the bed of the truck, flattening myself down to listen without being seen.

"—don't have anything major to report yet." Agent Sykes's voice. "But I think I'm almost there."

"You should send your target along to HQ," the police officer responded. "They're getting impatient."

"Absolutely not. This was my capture, so it's my interrogation."

"I'm just the messenger, sir."

"Well, here's a message: HQ can wait. The dogs are active right now—and if my informant is correct, they're already hunting for the Shiba."

"Sounds like a good reason to secure the target."

"Trust me, I'll bring in better than a small-time hacker." I could hear Sykes's smile in his words. "I'd advise them—and you—to be patient. Bellville is a treasure trove. And when we crack it open, we'll be heroes."

The police officer sighed. "All right. Yeah. I'll keep you updated if I hear anything else."

"Good. Very good." A short moment of silence. "What do you know about the Pulaskis?"

I froze. *Oh no.* "Spencer's family goes back three or

four generations. He met Laura in school, I think. They moved back here to raise their kid. Tomorrow's got good produce."

"And the kid?"

"What about him?" The officer sounded confused. "Oh, you mean the dog?"

"I find it suspicious he suddenly needs a service dog when canine activity is rising in the county."

". . . You think the kid is faking?"

"These creatures have kept themselves secret for decades. Maybe centuries." His smile had dropped—he sounded almost *scared*. "I think we shouldn't write off anything."

They said their goodbyes. Agent Sykes stepped back out of the car—I ducked down into the truck bed, so I couldn't see anything. I tried to calm my heartbeat as I thought through their conversation. Oscar suspected me and Tonio—but he didn't seem to have any real evidence. And Shadow was right—he was planning to catch more dogs looking for Jpeg. Going into that house without a cover was a trap.

And, worse, even the *police* were working with him. At least one officer was. Which made sense—the DNI was part of the government. But if there was one, maybe there were more. We couldn't trust any of the adults in Bellville. Sykes said he had an informant— dog? Human? There was no way to know.

I waited until I heard the beeping panel, the sound of three locks, and then the door opening and closing before I climbed back out. Leila looked like all the energy had been drained out of her as she underspoke. *It's true. All of it is true.*

I nudged her with my nose. *This is* good *news,* I said. *We know she's still in town. And he wouldn't be so careful about his house if there wasn't something important inside. We can still bring her home.*

We can save her from those humans. Leila rolled her shoulders in a sad shrug and started walking away. *But I don't think they'll ever let her come back home.*

They? I considered her words. Oh. Dog Court. I hadn't even thought about that. They put me through a trial for communicating with Tonio, but—getting caught by the humans for hacking? Letting herself become a trap for other dogs? Forcing them to call on me and Tonio to try to stop a potentially irreparable breach of the Law? I remembered Shadow's words: We cannot solve this problem by creating a bigger one. Shadow talked about "saving" Jpeg to motivate me, but . . . what was Dog Court really going to do with her?

I want to go in there right now.

I know. I sighed. *But you heard him—we have to be careful. Tonio has the best chance of any of us to get inside.*

The second you learn something, you tell me.

The millisecond!

And if there's a way I can help . . . Leila gave a little meaningless whine. *Please tell me. I want to save* her, *for once.*

I won't let them take her away, I insisted. *I'm confused about a lot of things, but I know you two should be together. That's what I want.*

Leila wagged her tail slowly, batting at fallen leaves on the sidewalk. "Glad to hear it."

— 18 —

Despite my fears that Tonio had gone too far in art class, lunch continued like normal the next day. Parker even went out of his way to find Tonio in line and walk him to the table—a thoughtful gesture I was surprised by. He knew Tonio would need it. Tonio, for his part, was losing his confidence from the previous day and woke up a bundle of raw nerves. Parker's casual smile and easy demeanor reassured him quickly. I couldn't tell Tonio about what I'd learned from our trip to Sykes's house . . . but he didn't need to know. All we could do was stay focused on our mission.

After school, play practice was running about as smoothly as I think it's possible for play practice to run in a middle school. We were rehearsing on the actual stage now! Tonio and I sat in the audience as they worked on act 1, which we weren't really a part of. Parker was already off book, so he was able to cast his lines proudly into the audience.

"The doe moves too fast!" he proclaimed. "It only shows up in pictures as a blur—and the light of my phone screen awakens it from any slumber. How am I supposed to get a clear shot?"

"How, indeed?" Coop chirped, as Hermes. "Need a hand?"

"I dunno, any bright ideas?"

"I'm the god of them, kid, and I've got one here for you." Hermes held out Piper's camera, which he'd borrowed as a prop.

"What . . . is this?"

King Eurystheus boomed a great laugh. "Why, it's a camera, my boy! Haven't you seen it before?"

Heracles spun it around in his hands, face full of wonder. "It looks just like the icon for the photos app!"

SLAM! The theater doors swung open. Surprised, Parker let go of the camera and sent it skidding across the stage—it fell off the edge and several feet down into the audience with a *crunch*.

"ALL RIGHT," Mia yelled from the doorway (at the same time as Piper yelled "My camera!"). "WHICH ONE OF YOU NERDS HAS THE KEY TO THE BATHROOM?"

Immediately, Tonio stood. "Mia? What are you—"

"NO," Mia continued yelling, walking down the aisle. Devon appeared hovering by the door, details obscured by the shadow. "I *KNOW* YOU DON'T HAVE IT." She held up a finger in his face to silence him. "BECAUSE YOU'RE SO SCARED OF THE GERMS YOU JUST HOLD IT ALL DAY. RING, RING, MRS. FELDMAN."

Mrs. Feldman looked confused, but I suppose she appreciated good drama. "Ring, ring, Mia."

"SO, SOMEONE ELSE IN HERE MUST HAVE THE KEY!" Mia headed down the aisle now and climbed up onto the stage. She pointed at Parker accusatorily. "IS IT YOU?"

Parker rubbed his chin. "We're in the middle of rehearsal," he said.

"So you are!" Mia looked around in mock astonishment, looking every bit like she belonged on the stage. She brought her voice down to a normal level of expressiveness and projected through the audience. "And yet, I am *desperate* to use the science hall bathroom." When none of the kids spoke up, Mia made her way to the audience and began shaking backpacks.

"What's going on, Mia?" Mrs. Feldman asked.

Mia rattled a red bag, shook her head, and set it back down. "Earlier today"—she cleared her throat loudly—"SOMEONE locked Devon Wilcrest in the science hall bathroom. Which means they must have kept a bathroom pass!"

I looked at Tonio—who looked at Piper and Miles. They were both trying to keep a straight face, but I could tell they knew something. My ears turned back and flattened as far as they could. *Cowards.*

"He was waiting—not this one—for *two hours*— aHA! Oh, no, just house keys, sorry, Weston—before I

177

got home and checked the voice mail there." Mia's head swiveled to find Piper and fix her with a glare. "And he was in there because *you* said there was something in his braces."

"Miles told me to!" Piper blurted out. Mia's eyes shot an inch over to glare at Miles.

"Tonio, did you know about this?" she asked.

Tonio, hands shaky, shook his head. His heart was racing.

"AS I SUSPECTED." Mia looked back toward the doors. "You see that, Devon?"

I turned to look in the doorway. Devon, silent and shadowed by the light from the windows behind him, nodded.

"It was Parker's idea, too," Miles mumbled.

"No, it wasn't," Parker snapped. "I *told you* it was stupid."

That got Mrs. Feldman's attention. "Parker, what did you do?"

"Nothing!"

Mia forced her way down the aisle of seats until she was standing over Miles. She held out her hand, but Miles crossed his arms and didn't look at her. I grabbed his backpack between my teeth and lifted it up to Mia, who took it and patted me on the head. "Good boy."

"Tonio told me to leave him alone," Miles said quietly. "So I did."

She rummaged around in his backpack and came up with a key attached to a wooden block that said BATHROOM PASS on it in marker. "Your son and his creep friends did this." She threw the block to Mrs. Feldman—the key jangled in the air. "And they've been bullying Devon nonstop all semester. If no one's told you yet, *somehow*, now you know."

Part of me was so proud of Mia. And part of me thought, *No, no, no*—Mia was ruining everything! She was embarrassing the Drama Kings, pushing them away from Tonio and getting them into *trouble*, which we would never be able to come back from. I was trying to think of some way to salvage it when a hissing sound above me reminded me I had a job to do.

Tonio was tugging at his shirt—his eyes were flitting frantically between everyone in the room, who were either watching Mia in awe, Parker in surprise, or Tonio in concern. His breath hissed as he fought for air—one hand pulled at his collar while the other squeezed into a fist, stabbing nails into his palm. He was having a panic attack, and he needed to sit back down, but he was too lost in fear to realize.

Free to step in as a service dog, I weaved in front of Tonio's legs and pushed at Piper and Miles, forcing them to give Tonio space. I turned around and moved my weight onto my hind legs so I could push him into his chair. Soon Mia was there, too. She saw what was happening and scooped him up like a bag of dog food in both arms. "Let's go, Tonio."

"Fifteen-minute break!" Director Feldman yelled. "Parker, Miles, Piper. Backstage. *Now.*" The cast erupted into noise at the permission to move but thankfully kept their distance. Tonio whimpered at Mia's collar, arms around her neck, as she hefted him back through the doors and into the light of the hallway. I shuffled along at her ankles, dragging my leash and drooping my tail.

Mia led us to an unused rehearsal room—the same one we'd auditioned in, with the wall-length mirror and the squishy floor. She set Tonio down against the bare wall and sat beside him, leaving a little space. Devon sat near his other shoulder, and I sat in between Tonio's legs while he rode the waves of the panic attack.

He hadn't gone through one this rough in a long time. He kept spreading and closing his fingers to check if they still worked, which happened in his worst panic attacks—his hands felt numb and tingly, which made him think there was something really wrong. I nudged him with my nose so he'd start petting me and let the feeling of my fur reassure him his hands were still working.

"It's okay, Tonio." Devon spoke softly. "You're not in trouble."

"Your *new friends* are, though!" Mia added.

"*Mia!*"

Gradually, Tonio calmed down. He released his grip on my neck fur and relaxed into the floor as the panic attack subsided and his body realized he was as safe as he was going to get, for the moment. "Sorry, y'all," he mumbled. I settled on the floor and watched them in the mirror.

Devon shook his head. "You don't have to apologize!"

"Not about that, anyway."

"Mia!!!"

She shrugged, barely moving the giant hoodie she must have borrowed from one of her dads. Devon shrank away under her tired look. "I'm just saying. You two have stuff you need to talk about, and I'm sick of being in the middle."

"I'm fine!" Devon said.

Mia rolled her eyes and repeated, mocking: *"I'm fine! You smell like boys' bathroom, and your eyes are still red."*

"He did it to get back at me," Tonio realized. "For sticking up for you."

The other kids didn't say anything. Finally, Tonio looked up at the mirror—so he could see Devon as if he was on the other end of the room and not right next to him. "She said they've been bullying you all semester?"

Devon shook his head. "Not really. I'm totally—"

"Yes," Mia interrupted, "is what he means."

Tonio rubbed at his eyes. I saw him suddenly remember: "Your locker. What happened before?"

181

I could see Devon try to process how to talk around this—he was rarely forced to talk about anything serious, and he obviously did not like it. "Miles and Parker pushed a bunch of pictures from magazine ads through the holes, so when I opened my locker, it was full of all these shirtless guys."

"*So many,*" Mia clarified, "that they flew out of his locker when he opened it, filling the hallway with them and making everybody think Devon put them there."

"And maybe I would!" Devon looked frustrated with Mia. "I actually thought it was funny!"

"*So funny,*" Mia said, "that he made me promise not to tell anyone about it. Tell him about the glitter."

Devon groaned. "Mia, please!!!" But at the look she gave him, he mumbled: "Fine. When I finished cleaning that up, someone put a tube thing inside. And when I tried to open it, glitter blasted everywhere."

"And *still* he made me stay quiet. But not this time. This was the final straw."

At that, Devon scrunched up his face. "I didn't really *know* who did it—"

Mia held both hands up toward his face and shook them with a frustrated, quiet yell: "Aaaaaaaaaaaaaaaahhh!!!!"

"So . . . you were lying." Tonio watched Devon, eyebrows knitted together in disappointment. "Every time we talked about this year being better, you were lying."

"It *is* better!" Devon insisted. "Because we're friends now!"

"Then why couldn't I know?" Tonio said, more sharply than I expected. "Why did Mia get to know about this, but I didn't? If we're friends?"

Air-conditioning clicked on—a light whir filled the room, and the smell that always comes with artificially chilled air. Devon took a long time to answer, but Mia didn't step in for him this time. "Well . . . she was there when it happened, and I thought, no reason to make you worried, too. I can take it."

"And I can't." Tonio's jaw set seriously. "Because you're tough, and I'm not."

"No!" Devon leaned forward. "But I know the stuff that bothers you *really* bothers you, and you've been so much happier—"

Mia raised a finger. "Until recently . . . but we'll get to *that* in a second! Keep going."

"—and I'm really fine! So there was no reason to tell you."

"But I don't want things to *seem* okay." Tonio echoed something he'd said in a therapy session with Dr. Jake. "I want them to *be* okay."

Mia offered everyone a piece of gum, but no one took one except for her. "Before you get too hard on Devon, I'm not sure he knows the difference."

Devon was frozen now, clearly working very hard to

183

keep his body still and calm—but I could hear his heart race and see the subtle changes of his face heating up. "I do know the difference."

"Then you should have *told* me!" Tonio snapped. And then Devon was crying.

"I'm sorry!" he blurted out. "You're right! I'm sorry!" And immediately, Tonio's face completely changed—he went from frustrated and hurt to realizing what I was realizing: He was getting mad at Devon for the way he *dealt* with being bullied instead of being mad at the bullies. It wasn't Devon's fault he was in this position—he never should have had to make that kind of choice.

And my anger at Mia was the same thing. I was getting mad at these kids—or getting mad at myself—for not handling this situation well, but we were reacting to totally inappropriate behavior from Miles and Parker. No one should *be* a bully! This wasn't Mia and Devon's fault, or Tonio's fault, or my fault—it was theirs. Sure, I thought we all could have handled it better, but we shouldn't have had to "handle it" in the first place.

"No, you're right." Tonio nodded. "Thank you for thinking about me."

"*That* can't be true," Mia countered, "because if you were both right, I wouldn't be here, missing out on my dad's famous hamburgers."

"Mia told me I should tell you," Devon admitted, wiping at his face—his crying done for the moment.

Tonio chewed at the inside of his cheek. "I just . . . I *hate it* when people change things because of my anxiety. It's bad enough that it's in my head. It doesn't need to be in yours."

Other people are going to care about you, I underspoke to him. *You can't stop that.*

He nodded. "I'm glad you guys care about me. But I'm not the only one that matters, and I should get to help you sometimes, too." I felt a sudden fear—I was doing the same thing. I hadn't told him about Jpeg for the exact same reason. If he was even mad at *Devon*, then—

"You did help!" Devon lit up, remembering. "Oh my gosh, when you told Miles to shut up!!!"

Mia grinned. "Top-ten moments of my life. *Easy.*" They laughed, and Tonio smiled sheepishly. "So wait, you *would* put those shirtless guys in your locker?"

"They're very high-quality pictures!" Devon shrugged. "I kept some. To reference for my stories, of course. Want to see?"

Tonio nodded, but Mia said, "Maybe later. And I'm sorry, too. We should have told you."

Devon smiled. "Yeah. No more secrets."

With a flourish, Mia presented her pinkie. "Triple pinkie swear?" Before I could say anything, both boys nodded seriously and tucked their pinkies all together. *No, Tonio, not the pinkie swear, you can't—*

"GREAT!" Mia released the pinkies and stretched.

"Now that *that's* out of the way, Tonio, what in the world is going on with *you*?"

Tonio blinked, surprised at the abrupt change in topic (and at Mia's sudden arrival right up next to his face). "Huh? Oh, I, uh—"

"Nope!" Mia pointed at her pinkie. "You *just swore.*"

I resisted covering my face with my paws. *You fool!* I thought. *You fell right into her trap!*

"Dr. Jake—"

"Doesn't explain why you're sitting with them at lunch."

Devon scratched the back of his neck. "And . . . Jason told me he saw you talking to them, when they were messing with Kimberlyn."

"And Roel."

Ack. Tonio's eyes were wide, and his expression wasn't chill at all—he felt guilty, and it was obvious. When he looked at me, I scrambled to underspeak: *You can't tell them!* With our mission already a failure, we couldn't *also* reveal the truth about dogs to two more kids. Who *knows* what Dog Court would do.

He couldn't underspeak back with all their attention on him, but he nodded once, slowly. I was confident Tonio understood: He wouldn't give away our secret so suddenly, even with a pinkie swear on the line.

But with both of his best friends staring at him, he had to say *something.* "You're right." He swallowed hard

186

and looked at them. "I'm the one who told them about Kimberlyn's anger management and Roel's stuff with the app game."

Devon's eyes widened. Mia looked immediately furious. I could smell the sweat on Tonio—these were serious crimes. They'd have good reason to be upset with him.

"I thought maybe I could be friends with them, and it would do something good." He avoided eye contact, just in case he would betray the truths he was hiding so close to a pinkie swear. "But that was stupid. I hurt people. And I'm sorry I didn't talk to you guys about it."

Another breath to say something else. The hackles of my fur rose as dread crept along my spine. *Careful, Tonio*, I underspoke. *Remember the mission. We still need to—*

He gave me an apologetic expression and shook his head.

"It's not worth it anymore. I give up. I'm going to quit the show."

— 19 —

I panicked. Tonio couldn't quit the play! *I understand what you're thinking,* I underspoke as they headed into the hallway. *Mia and Devon might keep asking questions if you don't really show you care about them. I totally get it. But you can't quit! This is our mission! If we don't succeed ... well, I don't know what they'll do, but it might be what they threatened over the summer: I could be sent away, and you could be assigned a watchdog for the rest of your life. We need to try and—*

"Tonio, is Buster okay?" Devon nudged his shoulder. "He seems kind of twitchy."

"Hm, really?" Tonio shrugged. "I'll check him for fleas later."

Mia clicked her tongue. "We can set you up with a goop that gets rid of them, if you want it."

I do not have fleas! But he still wasn't looking at me, and I couldn't be too obvious in front of the other kids. Tonio told them he'd catch up with them tomorrow and then headed back toward the theater to find Mrs. Feldman.

Tonio, please, let's talk about this! I pleaded.

He ignored me, eyes straight ahead. Suddenly, I was aware of how much I depended on him to feel like I mattered. If he didn't look at me, I couldn't speak—and if he didn't listen to me, I couldn't do anything. Because he was a human, and I was just a dog. It felt a hundred times worse than before we were friends, though, because he was doing it on purpose. He was forcing me to be silent.

Tonio pushed open the big door to the theater—Mrs. Feldman was waiting near the entrance for him, hovering over an uncomfortable trio of kids. Miles, Piper, and Parker all looked at Tonio with the unmistakable look of aggravated awkwardness—not a good sign. We needed to get out of there. I pawed at his leg and whined, but he shook me off without looking down.

"Is he all right?" Mrs. Feldman asked.

Tonio nodded. "He just needs to use the bathroom."

She accepted this easily and turned her focus on him. "Antonio, these three have something they'd like to say to you."

"Sorry," the trio mumbled. When Mrs. Feldman wasn't looking, Miles openly glared at Tonio. He, at least, clearly resented getting in trouble. Piper looked genuinely nervous to be under adult scrutiny, and Parker had transformed his whole body into a shrug. Through all of it, Tonio kept his face flat and focused.

"You—" Tonio started, and I knew I couldn't let him

finish. Not if there was going to be any chance of Parker working with us. I hopped up on my hind legs and pushed on Tonio's shirt.

"Buster, *down!*" he chided.

I barked back at him, which surprised all of them. But Tonio needed to listen to me. Mrs. Feldman frowned. "Maybe you should take him outside?"

Tonio tugged at my harness and pushed me down to the ground. "I just haven't been keeping up with his training, is all. Sorry. Bad dog! Down!"

Don't you "bad dog" me, I underspoke. *We have a job to do! Tearing up your only connection to them will mean there's no coming back.*

"This will only take a second," he said to the humans, still ignoring me. I don't think he paid attention to a single word. "Thank you, Mrs. Feldman, for casting me in your show. But my friends matter to me, and I can't trust the cast anymore."

Mrs. Feldman's eyes widened in fear—her director hat suddenly on, she was worried about the show. "Oh, Tonio, you can't quit! You and Buster are doing so well!"

That's what I'm saying.

But Tonio shook his head. "I'm sorry. I have to." He looked right at Parker and visibly swallowed. His face was red, and his heart was racing, but he had something he wanted to say. *Please,* I begged, *let's just go. Just stop there. We'll figure something out.* But my poses were to

190

no one, and Tonio kept his eyes on Parker. Exhausted from his panic attack and emotional conversation with his friends, Tonio seemed practically calm.

"All of my friends are scared of you. I almost left school because of you." That was hard for Tonio to admit. No one other than Mia and Devon knew how close Tonio had come to giving up completely. Parker's face didn't change, but I saw the hairs on his arm stand up—Tonio's words were getting to him. It was the most like Hades Tonio had ever acted—not that it mattered now.

"I thought I could change something. I thought, maybe, if I did *exactly* what you wanted, you'd stop being horrible. But I was wrong." Tonio squeezed the leash between his fingers and looked at Miles and Piper, too. "All of you think you're safe from each other, but you're not. None of you are real friends. But I *have* real friends, and I'm not going to let you hurt them again. Ever."

Director Feldman's hand was covering her mouth— she looked stunned, and I think she really had no idea what Parker was like to other kids. How could she know? As far as I knew, they managed to avoid getting in trouble, and it's not like they were going to go home and say, *Oh, my day was fine. I was a bully.*

Miles stepped forward from the trio. "Quit trying to get us in trouble. Sorry your friends can't *take a joke*."

Parker put a hand on his shoulder. "Shut up, Miles."

Miles jerked his shoulder away. "Why? He's making us look bad for no reason."

"All right, that's enough." Mrs. Feldman put her hand down and sighed. "I won't keep you here, Tonio, you can go home. I'm sorry about this. It sounds like Parker and I have a lot to talk about."

"You're just going to believe *him*?" Miles gasped.

"And I'm going to have a conversation with your mother as well, Miles." That *did* shut him up.

"I really am sorry," Piper mumbled. "I didn't know it would be such a big deal."

Tonio turned to her and looked almost apologetic. "Yes, you did." He looked up at the ceiling—as far away from me as he could go, I noted—and clenched his jaw for a moment. I imagined Jpeg, somewhere, getting locked up in a cage forever. "Just leave us alone, okay?"

Nobody was sure what to say to that, and Mrs. Feldman was ready to regain control of the rehearsal. She ushered the trio back into the theater, and Tonio fled out the doors. I tried again to speak to him.

Tonio, I know you're upset, but you have to listen to me. There's more to this than you know.

No response. Not even slowing down to look at me as he tugged me along out the door. Never have I wanted a human mouth as much as that moment.

Please. I can't just give up.

A few people were walking outside, running final

errands in the square before they settled in for the night. "Ring, ring!" Tonio waved to an old lady we delivered groceries to sometimes.

I know you're not ignoring me to be mean, I know you're scared, but I'm not mad at you. I just need you to listen.

When I tried to stop, he pulled on my harness. I couldn't make a scene in public, so I let him tug me up the stairs to our home. I wanted to cry.

I tried to get his attention one more time, half-heartedly, when he unlocked the door—but he ignored me. The house was empty and dark. He unhooked my harness and headed upstairs without looking back. I ran along behind him and slipped into the door as fast as I could.

My laptop was under the bed. I bit down on it and slid it out, then pushed it open with my paws. The screen lit up onto a word processor, so I typed fast. When my message was done, I pulled my laptop up onto his bed and started barking.

He was changing into more casual clothes and groaned from the closet. "Buster, no. I don't want to talk right now. I'm sorry, but I need some time."

No, I thought. *You don't get to decide I have no voice just because you don't want to hear it.* And I kept barking. Loudly.

Finally, he looked at me. His eyes were brimming with tears, and he had the same hollowed-out look he'd had the other day. But I'd already waited too long to tell him this, and—well, I was mad. We were supposed to be partners, and that meant he couldn't ignore me when I had something important to say! I kept barking, filling the tiny room with big noise, and pointed with my paw at the laptop.

"Fine. Fine! Stop it!" He pressed his palms to his ears and returned to the bed. I stopped yelling, and he read what I had typed:

TONIO, I UNDERSTAND YOU'RE UPSET. BUT OSCAR SYKES KIDNAPPED JPEG. OUR PLAN IS THE ONLY CHANCE TO FIND HER.

The room was especially silent after all that noise. Tonio read and then reread. He looked at me with a queasy expression on his face. "What?"

Now do you understand?! I posed. *This is why I was trying to stop you!*

"Is this true?"

Of course it's true! I posed back. *Why would I lie about this?* The question was confusing. I thought, when he read, he would understand that he'd messed up—that he should have *listened* to me, and then everything would have been fine—but instead, he was mad. He turned a face on me like I'd never seen before—a full growl. Eyebrows diving into his nose and mouth open in fury.

"How long have you known this?"

A few days, but I—

"*Days?* And you didn't feel like telling me?"

Shadow told me not to. She thought—

"The same thing Devon thought. I'm too anxious to know. And you agreed with her."

You were having a hard time. And since your plan was working, I didn't want to . . . I was using the same language as Devon. But I'd already started . . . *make you worried, too.*

"Because my anxiety would ruin the plan, like everything else." Tonio choked on the words but swallowed back the tears and his voice came back stronger and angrier than before. "You know, all y'all—especially you—keep saying how much you *believe* in me, how there's *nothing wrong* with me, how *proud of me* you are. And none of you actually believe it!" He shook his head in disbelief. I tried to underspeak, but he started talking and stopped looking at me.

"And that's because it's not true, is it? Judge Sweetie doesn't want *me* to solve this problem; I'm just all she has. I'm only a Farm agent because *you* told me about dogs—which you did because I was too messed up to solve my own problems. Even the idea that I pay attention to people, or I care about people more than other kids do—that's all stuff you made up to make me sound good, isn't it? To make me sound like a perfect little kid that you had to save." He laughed for a second and turned away from me toward the window. "But what have I *actually* done? I've hurt Kimberlyn. I've hurt Roel. I've let my friends get hurt because all I do is cause problems." He coughed and took a second to breathe, all heavy and ragged. "I didn't ask for any of this! I wouldn't have tried to be friends with Devon, or become an agent of The Farm, or gone through any of this if it weren't for you *using* me to feel like a hero and to do all the things you wish you could just do yourself. And you, and Devon, and everybody keeps pretending like I'm better, but really you're just lying to me. Doing the exact thing I TOLD YOU I didn't want my parents to do, that I hate more than anything, because you don't really believe I'm better. You don't really believe I'm a good partner, just like Devon doesn't really believe I'm a good friend. I'm just the one all of you got stuck with. And you know what? All of you are right. I agree."

He whipped around and picked me up so fast I didn't resist at all—I was heavy enough that it was a bit of a struggle for him but not impossible. He walked outside his room and set me down in the hallway.

"I can't do this. I can't be a real friend, I can't be a secret agent, and I can't save Jpeg. I'm not the person any of you want. So go tell them! Tell them I ruined the mission." He moved back and grabbed the door. I stepped forward, but he blocked the way. "Find another human who's more like you."

The door didn't slam—it didn't have to. When he shut it, he knew I wouldn't be able to open it myself. Not easily, anyway. I had tried to interrupt him—had tried to reassure him that none of that was true, that he was letting anxious thoughts overtake what was really going on—but I couldn't get him to listen. I had broken his trust.

I whined at the door and lay down with my nose by the crack. I heard muffled sounds of crying, which Tonio was trying to keep quiet with a pillow. I heard the sound of my own heartbeat, thumping into the carpet.

This was exactly why I hadn't told him—but I had to admit, this was *because* I hadn't told him. I hadn't trusted him. And even just then—I hadn't thought about his feelings. I had jumped straight back into the mission and told him about Jpeg at the worst possible time. I was a terrible service dog and an even worse friend.

But deep down, all these feelings were smaller than a feeling I felt *very* guilty about: This still wasn't as important as Jpeg's safety. I could repair things with Tonio once that was figured out, and if Tonio didn't want to work with me, I had to go somewhere else. *I'm sorry*, I thought. *I promise we'll work this out later.*

The front door of the Pulaskis' house was easy at least. I left it open a crack and headed down the front steps. The jangling of my collar felt loud in the dark, empty street—so I stood on my hind legs at the bottom of the stairs and caught it on the pole. I leaned away with all my weight, hoping to undo the buckle. The collar ripped along the opposite edge, ruining it. Another thing I couldn't fix right now. I set off through Bellville square, avoiding the streetlights and heading toward the highway.

Shadow, I hoped, would know what to do.

20

I got lost immediately. Getting to the highway was easy enough, but the woods along the side of it all looked the same to me and seemed to stretch on forever. My farsmelled nose made it hard to pick up any dog scents—plus, I hadn't been back other than the one time, and Shadow had a difficult smell to track. I tried following disturbances like broken branches and crushed leaves for a while, but those paths could have been made by deer, or squirrels, or anything. I ended up going in circles.

Embarrassed, I really only had one option: I had to howl. Obviously howling plays a very important part in passing information between dogs, but I was going to have to do a panic howl, which is the worst kind. I wasn't even sure my voice would still do it, it had been so long. I hadn't howled since—well, I realized with a twinge of shame, it was such a *dog* thing. So much of being a service dog meant giving that stuff up, because it didn't fit in with human society. If I howled out the window every night, Tonio's family would think it was annoying. So I didn't.

I'd barked earlier, though, so at least I was warmed up. "Rooooo?" I tested. A small sound, like an owl. Or a little ghost. "Aaaarrrroooo?" I did again, just noise, focused on what it felt like in my lungs. And then, feeling a little more confident, I dug deeper into my stomach, tilted my head back, and really *howled*:

"THIS IS BUSTER!" I called. "I'M LOST!"

My voice echoed through the forest. A few birds woke up, chirped angrily, and fluttered away to find a quieter spot to sleep. But there was no response, so I tried again.

"THIS IS BUSTER! I NEED HELP FINDING YOU!" I didn't know Shadow's situation—or how secret she needed to be—so I didn't want to use her name, just in case. I had to feel confident she'd hear me and respond—but there was no answer. Only silence.

Well, I'd tried, and I'd added another embarrassment to the end of an already-bad day. Maybe Tonio was right—I was just playing at being a hero. No one seemed to actually believe in *me*, anyway, for all of Tonio's talk about us believing in him. Jpeg and Leila always said I was too nosy, and Dog Court declared me guilty *twice*, which meant that I was even bad at being Bad. Maybe I *had* just been pretending. Hoping. And getting everyone else to play along with sheer luck.

Finding my way home would be tough now, because I was totally lost—but at least I could follow my own scent back to the highway. I turned to leave and started walking. But the second I crunched a single leaf—

"AWOOOOOOOOOOO." No information, just a pure howl—a perfect tone with no growling, a powerful volume that seemed effortless. The smooth kind of howl that even a human wouldn't complain about, because it was so beautiful.

That had to be Shadow.

Certain she wouldn't give me another chance, I took off running toward the sound. I put all my focus into keeping my running line directly straight—no wobbling or turning—so I could make it to the source. My heart pounded in time with my paws against the dirt, and I got right to the edge of exhaustion—

And burst into a clearing. The backyard behind the old house where I'd met the puppies—with the shattered dog kennels to one side, and the poorly kept lawn. The moon wasn't as bright today, but I recognized everything. And—*ah!*—Shadow was right in front of me, in the center of the yard, somehow the last thing I saw.

"You shouldn't have come here on your own." She slid forward in a flash and sniffed me and then my trail. "Did anyone follow you?"

"I don't think so." I dipped my tail, embarrassed. "But I didn't check. I didn't think anyone would—"

In another flash, she was off—following the trail I'd left. I stood awkwardly in the yard until she returned.

"No one. Good." She paused, corrected: "Lucky. What do you want?"

No use talking around it. She could probably sniff out my thoughts, anyway. "We failed. Tonio quit." The weight of it—the truth of what had happened that day—finally sank in. I got swept up in the feelings and couldn't stop: "I tried to stop him, but he was upset—and when I told him about Jpeg, he shut me out—so I thought, *I* can't give up, we have to save Jpeg, and you might know what to do!"

Shadow led me to the house. We entered through the doggy door, and she motioned with her chin for me to flick the light switch above the washing machine. No puppies this time—the whole house was eerily empty without them and looked even older and dustier than before. I shivered in the cold. "Do you . . . live here?"

"For now." She sat in the middle of the living room and watched me, black fur seeming to absorb light from the yellow light bulb on the ceiling. "Tell me what happened. Slower."

So I caught her up. I told her what was going on—trying not to feel embarrassed under her gaze as I described the human dramas of middle school, which she clearly felt only contempt for. (*Is there something wrong with me?* I thought as I spoke. *That these things matter to me?*)

"And so," I finished, "we need to try something else.

Switch to plan B. I'll do whatever we have to do to save Jpeg—but I don't think Tonio can help us anymore. So give me orders! A new mission! Anything!"

Shadow tilted her head and finally spoke. She never spoke with anything I would describe as gentleness, but she did seem hesitant. "Buster, you don't understand. There is no plan B."

That didn't make any sense. "There are more Farm agents, right? I don't care how scary that guy is. He can't stop us if we all show up at his house. Or there has to be evidence of where they took Jpeg—if we start investigating directly, maybe—"

"No, Buster." She said my name a second time, this time with more force. I stopped talking. "Jpeg got captured because of her own mistakes. You and Tonio were an *opportunity* to find her—an opportunity that didn't involve risking any of our important agents. Currently, there are no other options Dog Court is willing to pursue."

"But she's a dog!" I argued. "She's one of us! What if they torture her and find out she's smart? They could— that could reveal us, right? Doesn't Dog Court want to stop that?"

Shadow twitched her tail *no*. "One smart dog is an anomaly. *Two* is a pattern. Even one more compromised agent can make it worse."

"But—"

Shadow placed a paw on the side of my neck—the

most personal gesture she'd ever used in front of me. "You feel guilty. You shouldn't. This is your human's failing, not yours."

"Of *course* it's my fault!" I whined. "I'm not a hacker, like Jpeg, or a spy like you. I'm not strong like Leila, and I'm not smart like Lasagna. But I thought I could be a hero, just because I *wanted* to be. I thought I could change the world."

Shadow watched as a tear rolled down my nose—I was too nervous to pull away from her and too emotional to keep it in. She made no move to do anything about it. "You know, the humans don't believe we cry. Just another way we aren't like them."

I nodded. She stepped back to give me some space. "I *do* think you're a hero, Buster."

That was surprising. Other than maybe Tonio, no one had ever said that to me since the Miracle Dog debacle. Just that they thought *I* thought I was. Or that I was acting like one. Not that I *was* one. And I was definitely surprised *Shadow* thought so. She continued: "Being a hero is not so difficult a thing. You need only change the world for the better, which I believe you want to do. That is enough. But you have been misdirected.

"You will not find heroism in these small things you're worrying about. You will not change the world by being *polite* or stopping a fight between children. Saving Jpeg won't make you a hero. The *purpose* you are looking for will come from dedication to *important* changes—and to action that protects all of us. Even if that action is inaction, for a time." A car, driven by a human from the neighborhood, rolled by. Shadow ducked down as the lights hit the window, so I did the same. "I believe you have the correct drive, and I am disappointed that you have spent so much time worried about humans. But soon, we can make you a real Farm agent."

My head tilted. I didn't know how I felt about everything she said, so I focused on the last part: "What do you mean, 'real'?"

Her face barely moved, but—I thought perhaps she was smirking. "You think you and your boy have been Farm agents? With no training and a summer of sleeping and crying as your only experience? No." She began walking back to the laundry room—toward the back door. "This was a test—for your human—and he failed, which we'll deal with. But *your* training hasn't even begun."

I didn't know how to respond to that. She was saying that I would leave Tonio . . . but still be a Farm agent? That she believed I *could* be a dog hero? After so much time as a dog everyone made fun of or hated after my time in the Court—it sounded nice. I could make a difference, and I wouldn't have to live only through Tonio. I would get to make my own choices.

But only in the Dog world. I'd be setting aside humans forever.

Before I could get my thoughts in order, Shadow pushed open the doggy door. "Go home. Rest. Say your goodbyes, if he'll listen to you. I'll inform the Court of the mission's failure, and we'll contact you in the next few days. Understood?"

I bobbed my head. "Understood."

"And, Buster . . . your parents would be proud of you."

My *parents*! I'd forgotten—I needed to ask her about—but then I was outside, and she was gone. I looked again at the pile of broken kennels. *I could be doing that. Saving puppies, being a spy.* I imagined myself roaming silently through the forest, perfect sense of direction, losing all the bad guys on my tail. I wondered if my parents had done that. It sounded *amazing*.

Still, there would be no Tonio. Not anymore. And even though we were fighting—he was my best friend! And I *did* care about him, even if Shadow didn't.

I can't be a real friend, I can't be a secret agent, and I can't save Jpeg. Tonio had said it himself. He couldn't do it. And if it was what I wanted . . . well . . .

Finding my way through the forest was easier the second time. I thought, the whole way, about how to say goodbye.

The house was sleeping when I returned. I fell asleep quickly on the living room couch and dreamed—the first dream I remember having in a long time. I was a bear, and I was having tea—at a table that was also the moon—in a beautiful field. At the other side of the table, also drinking tea, was one of those big bear traps they're always stepping into in old cartoons. The bear trap picked up a cup and dumped the tea through the teeth of the trap, sending it splashing into the grass behind it.

Where the tea hit, the grass transformed—from blades of green to shards of broken kennels. The change rippled out across the field, until it was nothing but plastic and metal as far as I could see, reflecting the light of the moon-table.

"Could you hand me the sugar?" the bear trap asked. I knew that if I gave it the sugar, though, it would trap my paw between its teeth. Still, if I didn't, I would be a bad host. It would be impolite! And it wasn't as if the bear trap had its own hands to grab the sugar. I resolved to give it the sugar, even though I knew I would lose my paw.

My big bear heart pounded as I picked up the bowl of sugar, and my paws were so shaky that it got all over the table. "What a mess!" the bear trap said as I apologized. Unable to give up now—but terrified to lose my paws—I leaned over the moon-table *closer . . . closer . . .* but the moon kept expanding, and gravity kept getting weaker and weaker, until I was floating slowly across a giant crater on the moon's surface. I realized with a sinking feeling that the trap had grown, too, and now it filled the entire crater below me.

The moon's gravity started pulling me downward, and I knew now that the trap was going to close over my whole body, and I never should have given it the sugar. Directly below me was the metal disk that would trigger the trap, and there was nothing—not even wind—between me and it. Only a matter of time before I was swallowed entirely.

WHAM! Someone slammed into my shoulder, knocking me away from the center and floating, weightless, out of the crater. I spun around to look and saw Jpeg, in an astronaut suit with a big glass dome head and everything.

"Ты хорошая собака!" Jpeg barked, voice crackly through a speaker on the suit.

"What?" I yelled back as I glided farther away and she began to fall, rapidly, toward the bear trap's trigger. *No, no, she needs to get away from there, I've got to change course. How do I—*

"You're having a nightmare!" Tonio was pushing at my stomach, concerned. "You're gonna wake up Mom and Dad." Startled, I looked around—it was still the middle of the night. The only light was coming from a glowing alien baby in a jar, a replica of something from one of Mr. Pulaski's favorite movies—it made Tonio look dim and green, kneeling next to the couch.

I rolled over and stood on the cushions to under-speak. *Sorry.* He squinted to see my movements. I was relieved to see him, rather than a bear trap, but I wasn't sure what to say. The last thing he'd done was lock me out of his room. *I was thinking about Jpeg*, I admitted. Our agreed-upon sign for *Jpeg* was a very quick patter with both paws, close to the word for typing. It made a silly squishy sound on the couch.

"Me too," he whispered, pushing at his sleepy hair to get it out of his face. "What happened to her?"

That guy we saw at the Beamblade Dog League—that felt so long ago now!—*was Oscar Sykes. Wearing a disguise.*

Tonio's eyes widened. "I told you I had a bad feeling about that guy!"

I'd forgotten about that. *That's true. You did.*

We sat in silence for a moment. I looked around at all the little statues and trinkets covering all the sur-faces of the room: superheroes, spaceships, and strange fake technology as lamps and on display; records hang-ing on the wall of Mrs. Pulaski's favorite bands; and in one little box under the TV, a small collection of Beamblade heroes Tonio got the Christmas before I met him. Apparently, Roll the Ice sold surprise boxes with random hero figures, and Tonio was scared to buy them if he didn't know what he would get, so his parents ordered the complete set online.

"Where did you go tonight?" he asked.

To talk to Shadow. I told her you quit.

Tonio looked away but nodded. "Does she have an idea? Or a plan?"

I posed *no* when he looked back to me. *We were the only chance to find her. They don't want to risk another dog.*

"But they wanted to risk *us*."

I rolled my shoulders in a shrug. Part of me wanted to comfort him—to tell him things would be okay, like always—but this time I knew they wouldn't be. And part of me was still mad at him.

He swallowed. "I'm sorry, Buster. I didn't mean what I said. It's like you said about Devon: I can't stop people from caring about me. Even if they don't do it the way I want." He kept his eyes away from me, staring at the dark screen of the TV in front of the windows, so I knew he wasn't done talking. "I'm mad at myself, not you, and I don't think you're using me. I think Dog Court is using *both* of us."

What do you mean?

"Do you remember why we agreed to do this? To be Farm agents?"

So we could stay together and live normal lives.

Tonio nodded but used his finger to do the Underspeak for *And?*

To prove that Dogs and Humans can work together?

"Yeah! But here we are, and on the *first* job they give us, we're in the same bad spot you were in, just together. We can't tell anybody anything, we're lying all the time, and we haven't been able to live normal lives at all. And now Jpeg is in trouble, with no way out."

Because we failed.

"No!" Tonio yipped, then brought his voice back down with a nervous look up the stairs toward his parents' room. "Because they won't let us do this our way in the first place!"

Our way?

"Tell Mia! She cares about Jpeg *so much*. And Devon. Get Leila and Mozart and everybody and all work together."

That's too dangerous. We have to be careful, or more dogs will end up like Jpeg.

He gave me a frustrated, surprised look. "When did you start thinking like that?" he asked. "I thought you wanted things to change, too. For dogs and humans to help each other."

I do! I insisted. *But it might not be the right time. If the DNI is abducting dogs, and if—*

"This is what I mean!" Tonio held both hands out, palms up, like he was begging me to listen. "I think this is what Dog Court *wants*. They want you to give up so they don't have to change."

I— No. No way! I couldn't believe that. I *don't* believe

that. *Sweetie believes in this. I know she does! And Shadow—she says I'm going to train like the other Farm agents, and then I'll be able to help as a spy, or—*

His face, just moments ago pleading for me to listen, hardened into anger. Then, in another instant, into carefully blank nothingness. "'Going to.' So you're leaving."

Oops. *I didn't mean to tell you like that. But . . .*

"It really happened." Tonio lifted off the ground and looked down at me. "I thought it was just my anxiety— you *said* it was just my anxiety—but I was right. I messed up one time, and I've ruined everything. *For all humans* and all the dogs that were counting on me. And now you're leaving."

You said *you couldn't be an agent anymore!* Now I was mad, too. *You said you didn't want to do this! But* I *do!*

"I was upset!" His voice was rising again. "But I'm not allowed to be upset and be an agent. And I'm not allowed to be anxious. And I'm not allowed to know what's actually going on, in case I get upset or anxious. 'You don't have to be perfect, Tonio,'" he mimicked. "That's what you said. 'You just have to be yourself!'" He made a gurgly noise in his throat. "I'm anxious all the time! If I can't be that *and* an agent, then why make me one in the first place?!"

I was about to answer, but a door opened upstairs. "Tonio?" Mrs. Pulaski called, voice dripping with sleep. "Is't you?"

"Sorry, Mom!" he called back. "Just . . . practicing lines!"

"Isstoo ayem."

"Oh, gosh, I'm sorry."

"Yokay?"

"Yeah, I'm really fine. I'll go to bed now."

She mumbled something completely indecipherable and shut the door.

Tonio, you're right. It's my fault. I should have told you about Jpeg.

He switched to Underspeak, but his posture made it clear the conversation was almost over. *But now that I messed up, you're going to go join the people who* aren't *going to save her?*

I didn't have a choice! Not anymore. So I didn't answer right away, and he sighed and headed toward the stairs. Two stairs up, he paused and turned around.

"You know what's funny? When you get a dog, one of the things they say is that you'll have a friend who will love you no matter what. They think dogs aren't people, so they say you get someone you can always depend on."

He shrugged. "I'm glad dogs are people. But it's a little sad that doesn't exist."

— 21 —

I woke the next morning to the phone ringing. It was Saturday, so we'd slept late, and Mr. Pulaski had an employee who worked mornings for him, so everyone was home. The jingling melody of the phone was a surprise—both because a call to the landline was rare, and also because of *who* was calling.

"TOOOONIOOOOO!" Mr. Pulaski sang up the stairs, one hand patting me on the couch. "Parker's on the phone for you!"

Whoa, what? I stood up and propped my front legs on the back of the couch so I could reach Mr. Pulaski's hand. I gently bit down on the phone with my jaws, and he let go with a laugh. "Sure, Buster, you can take it to him. Good boy."

I ran the phone up the stairs to him, excited—until the silence of my missing collar reminded me of the day before. Our mission was over. I paused beside Tonio's cracked-open door—but it wasn't like we could hang up on him now. And maybe—*just maybe*—there was still a glimmer of hope for saving Jpeg, if not our friendship. I walked inside.

Tonio groaned. "I *hate* talking on the phone."

I began underspeaking back, but Parker's voice said: "I would have texted you, but you don't have a phone."

"Dad didn't mute it?!" Tonio hissed.

Parker said, "Nope." Tonio took the phone from my mouth, wiped it on his shirt, and put it up to his ear. (I could still hear Parker clearly.) "I got to hear Buster's saliva *right* in my ear."

"Gross. Sorry."

"It's whatever." Tonio waited for him to continue, but he didn't.

"You called me?" Tonio's face went red. "Wait, I . . . Uhhhhf course you called me. I meant why?"

Parker took his stumbling without comment. "I have a nice reason and a real reason. Which one do you want first?"

Tonio looked at me. I thought we could use something nice. "Nice first," he said.

"I want to apologize. For everything." The rumble of a car drove by Parker—he must have been somewhere outside. "Miles was lying when he said it was my idea. I wanted to stop him, but . . ." A breath. "He gets really intense sometimes. It's easier to stay out of his way."

Squeezing the phone between his ear and shoulder, Tonio underspoke to me. *That was* not *an apology*, he signed. *And I don't trust him. But I'm doing this for Jpeg.* "Thank you."

For Jpeg? I thought. Tonio's attention returned to the phone, but I felt my heart fill with complicated emotions. Even though he was mad at me—even though I'd told him it was over—he wasn't giving up on Jpeg. And if Parker was reaching out to us, maybe we *did* still have a chance.

"You're pretty cool," Parker continued, voice as confident and believable as always. "And I know everybody likes having you in the show."

"Thank you," Tonio repeated, face burning a deeper red. "What's . . . uh, you said there was a real reason?"

"Yeah." A sigh. "You know how I'm grounded?"

"Yes?"

". . . . ."

"Are you still there??"

". . . . . . . mymomsaidican'tgotothefallfestivalunlessi gowithyou."

"Huh?"

"Everyone's going to the festival tonight." *Already?!* It had really snuck up on me. I guess I had seen them putting up decorations a few days before. "But Mom said I can't go unless my 'apology is good enough' that you want to go with me." Another sigh. "I know it's stupid. But if you'll just come get me tonight, I can leave you alone once we get there. I don't want to miss everything. I've already called Devon and Mia and apologized."

Tonio was frozen in his desk chair, staring at the

ceiling. He didn't look to me for advice, and even though I wanted to save Jpeg, it felt like I'd forfeited my right to suggest anything to him anymore. I was going to leave. And—I still feel that way. I *am* going to leave. I think.

(Honestly, and you can cut this, Lasagna, I'm starting to get really nervous. I've been writing so much of this waiting for Tonio . . . and I'm worried about him. It's so weird to be in this room alone, and even after all of this, that *he* would be the one to risk himself, while I just sit here, writing. I had to say that somewhere. Sorry.)

"Are *you* still there?"

"I have conditions!" Tonio blurted out.

At that, Parker actually laughed. My tail wagged.

"Okay. *Let's make a deal.*"

"I'm going in early with Devon to help Mia and her dads set up. You have to come and help, too."

"I can do that."

"And . . ." *I would ask for a sleepover*, Tonio underspoke, *but I would sound crazy. There's literally no reason I would want that.*

We don't want to warn Sykes you're onto him, I agreed. *It has to be casual.*

"You have to promise to stop messing with my friends. Forever. And if Miles tries to mess with them, you have to stop him."

"I can *try*. I'm not his dad."

Tonio nodded, even though Parker couldn't see it. "If you want to go to the festival, those are my terms."

I was impressed. Tonio was threading the needle perfectly—he was finding a way to include Mia and Devon, fix their bullying problem, *and* get closer to Parker. All without really having to give anything up— Parker had set his own trap, getting grounded and letting Miles and Piper trick Devon. It was really smart.

And . . . Tonio is *always* smart. He's always thought- ful. He's anxious, yes, but—this was why I wanted to be his partner in the first place. How did I forget that? Why have I been so ready to give up on him? When I see you again, Tonio, I'm going to give you an apology. A real apology, where I even say I'm sorry.

"Deal," Parker agreed finally. I imagined them shak- ing hands in a fancy office, resolving a middle school dispute with a company merger. "If you make sure Mia doesn't beat me up when we get there."

"Oh, she wouldn't—" Tonio stopped, thinking. "Actually, yeah, I'm going to call her."

They settled on a time for Tonio to come get him, and hung up.

I started underspeaking, tail wagging. *You did it! This is amazing. I can go tell Shadow we're back on track, and—*

Tonio shook his head. "I'm doing this for Jpeg. Not Dog Court." He swiveled his chair around and grabbed a pencil to do some drawing. "I thought about it, and I know for sure: I don't want to be their agent anymore. So if that's what you want, nothing's changed. You can go with them when we're done."

He wasn't looking at me anymore, and I didn't have anything else to add, anyway. He was right; if he was really done with Dog Court, then we did have to go separate ways. Nothing was different.

I squeezed into the closet to work on this report and tried to focus on what to do when we got to the festival.

The Bellville Fall Festival was the largest Bellville-specific event of the year. Visitors and vendors from nearby towns were already parking all over the square and side roads leading to the Lin Family Shelter and Dog Park—Mia's family hosted the event on their land, but technically it was organized by the town itself. The mayor would be there, along with almost everybody in Bellville.

Tonio hadn't gone for a few years, because his parents started keeping him away from crowds when his anxiety worsened. This was his first time back—and it was supposed to be triumphant, exciting, but instead it was melancholy and intimidating. (Not that Tonio's parents realized.)

"You look so *cute!*" Mrs. Pulaski had helped Tonio shave the side of his head back down, and they dressed him up in an outfit I'd never seen before: a light blue button-down shirt and khakis with a plaid bow tie. He looked *so* South Carolina. Before I could protest, though, his dad gave me a present, too: a matching plaid collar with a bow tie on it. "Buster's first Fall Festival! Pose for pictures over here."

We stood in front of the floating alien baby in the living room. I sat beside him and lifted my chin to pose for the camera while Tonio stood silently beside me. "Come on, smile!" Mr. Pulaski cheered. He was dressed up, too, with a blazer over a comic-book movie T-shirt. "You look great!"

Tonio tried to smile. After a few shots: "Okay, now kneel down next to him!"

He did. We were on the same level now. I looked sideways at him, but he didn't look at me. We hadn't really talked since that morning. "Awww. Give your best friend a big hug!" *C'mon, Mom!* I thought. But Tonio listened, and he wrapped his arms around me and hugged, putting us cheek to cheek. *So awkward.*

"Look at Buster! He loves it!"

Tonio let go and stood up after a few shots. "Mom, can we go? We need to pick up Parker."

"Sure, sure." Mrs. Pulaski put her phone in her pocket and hugged her husband. She was dressed up, too, in a sense: same faux-leather jacket, band shirt, and jeans, but today her big boots had shiny studs on them.

"You'll be happy to have pictures when you're older, you know." Mr. Pulaski hugged Tonio, too. "We have hardly anything of your mom when she was a kid."

Mrs. Pulaski lifted her palms up. "My parents weren't very sentimental, I guess."

"And so now she's completely forgotten what it was like to be a child." He shook his head sadly.

"How many times do I have to tell you, *I was born twenty-three!* See you in a bit." She opened the door, grabbed the keys to the nice car, and waved us out. Tonio hooked on my harness quietly, and we headed to Chime Hollow.

"What did you say his house number was?" Mrs. Pulaski asked Tonio when we arrived.

"415." She punched the number into the panel by the gate. It rang, like a phone, several times. Finally, someone picked up.

A man's voice: "Yes? Who is this?" It was definitely Oscar Sykes, even garbled through the speaker.

"Laura, Tonio's mom. We're here to pick up Parker for the festival!"

Muffled conversation, then: "Is that dog with you?" Mrs. Pulaski made a face at his tone. She turned around and mouthed to Tonio, *That dog!*

"Yep. Tonio told me about your allergy—we vacuumed

the seats this morning, and Parker will be sitting in the front seat. Is that okay?"

"Mm." A pause. "The gate is broken. I'll send him out to meet you." We watched a car, that exact second, drive up to the gate from the other side. It opened smoothly and quickly. He was obviously lying, but Mrs. Pulaski didn't push it.

"Okay. We're in the blue—" The panel made a clicking sound and shut off. "Minivan." She backed up away from the gate and parked along the side of the road. Tonio and I looked through the bars to the houses.

Parker pushed on a human-sized door in the gate and walked toward the car. He was dressed up, too, in a gray sweater over a green button-down—slightly less formal than Tonio's bow tie and moving with *much* more confidence. It was obvious he wore clothes like this more often than Tonio did—or maybe he was just natural with any kind of costume.

"Hi, Mrs. Pulaski!" Parker chirped, opening the front door and jumping in. He flashed a big smile to Tonio's mom, then nodded at Tonio. "Hey, Tonio."

"Hello."

"Parker! Look at you. You've gotten so tall!" He laughed and smiled big again, clearly turning his charm all the way up for Mrs. Pulaski. As they made conversation, I stared out the window.

Now we'd both seen our target: house 415 in Chime Hollow. Our big challenge was coming up: somehow turning an experience with Mia, Devon, *and* Parker into something positive—and turning this festival, our last chance, into sleepover gold.

⊸ 22 ⊸

We were dropped off outside the gate to the Lin Family Shelter and Dog Park, which was decorated in fairy lights and ribbons. A big sign on the part of the gate people walked through said *WARNING: DOGS LOOSE ON THE PREMISES. PLEASE BE CAREFUL NOT TO LET THEM THROUGH THE GATES.* And then in different, *very* recognizable handwriting: *IF YOU RELEASE THEM, YOU BRING THEM BACK. WE ARE WATCHING!!!! —Management.*

A dirt path led into The Farm, lined by trees that were already lit up in preparation for the evening. Tonio, Parker, and I walked toward the Lins' office and home to find Mia and Devon, marveling at how the place transformed: A ton of those canopy tents and tables were set up all along the path and across the dirt field, and there were *way* more humans around than usual. The festival wasn't even open to the public yet, but adults from miles around came to sell art, jewelry, clothes, food, and all sorts of other things.

"You should do a booth here one day," Parker suggested, nodding to someone hanging up portraits of celebrities made out of household objects. "People would totally buy your art. Your little cards or whatever."

Tonio blushed. "Mia says that all the time. But I think it's because she wants to be my 'agent.'"

"Aw, she's already called it?" Parker snapped his fingers and mouthed, *Dang*, which made Tonio laugh. "When did you and Mia become friends? I feel like you never really talked to anyone."

"Everybody was at Camp Sticks and Bugs this summer, except for us and Devon." Tonio squinted at Parker. "You're a Cicada Scout, right?"

"Hercules Beetle this year, actually. I found rabbit tracks and got the badge to push me over on the last day. Super lucky."

"I thought that was before Cicada?"

"No, it goes Caterpillar, Cocoon, Butterfly, Cicada, Hercules—though really it should be Heracles—Moth, and then Mantis."

"That's funny!" Tonio announced. "You're Heracles in two different ways."

"Yep." Parker kicked a rock on the road. "Is Mia why you didn't quit school?" Tonio stiffened, but Parker kept his calm posture. "You said you almost quit because of me."

"Uh, yeah. I . . . it was a lot of reasons, not just you. I was mad."

Parker stopped on the side of the road. Tonio stopped, too, when he noticed. "I've been thinking about it, and

I can't figure it out. I never messed with you. When you asked me to promise not to, I was like, 'I already never did.' Is that wrong? Did I ever mess with you?"

Tonio was visibly uncomfortable with where this conversation was going. "No, not *me*."

"Right." Parker shrugged. "I know it sounds fake now, but I tried to make sure Miles never did, either. Your mom was always really nice to my mom, and we used to be friends. So I know it wasn't because I was bothering you. The only bad thing that happened was you threw up on Devon at yearbook signing, right? Before that, nobody ever even talked about you, 'cause all you did was sit there and draw. And then we all come back for sixth grade and now you're best friends with both of them and you get to bring a dog with you everywhere." He looked at me, at the end of a loosely held leash. "So I figure it has to have something to do with that, right? When you threw up. How is that *my* fault?"

I watched Tonio weigh how much truth to tell Parker against how uncomfortable he was willing to be. He settled faster than I expected. "You want to know so you can make fun of me."

"Don't you think, if I was going to make fun of you, I would have done it by now?"

"You called me short," Tonio recalled. "And you said I looked like a tomato."

"While you were *running*! And that's barely even

scratching the surface. I could say *so* much stuff about you, but—" He paused. "I mean, not *that* much."

"Uh-huh."

"I'm asking for real."

Tonio sighed and looked nervous to tell him something close to the truth. But he summoned up confidence—all on his own, without needing any input from me—and spoke. "That class was a nightmare. For *everybody*. You and Miles kept picking on Devon behind his back and then doing the same thing to anybody who tried to help him."

For the first time, Parker seemed uncomfortable. "It wasn't that bad. We were just, like, class clowns. We were making people laugh."

"You were making people *scared*," Tonio insisted. "They started laughing to get on your good side." The look on Parker's face made me think he hadn't considered this, which seemed impossible. Tonio, apparently also frustrated by that look, pushed harder. "I watched it happen to everyone, except Sloan—because you're scared of Mia."

"I'm not scared of Mia."

"You *asked me today* to make sure she didn't kill you."

"But that was a joke—"

"Okay, then why don't you mess with Mia like you mess with Devon?"

Parker shrugged. "She got so *serious* about it, and it was just jokes."

"She was the only one who fought back! And Devon did the opposite of fight back." Tonio shook his head. "You weren't just making people laugh; you were targeting the ones who were easy to target, and Devon was easy because he didn't know anybody."

Parker didn't say anything.

"I never stood up for him, and I hated myself for that. I hated that there was nothing I could do, and I was scared of what would happen if I *did* do something, and every second in that class was horrible for me."

"Then why did you start talking to us? If we're so *terrible*."

Tonio looked at me for the first time in this conversation, just for a second. I expected to hear him come up with some sort of lie, but instead he said, "I thought I could make things better. You have a whole . . ." He made a sphere with his hands. "A whole *system*. You have older friends, so you look cool, and you have Miles to do whatever you want so you always have backup. You pick people to make fun of who are already uncool—like Jason, or Kimberlyn, or Roel—and other people don't stop you, because they're scared of you. And if they're too cool for you to trick, and too smart to be scared of you, you make them part of your group. Like Piper."

Back when I first met him, Tonio used to only get on a roll like this when he was safe and hidden in his room—showing me that his mind *always* worked that fast, always had thoughts like this ready to go, but was usually held back by his fear. It also was usually triggered when he really needed to unload his anxious thoughts, but this time—it was like he was finally getting to say something he'd held inside for years.

"I thought that if I joined you—if I became a part of your little bully world—I could change it. Even before this year, I imagined how I could save Devon and the rest of the class by standing up to you." He stared at the ground between them. Parker watched the top of his head. "The worst part is that I really thought I *could*, if it wasn't for my anxiety, but now I know that was wrong, too, because I *did* try, and it didn't work. It wasn't worth it."

Parker adjusted the sweater around his collar. He gave Tonio a dubious look. "You make it all sound like such a huge deal, but it's just, like, jokes."

"Maybe to you. Not everyone has the same brain you do."

"And all that stuff about a 'system' is wrong. I don't do any of that on purpose. My friends are my friends."

A woman walked toward the booths, carrying a stack of boxes that swished like they were full of sand. Tonio waited for her to pass. "You don't have to do it on purpose to do it."

Irritation flashed across Parker's face. He shrugged it off, but I could hear his heart pounding. "Okay, well, you answered my question." He jerked a thumb toward the office. "Can we go?"

I looked up to Tonio, expecting our normal check-in swap of glances—but he didn't look down. His jaw clenched, a glare at the back of Parker's head as he walked away. "Yeah, okay. They're probably waiting for us."

Mia met us outside the office with a smile and threw neon-yellow safety vests at both of them. (Parker's a little harder than Tonio's.)

"We have to wear these?" Parker asked.

"Yep!" Mia kept her big smile on as she answered. "They'll make sure you're visible all night as an Adoption Helper."

"All night?"

"Oh?" She brought her eyebrows together, as if concerned. "That's what Tonio and I'll be doing. Did you want me to call your mom and tell her you plan on ditching us as soon as the festival starts?"

"No, I'll wear it."

"Because I'd be happy to."

"I said I'll wear it!"

Tonio had already put his on. Parker rolled his eyes and slowly pulled his on, too. Mia was wearing a dress with an autumn leaf pattern under hers—the brightest yellow of the flowers actually sort of matched, which told me she'd planned it that way. Parker, with his gray sweater and neon-yellow vest, looked radioactive.

"Great!" Mia clapped her hands together and whirled on her heels. "Everyone else is at the barn."

Devon waved as we got closer to the barn. He started to head toward us with a concerned look on his face, but Mia didn't let him slow us down. "Uh, hi, Tonio!" Devon smiled in a way that scared me in the opposite way Mia's smile did—he usually *would* be smiling, so his difficulty showed that something was going on. "And . . . Parker. Um, okay, we're not gonna stop, I guess, so—"

Now, as I looked past him, it was obvious the other figures wearing safety vests weren't Mia's dads. They were kids. As each of them turned to look at us, I saw:

Another green shirt, like always. Roel, who Parker had done a "collection" for after Tonio told him about his accidental in-app purchases;

A beanie over blue hair. Kimberlyn, who'd given Parker a bloody nose after he bullied her using Tonio's information about her anger management;

And a very well-tightened belt on a fidgety frame. Jason, who had watched Tonio befriend the Drama Kings after Parker managed to socially pants him without actually pantsing him.

"I asked some friends to help out tonight," Mia explained. "I hope you don't mind!"

Yikes. This whole *farm* wasn't big enough for the

tension between this group. Roel, Kimberlyn, and Jason glared at Parker, who looked from each of them to Mia, who smiled a big fake smile at Tonio, who looked at Devon, who sighed, a helpless expression on his face.

"What's up?" Parker asked finally.

"Oh, nothing. When you called earlier, I thought . . ." Mia leaned against the wall of the barn and crossed her arms. "Devon and I are fine. So I figured you might also like to apologize to some people you *actually hurt*. Both of you."

Parker rolled his eyes and spoke—which was good, because Tonio had frozen completely. He pointed at Kimberlyn. "You attacked *me* for making jokes. I still have a bruise on *my face*! Aren't we even?"

"I had to go to ISS for three days, you jerk! And I got grounded!"

"Well, Roel—I was *helping* you. We raised like thirty bucks."

"And a bunch of kids told their parents, who called my parents to 'ask if they could help.' My mom just wanted to forget it. You made her cry."

I saw desperation start to appear in Parker's eyes. But—how was this possible? Could he really not have realized he was a bad guy?

"Jason, nobody even remembers the pants thing anymore. And—Miles was going to *really* do it, but I told him he didn't have to! I saved you from it."

That got a laugh from Jason. "I *wish* that was all you did to me this year. Don't think I forgot when you took credit for finding those tracks at Sticks and Bugs." Parker winced and glanced sideways at Tonio. "*I* should be a Hercules Beetle Scout, not you."

Here it comes, I thought. *This is when he does what he's done with everything else: push the blame away. Tell them about how he couldn't have known their secrets without Tonio's help.* Tonio was staring past them all, into the barn wall, breathing heavy. He was waiting for it, too, and trying to keep himself from panicking.

"Well . . ." Parker began, quiet and grumbly. ". . . I don't know what Tonio has to apologize for. He was only helping me to protect his friends."

Kimberlyn and Roel looked confused, too. "Yeah, Mia, what did you mean? Tonio didn't do anything." But Jason had seen. He watched Tonio's face.

The words snapped Tonio out of his head. He turned to Parker with an unfiltered *Are you serious?* look on his face. Pure surprise. "No!" he yelped, then brought his voice down. "I mean, uh, well, I mean no." He forced his eyes up to Jason, and Roel, and Kimberlyn. "Mia's right. It's my fault Parker and Miles knew anything about you two." He forced himself to look them in the eyes. "*Your* mom talked about the anger management to my dad. And I helped do grocery deliveries for *your* family, so I knew about the money."

Roel and Kimberlyn both made the kind of face you make when you realize something didn't make sense at the same time you learn why it *does*. Jason nodded.

"I used your stories to make myself look better, which is the same thing Parker does." Parker narrowed his eyes at this small betrayal. I felt a *little* bad for him—he had reached out to Tonio for some solidarity. "Actually, I think what I did was worse, because I thought I could keep it a secret. I'm sorry."

Neither of them looked like they knew what to say. After a moment, Roel said, "What's *your* thing?"

Tonio's head tilted. "My thing?"

"Yeah!" Kimberlyn nodded along with her friend. "You know both of *our* secrets. What's yours?"

Tonio's face turned red immediately. "Oh, I don't— Secrets? I've never—"

Mia spread her arms and beamed. "What a great idea! It's only fair."

Oh no. Tonio, we can't tell them! I started to dance nervously on the dirt, but Tonio wasn't looking at me. "Okay," he said. "But I'll only tell you two." He handed my leash to Mia, making it clear I wasn't coming along. The three of them stepped down to the end of the barn, and Tonio leaned over to whisper into each of their ears in turn.

I was panicking. He couldn't!!! If he told them the truth about dogs right now—even ignoring all the *other*

234

reasons it would be bad—the whole evening would become about that. We'd have no time to make things work with Parker! I needed to get over there and—

A big laugh from Kimberlyn rang through The Farm as they walked back. "Okay, that's *adorable*."

"Honestly," Roel said with a thoughtful look, "better than I expected, secret-wise."

"Good luck!"

Mia, for all her tough acting lately, looked *very* relieved as the other kids came back happy. There was only a tiny crack in her confident poise, but I saw it: She'd been worried. Worried that Tonio was in too deep with Parker, and that his answers at the theater were for show. She exchanged a look with Devon, who smiled. Tonio was earning back their trust.

But what secret was *I* not allowed to know? I could tell Devon was curious, too. But . . . I guess it was Tonio's choice. And if it wasn't about dogs, he was allowed to tell other people secrets I don't know. I guess. Even though I'm his best friend and I am *extremely curious*!!!

Parker's brow was stabbing down into his nose, and he spoke by practically spitting out the words. "Is it true," he asked, "that me and Miles made fifth grade awful? For everybody?"

"Yes," Mia said, while Devon said, "No!" and the other kids considered their answers.

Roel shrugged. "I wasn't in your class." Jason

nodded—he wasn't, either. So eyes went to Kimberlyn.

She pulled her beanie off and scratched at her head—blond hair growing out at the roots. "I used to go home every day and yell about you to my brother."

"No way it was—"

"Every. Day."

Watching Parker's reaction was unlike anything I'd seen before. When Tonio thought he did something wrong, he tended to get sad or scared. But Parker looked *really, really mad*. His face was red and kept moving back and forth from glaring anger to confusion. The whole group seemed to lean away from him, nervous about how he was going to lash out. He'd always seemed so chill—but he'd never been powerless before. He'd never been in a group of people who weren't on his side.

As the seconds dragged on in a way that felt like hours, I realized he was trying to keep himself under control. He wasn't going to lash out—he was trying to listen, and it was *hard*. I could almost laugh, not so much because the situation was funny but because of how different he was from Tonio and Devon, who would take basically any criticism and immediately believe the criticizer was right. Parker was so used to being confident, so comfortable with his superiority, that he had to fight himself to accept notes. *He'll have to work on that if he wants to keep being an actor*, I thought.

"What do I have to do?" Parker barked, looking at Mia, making it clear he couldn't handle more attention right now. "As an Adoption Helper?"

Mia started to say something, but Devon spoke first. "Yeah, Mia!" He smiled and gave her a pleading look to let it go, for now. "How do we help?"

The other kids seemed ready to give Parker a minute, so Mia nodded and pulled a bunch of differently colored collars out of her back pocket. "OKAY! So. The Fall Festival is our biggest adoption night of the year, and the shelter needs even more than usual to afford to take care of all the new dogs this season. If you've been before, you know that we let the dogs roam around and meet people who might adopt them naturally." She wiggled the collars in her hand. "That's where the collars come in."

"A red collar means the dog is already adopted or lives here with us. They're not adoptable. A green collar means they are adoptable, friendly, and healthy! All adoptable dogs have their shots and everything, but—" She held up a yellow collar. "Yellow means the dog has special needs, so we probably won't just adopt those dogs out right away. Blue collars mean they're adoptable, but that they're shy or wary of humans—so people should be a little more careful with them and ready for that. Finally, purple means they're totally adoptable, but that there's at least one other dog that has to go with them.

"Your job is to help people who might want to adopt one—and by help, I also mean *convince*. We're kids, so we're allowed to be a little annoying about it. There's a big pile of complimentary leashes in this box for you to keep with you. If someone approaches you because of your vest, you check the dog's collar and inform them what it means, then give them a leash and lead both them and the dog back here, where my dads and the people from the pet store can set them up with a take-home kit. If they ask—"

"I'm sorry!"

"Uh—"

"I didn't know I was this bad." Parker was staring at the ground. "I thought, uh . . ." He rubbed at his nose and looked up at the sky. "I thought people liked me. But you're right." He shrugged, obviously struggling to add some element of casual coolness into this emotional announcement. "I'm obnoxious. Sorry."

Every word still sounded like he was *mad*. It didn't sound sincere, the way all of his lies did. Something about that, though, made me feel like it was truer. He wasn't disguising his feelings—he felt bad because he was listening to people tell him he was bad. That made sense to me, a well-documented Bad Dog.

The other kids were slow to speak. I think it was hard

for them to simply accept an apology from someone who had hurt them for so long. Mia, however, already had an answer prepared.

"You can make it up to *me* by getting some adoptions." She threw a pile of leashes at his face, which he managed to catch easily despite his mood. "So why don't we start with that?"

— 23 —

On the other side of The Farm, another conversation was happening.

"Okay," Leila boomed across a gathering of dogs hidden in the forest, "who actually wants to get adopted?" She'd teamed up with a few other dogs to sneak a bunch of red collars away and was passing them out to whoever wanted them. Blue-collared dogs who *were* shy but wanted to get adopted for sure swapped with green-collared dogs who were picky about which humans they might go home with.

Most of the dogs in the shelter this season were puppies who Dog Court had decided would be pets—I even recognized a few who'd arrived here after their stop in the house Shadow was watching over. And most of them *did* want to get adopted. That was the normal route— you usually got better food, a chill life, and you could take what you learned from your humans and share it with all dogs. It was easy to make it sound nice.

But . . . not all dogs are interested in that. And not all of us are cut out for a life that simple. Many of those dogs would be going back to situations with humans who needed help the dogs couldn't give—or, worse, they'd find out too late they were adopted by humans who weren't going to take care of them the way they'd promised, especially the puppies. Dog Court liked to say that was a symptom of humanity's cruelty, but . . . I think it's Dog Court's fault, too, for deciding to risk a few puppies to bad homes rather than open up the rest of Dogkind to the danger of humans who find out they're not alone. And maybe the Court is right? I'm so unsure lately.

I already had a red collar. Leila was wearing a purple one in honor of Jpeg. "Any news?"

"Yeah, good and bad. I . . . well, Tonio and I had a deal with the Court, and Tonio doesn't want to do it anymore, which means I'll probably be leaving soon. But he's still trying to save Jpeg."

She gave me a look with tiny eyes under the fur that piled up at her forehead. "*He* is?"

"He's not listening to me anymore. I think I let him down. There's not much I can do, anyway—it's kind of a human thing."

Leila stared into my eyes. She leaned forward and sniffed on either side of my face. "Hey, what are you—" She put a paw on my face and inspected the inside of my ears—her nose blew air into one. "That tickles!!"

She pulled back and gave me a sad look. "Someone trapped you."

I blinked, stunned. "My dream? Did you smell my *dream*?"

"What? No." Leila nodded to a puppy who barked hello, then looked back at me. "You smell like a mess. You're stressed, and you don't look healthy. I warned you about this." At my confused face, she huffed. "I *told* you that if you didn't figure out what you wanted, someone would lead you into a trap. And they have."

"I'm not in a trap!" I argued.

"But you're leaving *Tonio*? The boy you were willing to get *exiled for life* over?" Leila shook her head. "Somebody's got you leashed, and you're doing what they want."

"That's not true!" I felt heat rising in my body—I was doing *everything I could* to save Jpeg for her, and out of nowhere she wanted to tell me I wasn't making my own decisions? No. She couldn't talk to me like that, not when I . . .

. . . was being like Parker. I was getting mad. I needed to listen. Leila had no reason to lie to me, right? I could trust her. But my anger was telling me something—she was making me sensitive. I thought about all the advice Dr. Jake had given Tonio; I knew from him that when you had a big emotion, like worry or anger, you needed to ask questions. Figure out why you felt that way, not try to stop it.

"Can you tell me what you mean?" I asked.

Leila bobbed her head *yes*. "Buster, a few months ago nobody could stop you from helping the kids around here, and that was before any of them listened to you. What changed?" I felt another flare of anger. She couldn't possibly understand what had changed! Everything had changed! Tonio was mad at me—he didn't want to be a Farm agent, and if he didn't want to be a Farm agent, I couldn't do what I want.

What I want?

"Back then, I just wanted to feel important. I was nosy, like you said. I wasn't being a real hero, I was just pretending to be one."

"And how will leaving Tonio change that?"

"Dog Court has a place where I can be a real hero."

Leila bared her teeth at me. "Buster, I want you to think about what you said. *Leaving behind a human who needs you* will make you a *hero*?"

Anger again. Did she think I was stupid? I knew it was complicated—the whole *situation* was complicated, more complicated than anything I'd ever done in my life! You couldn't narrow it down to one simple sentence like that and act like you understood what was going on. Right?

But if the whole situation was complicated, why did Shadow's solution seem so simple? I felt so relaxed when

I thought about it: She would tell Dog Court the mission was over; I would leave this complicated situation and go off to be a hero. I would go make *big* changes, instead of these small ones. And I would be able to be somebody who made a difference, not someone dependent on a human.

"Tonio *told me* to leave; he said he didn't want to keep the deal with Dog Court anymore."

Leila gave me a look of exhausted patience. "Even if that's true, I'm wondering when you started listening to other people when they told you to give up."

She was right.

"There it is." Leila was watching my face. "You're finally thinking!"

"What do you think I should do?" I asked Leila. "You think I should stay with Tonio?"

"*I* think you need to make your own decisions." Leila shrugged. "Or you'll be right back in this same situation, again and again. You have to believe in something, Buster. You have to *want* something. Or other people are going to fill your brain with the things *they* want."

I thought about what Tonio had told me. *I think this is what Dog Court wants. They want you to give up so they don't have to change.* I didn't believe Sweetie wanted that, but maybe that's what *Shadow* wanted? Could that be true?

Leaving Tonio didn't help Tonio, and it didn't help Jpeg, and it didn't help anyone I knew. It helped Shadow, it helped the parts of Dog Court who wanted dogs to stay quiet, who I *know* I don't agree with, and it helped me. It made me feel like a hero.

I felt my anger break through, all at once, to shame. I was finally *actually* doing what everyone used to accuse me of doing. I was making decisions because I wanted to feel like a hero, not because I really cared about something. I care about Tonio, and Jpeg, and Mia, and Bellville. I care about *people*, and about the dogs who love them. I don't care about Dog Court! Sorry, Sweetie, but that's why I became a Bad Dog in the first place. It's why you hired me.

This was when I realized, too, I hadn't spoken to you since that first night. I'd only spoken to Shadow.

"Oh, wow," I gasped. It was like Leila had performed a magic trick. Suddenly—abracadabra—*I* was there. Where had I been? "Thank you, Leila."

"Ooh, I like that face." Leila's tail was wagging again. "You have an idea."

I did. It was a risky one, but this was the most important night of the mission. Why had I wandered away and left Tonio alone to it? And Leila deserved to be involved, too. Tonio might still be mad at me, and I might not be able to fix our friendship right away—but I could at least make sure the mission succeeded. *Our way*, like Tonio said. Not Dog Court's way.

"This is going to sound crazy," I explained, "but if we're going to find Jpeg, these kids need to have the best Fall Festival of their lives."

— 24 —

Gates opened for the festival, and suddenly humans out-numbered dogs on The Farm for the first time I'd ever seen. Hundreds of people walked around the booths, took hay rides in Jeff Lin's truck, and tested their luck at carnival-style games. Festivities trailed all the way from here to the square, covering the whole path Tonio and I took whenever we visited. The sun was going down early these days, so twilight was close to settling in— and a whole sky's worth of sparkling lights turned on, making the festival feel like the brightest place in the night.

The sound of crunching leaves underfoot mingled with laughter and music. Turkey legs, funnel cakes, and even a booth that only sold macaroni and cheese filled the air with smells I couldn't pick apart easily with my messed-up nose, but I didn't mind—each thing layered on top of the next beautifully until even my breath felt like pure *fall*.

I kept track of Tonio easily, thanks to the vests, and I could tell he was already growing anxious. There were more people at this Festival than there were in his entire school. The kids decided to split up to cover more ground, but Mia suggested they try to stay paired up, in case they had to help get a leash on a fast, or big, dog. Jason, Roel, and Kimberlyn stuck together—Mia and Tonio split to pair with Parker and Devon, respectively, since it didn't make sense to pair the two who knew the most about dogs together at first.

I knew this would only make Tonio more nervous—sending Mia off with Parker alone seemed dangerous for both of them—but that's what we dogs were here for. Leila looked to me for direction. "You know the situation better than I do. Which group is more important? You take that one, and I'll cover the other."

Leaving Tonio alone made me nervous, but he wasn't really talking to me anyway, and I was even more nervous to *face him* right now. Once this night had gone how I planned—once everything was fixed and the mission was complete—then I would apologize and show him all the work I'd done. For now, though, I needed to help Parker connect with these kids.

"You go with Tonio," I decided. "But if something happens—if you hear his heart rate even *start* to rise, or he looks like he might have a panic attack—"

"I'll howl for you. Don't worry." Leila gave me a reassuring pat on my shoulder that knocked me sideways with its force. I trusted her.

"Thank you." Mia and Devon were heading away from the crowds, which surprised me—I realized quickly they were looking for dogs.

"How many adoptions do I need?" Parker asked. "For, uh—for me to be—"

Mia cut him off. "Our record is thirteen—but this year, we have a bunch of new puppies somebody found last week. I want to beat the record. Let me know if you see any of them."

Ah. She's looking for puppies. I ducked behind a stall and howled—a sound that mingled in with all the other noises for the humans but would stick out for the dogs. "I NEED A FEW PUPPIES TO THE EDGE OF THE BOOTHS. CREEKSIDE."

When I caught up, Parker was trying to fill the silence between them. "I heard Sloan moved to Colorado. How is she?"

Mia was silent.

"One time, when I skinned my knee on the playground, she got like a whole kit out of her bag. 'We need to sterilize it, first, before the bandage.'"

"Don't talk about her."

"I'm just saying she was nice! But she was weird, right? 'Sterilize.' 'Bandage.' It was just like, a little goop and a Band-Aid."

Mia didn't answer him. A few puppies found their

way to my howl—the Akita and the Chiweenie from earlier. Parker gasped at the sight. "Look at them!" he whispered. "They're so *small*!"

"They're puppies." But Mia smiled, a little. The puppies cheerfully headed for the kids, but I jumped to catch their attention and posed: *Make them chase you! I'll tell you when.*

Tails wagging and excited to run, the puppies waited until Mia was leaning down to grab them—and then bolted farther away from the booths and toward the trees around the creek. Parker and Mia both ran after them, safety vests flapping in the wind. Mia dove for the Chiweenie, Parker ran for the Akita—and he tripped over her when the dogs switched directions and leaped away, yipping with laughter.

"Hey!" Mia yelled.

"Hey yourself!" Parker retorted, pushing off the grass and checking his hands for scratches. "Speaking of skinned knees." He made his voice smaller, lighter, but more serious: "We should sterilize these wounds."

Mia, checking her dress for grass stains, laughed in surprise. "You sound just like her!"

"I'm pretty good at impressions. I can make people think I'm my mom on the phone."

"So you're good at impressions of girls."

He shrugged a big shrug, with his whole arms. "I'm

an actor! You use the instrument you have, and the instrument *I* have is being twelve."

Mia laughed again. *I knew it*, I thought. Parker *was* charming, and he was best one-on-one. In situations where he didn't have to try to perform for multiple people—where he wasn't scanning a crowd for how to be the most powerful—he was just himself. All he needed was a little material, and some time. He'd win them over.

Now, I posed to the puppies. They ran up to sniff the kids' shoes and were quickly scooped into the air.

"She's going to be a doctor," Mia explained. "That's why she talks like that."

"Well, she's already a master with a Band-Aid." Parker tossed his head to the side, resettling his hair into its signature swoosh.

Mia's mouth curled into a mischievous smirk. "I bet I can get someone to fall in love with my puppy"—she adjusted her grip on the Chiweenie—"*way* before you can!"

Parker gave the Akita puppy a kiss on the forehead. "You hear that, baby? She thinks she's better than us!"

"I've been doing this since I was in diapers. I *know* I'm better than you."

The little Chiweenie yipped. "Let's kick their butts!"

"AS IF!" the Akita barked.

"You said it." Parker tilted his chin back and put on

his best Heracles voice. "I accept your challenge, Mia Lin. *You're on.*"

Devon gasped. "You won?!" After the puppy challenge, the two groups ran into each other and got reshuffled. Parker ended up with Devon thanks to an *extremely convenient* bit of chaos that Leila got Mozart to create, distracting Mia. Tonio saw me and didn't say anything—but he did put something together, because he volunteered to stay and help.

Which left Devon and Parker, headed toward the carnival games. "I was in a play last year where I was"—he did a fake British accent—"*a very sad li'l boy,* so I gave them some of that *me sweet dog 'ad these puppies, and if I don't find 'em good 'omes—*"

"*Oi could nevvuh wiv wif meself!*" Devon finished, grinning. Parker winced away from his accent like he'd been slapped, which just made Devon do it more. "*'Es 'ad aw 'is shots, gov'na!*"

"Please, my ears!" Parker was clutching the sides of his head and rotating away from Devon at his waist—his joking tone reassuring the other boy, even as he complained. "They can only take so much!!"

"Mia must have been so mad."

"She told me that, *actually,* I didn't win unless I got more adoptions than her all night. So I think she was fine."

They were almost where I wanted them. At my signal,

a frizzy-haired terrier named Zuzu leaped up onto one of the game booths—a ring toss. The man running the booth stood up from his seat and loudly cried, "Shoo! Shoo, you!" Zuzu stalled until the boys noticed and, in their capacity as Adoption Helpers, came to get her down. She listened as soon as they were there. *Perfect*, I posed. She wagged her tail and went to find her brother, Houdini.

Devon apologized, even though it wasn't his fault. They started to leave— *No! Look closer!* I wanted to yell from my position next to the funnel cake booth on the other side of the path, but there was nothing I could do. *C'mon c'mon c'mon*—

"Oh, whoa." Devon's hand went involuntarily to his heart. "No way."

"What?"

He lifted his other hand to point at one of the prizes. "Is that the starship Sincerity from *Sun Squadron: Nightrise*?"

Parker tried to find the words in the syllables. "You mean that stuffed toy?"

"Spoken like a real fan." The man at the booth—I realized I knew him! It was Keegan, one of the young adults who came to Beamblade tournaments. He had purple hair now, another piercing, and the crystal jewelry was a little different—but it was definitely him. "Hey, Devon."

"Oh, hi, Keegan. I . . . want that."

Keegan nodded. "Don't we all? But it's one of the grand prizes. You have to land five rings on bottles to get it."

"How many rings do you get?"

"Five."

Devon groaned. "I will never, ever be able to do that in a million years."

"They only give this version to our company. It's not sold anywhere else *I* know of."

"I have to have it!!!"

Parker didn't understand. "It looks like someone crocheted a bunch of dirty dishes together."

"It's my *favorite* starship. I could *hug* my favorite starship! I didn't even know they made these." He slammed some money down, grabbed the rings—and missed every single one. *Badly.* He was like Tonio when it came to hand-eye coordination, I supposed. These poor indoor kids.

A second try, same deal. Some of them didn't even touch the bottles. At the third offering of money, Keegan looked a little sorry for him. "Maybe you—"

"Devon." Parker rubbed the back of his neck. "If I get that for you . . . can we be even?"

"Even?"

"After the locker." He avoided eye contact. "And, uh. And everything else."

Devon looked surprised. He considered. "You're really going to stop? This isn't all some big trick?"

"It's not."

"Then, yeah." Devon smiled, braces sparkling. "We'd be totally even!"

Parker unbuttoned the end of his sleeves, rolled them up above his elbow. "You got it, *gov'na.*"

"I'm so sorry," Parker mumbled miserably. "I really didn't think it would take so long. Those bottles—there's something wrong with them. They're *lying*, somehow."

Devon squeezed the *Sincerity* so hard he could have punctured the hull, sending a thousand little astronauts flying into outer space. "Thank you thank you THANK YOU *thank you!!!*"

"Really?" Parker gave him a dubious look. "After *fifty dollars*?" But Devon waved away his concerns. It was actually getting dark now—they'd spent a lot of time at the ring toss booth, and not a lot of time helping with dogs. Parker noticed the time and sighed. "Mia's gonna be so mad we goofed off this long."

"Tonio!" Devon held the starship up above the crowd—and there he was, hovering awkwardly to the side while Mia asked passersby if they wanted to meet a very special Labrador. "Look!!"

"Is that the *Endeavor*?"

"The *Sincerity*! Parker won it for me."

Mia waved to get his attention. "Devon! Come pretend to choke so Paprika can save your life!"

He looked to the other boys and shrugged. "Duty calls!"

Parker cupped his hands around his mouth and yelled over the crowd. "IF DEVON HELPS YOU, IT DOESN'T COUNT!"

"WHAT?" Mia yelled. "I CAN'T HEAR YOU?"

"YES, YOU CAN!" He turned to Tonio. "Let's go look for some more puppies!"

They headed back out of the crowd, this time toward the old stable. Tonio watched Parker curiously. "That was nice of you."

"Oh, the toy? I guess. It took me like twenty tries. He spent fifty bucks!"

"He seemed happy." Tonio tilted his head thoughtfully. "I think Devon might be kind of rich?"

"Maybe he'll buy our food tickets, then." Parker pushed at the door to the stable, but it was locked. No dogs hiding in there. Tonio, not especially helping with the puppy hunt, dropped his hand to the side and made an Underspeak sign—*Good job.* He knew I was there. Maybe not exactly where I was (up in the branches of a nearby pecan tree), but he knew I was watching. I felt some relief—he was glad. My plan was working.

"Why did you want to come so bad?" Tonio asked.

"You've just been hanging out with us since we got here."

"I was gonna hang out with Miles, but I haven't seen him yet." *Thanks to me!* I'd assigned a bunch of red collars to the defense team—a whole squad of unadoptables were making enough drama to keep Miles from ever coming *close* to these kids. Parker headed around the side of the barn, Tonio a few steps behind. "Honestly, I *really* wanted to be somewhere I knew Oscar wouldn't show up."

"Because of the dogs?"

"Yeah. Ever since they got married, it's like we can't go anywhere without him showing up. He always pretends like he's doing something nice—bringing dinner or whatever—or like it's an accident, but I think he's checking on us. Making sure we're not doing something he doesn't like."

"When he came to rehearsal and called you outside."

Parker nodded. "It's like he's so scared, all the time, of *something*. But what are we going to do?? In Bellville???"

"Yeah." Tonio worked very carefully to not do his Lie Face. "Nothing ever happens here."

"Right. I dunno, it just doesn't seem like he even *likes* us. It's like we're part of his chores." He scowled. "Especially me."

"Why did they get married?" Tonio asked, which was

kind of a weird question, but Parker must have wondered, too.

"He didn't used to be like this. When they first met online, he seemed super cool—bought a bunch of presents, took us to Skopelos." At Tonio's face, he explained: "It's in Greece. Mom always wanted to go, because *Mamma Mia!* was filmed there." He paused a moment. "And she's never been married before, so maybe she wanted to know what it was like." A shrug. A pebble, kicked. "Seems bad."

Tonio wasn't sure what to say. He went with "I'm sorry," but was visibly disappointed he didn't have anything better. "That sounds hard."

They'd made a full rotation around the barn now. Parker leaned against it and crossed his arms. "Thanks." I held off on calling in any puppies—it didn't seem like Tonio needed my help. He was doing great. "Whenever you get mad at me, you sound kinda like him."

"What?!" Tonio was immediately alarmed. "I'm sorry! I don't—but he's so—"

"I never did anything to him, though. He's always saying I'm 'horrible,' or 'obnoxious,' or 'mean,' but for no reason." Parker's face was red now. "I didn't realize until you said something that maybe he's right. Or I *made him* right."

If Tonio didn't know what to say before, he seemed

even less sure now. I saw him clench one hand around the wrist of the other, behind his back—hiding his stress from Parker. After a few seconds of thinking, he said: "I don't think either of us are right." At Parker's confused look, Tonio tilted his head and scrunched up one side of his face like he was holding something sour in his mouth. "*People* can't be bad. At least, I don't think so. People can't be any one thing. And it sounds like he just uses bigger words for 'bad.'" His face settled, sourness swallowed. "I think if he's trying to make you feel like a bad person, it's because something's wrong with *him*. Not you."

I don't think Tonio was saying this to get on his good side. Tonio was being honest—and he was really trying to help. Parker looked unsure. "That's different than how you felt before."

"I was mad. And you guys had *done* something horrible."

"Sorry again."

"Thanks."

Tonio's stomach growled loudly in the silence. Tonio blushed, and Parker grinned. "Let's go see if *m'lord Wilcrest* will get us some mac 'n' cheese."

"You can't!!! If you ask, *he will do it*."

They went back to find the other kids, and I hopped down from the tree. *No dogs required.* Just Tonio, being the same person who made me feel better when the rest of the world said *I* was bad, too. And if Tonio was right . . . what did that say about the Court?

Several greasy food purchases later (Devon didn't have to pay—Kimberlyn and Roel had mysteriously found enough food tickets on the ground for everyone *as if they'd been put there on purpose*), all seven kids were sitting on two big blankets rolled over the dirt. A stage was built over the area dogs usually had wrestling tournaments in, and musicians had performed all afternoon. Now, as the festival was winding down for the night, fewer people were around to watch—but Tonio wouldn't miss this particular band for the world. Skyler from Roll the Ice was performing with her new group, Glass Mug.

"How many adoptions did you end up with?" Parker asked.

Mia grinned. *"Eight."*

"Eight?! I only got four!"

"Maybe next time, Feldman." Tonio noticed the *next time* with a little surprised smile. "What about you guys?"

"I helped out with one adoption!" Kimberlyn gave a thumbs-up. "I also met a nice big dog who caught me out of nowhere when I almost fell in the mud."

"Really big?"

"Yeah."

"That's Leila. She's the best."

"Jason and I each helped with two." Roel held up his phone and swiped past pictures of humans paired with dogs, as proof. "And this is crazy, but a black-and-white dog walked by carrying all the answers to our math homework?" He held up the paper.

Mia swiped it from his hand. "My dogs, my answers."

"That's fine. I took a picture."

"I wonder where Charmander found these." She must have written them. *Way to go above and beyond*, I thought.

"So that's . . ." Parker counted on his fingers. "Seventeen? We broke your record!"

"Yes!!!" Mia held up her turkey leg triumphantly. "Thanks, everybody!" Each kid matched her pose with mac and cheese, tacos, or corn dogs, then chomped down.

Glass Mug finished their first song. "This next song's for my friend Tonio!" Skyler yelled into the mic, guitar in hand. "He gave me the idea. It's called 'Thunderstorm Day.'"

The kids all cheered together, mouths full. Tonio was stunned. "Me?" he whispered. "A song for me?"

It was a bop. Devon was first to dance, I think, with Parker and Mia not far behind. Roel and Kimberlyn pulled Jason up and they did the wave in a circle. Tonio, stunned by the whole scene, watched and listened from the blanket.

"C'mon, Tonio!" It was Parker, hand out.

"No thanks."

"What? It's your song!"

"It's okay." Tonio smiled, a reassuring and genuine smile. He reached over and put a hand on my head. "I think all the noise is making Buster nervous. I'm happy to watch from here."

"If you're sure."

"I am." Parker rejoined the crowd of kids and started giving Devon directions on how to do a dance from some video game. I looked up at Tonio, careful not to knock his hand off of my head. He looked down at me, too, and smiled. I wiggled along the ground on my stomach closer to him and rested my head on his lap. He scratched behind my ears automatically.

"This is great," he whispered. "How did you do this?"

I rolled over and underspoke upside down, *Our way.*

Skyler yelled through the speakers as the kids crunched leaves with their dance in the twinkling lights. Tonio closed his eyes again and held on to my fur, head bobbing to the music. I snuck a bite of Mia's turkey leg. For a minute, we had a taste of what we had asked for to begin with: a regular life, where we got to be normal friends. Whatever else was going on with us, this moment was *perfect.*

After the song, sweaty and giggling, the group plopped back on the blankets around him. Parker cleared his throat and addressed the group. "Okay, everyone, I need to ask a favor."

"A *favor*?" Mia laughed. "For *you*?"

"I know, I know. But . . ." He bowed his head and clasped his hands together, begging. "My mom is going to *kill* me if Tonio doesn't come back to the show. It's next week, and we need Hades and Cerberus."

Tonio narrowed his eyes. Devon looked at him, concerned. "Only if you want to. I know you're nervous."

Parker's head bolted up immediately, one finger pointing to the sky. "But *you* don't mind?"

"Oh, I mean . . ."

Mia crossed her arms. "*I* mind. Even if you apologized, Miles didn't. It's dangerous for him."

Tonio looked between all of them, eyes wide. "I'm right here, y'all!"

"What if I make sure Miles leaves him alone?"

"You didn't do so great last time."

"Yeah, but—"

Kimberlyn leaned over. "He's Hades, right? And you're Heracles? I would *love* to see him yell at you in front of everyone."

"That's what I'm saying!" Parker looked pleadingly at Mia and Devon. "Let him yell!"

Devon shushed everyone. "Tonio, what do you think?"

"I think . . ." I saw something dawn on Tonio—a little flash of a realization that he hid from everyone else. "Even if I want to, I'm not off book. I stopped studying the lines, and—it's a dress rehearsal tomorrow, right? I'd mess it up."

Parker threw his hands up triumphantly. "That's easy! I can help you!"

"But it's so soon . . ."

"I'll help you right now! We can start this second!"

Mia sighed. "As long as there's no more weird tricks, you probably should go back. And I *would* like to see you dressed up in scary robes."

"Me too!" Devon cheered.

"Great!" Parker clenched a fist and pulled it toward him—*nailed it*. "How 'bout it?"

Tonio was keeping every single one of his muscles still and trying to sound *perfectly* normal. Like it was an idea he'd just had for the first time. "Can we go practice at your house tonight? My dad has to get up early for work, so—"

"Oh, my mom would *love* that. Totally." And there it was. After all of that—it was so simple. So quick. Parker tilted his head when a thought struck him: "You can't bring Buster, though. Oscar's allergies."

We exchanged a glance. As expected. *You can handle it*, I posed. *I know you can.*

Tonio took a long breath, then looked up and smiled. "That's okay! We can go drop him off, and I can get a change of clothes."

Mia clapped both of them on the back. "Great! Now let's try to get some more adoptions before everything shuts down."

"But we already broke the record!!!"

The kids slipped back into normal conversations, finished their food, and spread out for the last half hour of the festival. When it was done, Parker called his mom for permission and walked back home with Tonio. He packed a backpack, explained the situation to his parents, and said his goodbyes when Mrs. Feldman arrived to pick them up.

"This is it," he whispered in the last few moments in his room. "We did it."

I'm so proud of you. That was amazing!

He lifted his hand, and I put my paw in it. "For Jpeg."

For Jpeg. He stood up and pulled the backpack tight around his shoulders. *And, Tonio, I'm sorry. I think . . . I think I've figured out what I want.*

Tonio turned his head away a little and looked back from the corner of his eye. "Tell me when I get back, okay? I need to focus right now."

That hurt a little bit, but—he didn't trust my answer. He didn't know what I would say, and he was probably still feeling hurt by my decisions. We could handle it when we'd finished the mission.

Good luck, I posed. He smiled, nodded, and walked out the door.

I haven't seen him since.

Connection Available

Tonio's voice was tired. He'd been calling back and forth with the *Sun Squadron* badge for what had to be *hours* now, repeating numbers and codes and commands. Jpeg would give him another thing to say he didn't understand, the badge would reply with something that made even *less* sense, and then Jpeg would bob her head and tap her paws and make a little grunt in the back of her throat.

He could follow the rough pattern of what she was doing—she spent a big chunk of the time trying to see if she could get around the "intranet" and into the regular internet, but that didn't work. Then she had to check each of the devices individually for whether or not they were still connected *to* the intranet, somewhere, and if she could use that connection, while trying to avoid the device that their captor was carrying around. (Tonio understood this part, even though it was mostly numbers called "MAC addresses," because she kept pestering him for a more and more specific timeline of where he'd taken his backpack.)

Finally: "Connection available to: SoundULTIMATE portable speaker. Connect?"

Jpeg grunted, this time more positive-sounding to Tonio's ear. At her instruction: "No. Do not connect."

so, i found that portable speaker on the intranet, which means there's a few options: it's in this building, it's in some other DNI base we passed by, or it's at that agent's house.

Agent Sykes. So . . . Parker's house. "Parker used to bring a speaker for his mom to use!" Tonio remembered. "For rehearsal!"

Jpeg nodded. *that's probably it. it's the* only *device i've been able to find, which means it's our only real line to the outside.* She didn't have to say: Our only chance of being saved from whatever the DNI had planned for them.

"It's probably in Parker's backpack."

meaning our choice is to tell that human or not tell anybody at all.

Telling Parker he was trapped would spiral—on his own, Parker would probably go to his mom, who would go to Sykes, who would put a stop to it. He knew from Buster's warnings that Sykes was working with the police—which meant it wasn't even safe for Parker to go directly to them. They needed *dog* help, which meant Parker needed to know about Buster.

Break Dog Law or stay under DNI's control? "Ugh." Tonio did not want to be making this kind of decision!

And this was exactly what Dog Court was worried about, wasn't it? That's what Buster had said. They didn't want a bigger problem to grow out of a small one. Telling another human the truth about dogs would definitely be a "bigger problem," according to Dog Court.

"What do you think?" he asked Jpeg, who was watching him consider.

i'm already going to sky jail forever, probably, Jpeg underspoke, *but it's better than whatever these guys are planning. if you trust this kid, i say do it.*

So it would depend on Parker believing him—and actually helping him. Plus, he didn't want to ruin Buster's chances at being a real Farm agent. Tonio was the one who hadn't been careful enough. It's not like the DNI could keep him forever anyway, right? Eventually, Agent Sykes would have to explain where Tonio had gone. They couldn't just kidnap him and get away with it. Tonio hoped.

Jpeg seemed pretty sure there were bad things in store for them, though—she hadn't even mentioned what happened to her in the weeks before Tonio showed up. And she'd already worked so hard to make this possible—she really was a genius—so he didn't want to give up now.

But what if the speaker was with Mrs. Feldman? Or worse, Agent Sykes?

Or what if Parker was secretly working with him the whole time? What if this was all a trap?

Tonio took a breath. His anxiety was crawling in again, and he was thinking of the worst outcomes. He needed to keep it simple and think of the choice in front of him. Ask for Parker's help, or not.

He would ask for help. But what would he say? How would he convince him?

After a minute, he nodded. "Okay, let's connect. I think I know what to say." Jpeg repeated all the things he had to say to find the speaker, then:

"Connection available to: SoundULTIMATE portable speaker. Connect?"

"Yes. Connect." A little *bloop* sound of a successful connection. Tonio pushed right up against the bars of his dog crate. "Parker, this is Tonio. I can't hear you, but you should be able to hear me. I don't know what time it is, so I'm sorry if I woke you up. Um. If you're there, please turn this speaker off and back on, as fast as you can."

They waited. A long minute passed. And then: "Disconnected. Trying to reconnect... connection failed."

Oh no. Oscar might have grabbed it and turned it off when he realized what they were doing. Or maybe the speaker wasn't loud enough, so Parker thought it was just making random noises and turned it off? Tonio looked at Jpeg.

don't panic. wait a second, let's try again.

They waited for an excruciatingly long minute, then tried again.

"Connection available to: SoundULTIMATE portable speaker. Connect?"

"YES! Yes. Connect. Yes."

Bloop.

"Great. Hi, Parker. Okay. I don't think I have a lot of time. Oscar did *not* take me home. I don't know where I am. This is going to sound crazy, but I need you to find Buster and tell him everything that happened, okay? Buster, my dog. I am not joking. Do not—"

A much sadder bloop sound, three descending notes, played from the badge.

"—tell Oscar . . . Hello? Computer? Hello?"

Nothing. Jpeg huffed out a burst of air. *the battery died.*

Well. He'd said the important parts, anyway. Now it was up to them.

Parker's Report. TO A DOG. I MEAN, WHAT AM I DOING? WHY AM I TALKING TO A DOG? THIS IS CRAZY.

So, uh, yeah. We went to my house. I could tell Tonio didn't like it. I don't like it, either, but he *really* didn't like it. I didn't ask, but if I had to guess, it's because it feels like nobody lives there. Actually, we have one of those magnets on the fridge that says *Sorry for the mess, but we live here!* left over from where Mom and I used to live, and it feels like a total lie. There's no mess, and if I told you it was one of those houses they use only for real estate tours or TV show sets you'd probably believe me.

If you believed anything I said. If you understood anything I said. But you are a dog.

Anyway, uh, Oscar was really mad that Tonio was coming over, so he locked himself up in his office as soon as we arrived. Mom really wanted to make Tonio happy, so she hovered around for a while talking about whatever before going to send emails about costumes or something.

We ran lines for a while, and—I think Tonio actually knew most of his lines but was worried for no reason.

Kinda like at auditions when he kept staring at his script. He was distracted, though, and kept forgetting it was his turn to talk.

Once it seemed like we'd practiced enough, we played games in my room. Video games, I mean. Mostly he kept asking me questions and asking me to play while he watched, still all distracted. And then finally, probably at like eleven? We heard Oscar leave his office and head to his and my mom's room.

Tonio started asking questions, and he seemed really antsy. "What do you think is in the office?" "You've *never* been in there?" That kinda stuff. And I told him: It's just taxes! He works for the IRS. Nothing in there is interesting, and he locks it because legally he's supposed to. But Tonio asked me if I knew where he kept the key, and I said of course I do, who does he think I am, and he said: "Let's go look."

I said, "But I'm already grounded. I would be sent directly into forever-eternity prison for doing that. Also, maybe *actual* prison, because it's the IRS?"

But he said, "Blame it on me, then. Your mom will protect me, right?"

And I said, "No one will ever believe that it was you! I'm the bad kid, remember?"

And he said, "That's true," which didn't feel so good 'cause he said it like it was just one of those facts of the universe that everybody knew. He'd already given me the speech and all, I knew he didn't mean I was *bad* bad, I think he said, but who likes to hear that?

The more he talked about it, though, the more interested I actually was. It's kinda weird, right, that there's a whole room in my own house that I've never been in? And like . . . what is he going to do, call the tax police on his own son? Tonio pointed out that the tax police were probably just the regular police, and I said that I wasn't sure that was true, because I'm pretty sure my stepdad is the tax police. He shook his head seriously at that, which I thought was kinda weird, because it was funny, not serious.

I showed him the pair of boots by the front door that Oscar keeps an extra key in, and I was like, "Okay, we can do this, but *just for a second*. We look at the most boring room on earth with its single computer on a desk that's empty except for the wet ring from his last protein shake, and then we leave."

Tonio said of course, just a second, no problem, but he is honestly, like, when I'm paying attention, not a great liar? But I was like, uh, I guess if I need to get him out of there I can just pick him up probably, so I didn't worry about it too much.

The house was dead silent, so we had to be extra careful going for the office door right next to their bedroom. The key worked, though—I stuck it in the lock and popped the door open, no problem. Inside, though? *Lots* problem.

DOGS. Dozens of dogs—photographs, I mean. All over the walls. Tonio gasped at the same time I said, *"What?"* but he didn't seem *as* surprised as he should have been—right away, Tonio was looking around for something. I took the whole thing in, and the whole thing was *a lot*. He did have a computer on a desk, but the desk was covered in folders and papers stacked on top of each other. The photos, when I looked closer, were pinned to corkboards around the room—with sticky notes and pages of printouts pasted next to them. I looked at one—I think the dog was a Pekingese? The little blobby furry ones. The note next to it said *PATTY, CHICAGO: Anonymous contributor to literary journal traced to home. Owners never heard of the journal.*

I looked at another, two pictures of a pit-bull-looking guy. *GOKU/CHARLIE, AUSTIN/SAN ANTONIO: Family of Goku contacted local paper about a "You're a Winner!" pop-up ad on their computer that actually led to a large sum of money showing up at their house. Around this time, a pit bull appeared in the feature film WRONG TREE HILL. Double life?*

Then *SCOUT, CHATTANOOGA* and *BANDIT, PORTLAND: Phone call placed in the middle of the night between two houses. Owners entirely unrelated, but both houses had Jack Russells. Relatives?*

Next to that were a collection of pictures that were all smudgy—bad focus, like the bigfoot pictures, all of this kind of black swoosh. *THE IOWA TERROR, VARIOUS: Responsible for severe disruptions of greyhound racing activity, including somehow locking handlers in their own kennels. Unable to confirm this is a dog based on evidence, but there appears to be no other explanation.*

And there, by the computer, was BUSTER, BELLVILLE: *Identical to Buster "Miracle Dog" from article attached, disappeared about a year ago. Fire dog . . . to anxiety service dog? And such a far move. What's the story here?*

"Uh, Tonio," I said. "Why does my stepdad have a picture of you in his office?" Because right there next to the picture of you was a picture of Tonio, looking surprised, hands in kind of a weird pose, crouched between some dogs. The note said *Boy speaking dog code? Possibly coincidence.*

Tonio said, "Oh, does he?" while he opened a bunch of drawers all at once. "That's weird." Behind him, I noticed a closet was open—with a bunch of clothes I'd never seen Oscar wear. I was like, what's going *on*? But Tonio seemed busy, so I kept looking at stuff.

I checked Oscar's desk and opened the folder closest to the keyboard. It was a whole big set of documents about a Shiba named Jpeg, which is a funny name for a dog. I said so, and Tonio grabbed the folder from me and started flipping through it—but he got more frustrated every time he turned the page.

He said, "There's nothing here. I have to check the

computer—maybe he's sent an email, something—" and he clicked the power button on the tower and clicked around to get the monitor on. It was an old computer, so it took a while. I opened another folder—this one was for a husky named Pronto. A paper was folded up on top, and I figured, well, can't get any weirder, right?

The email was like, *Hello, Agent Sykes. I believe this information might be useful to you, should you follow the trail. Best, P.* And then there was information on some-thing about the United States government being hacked? Oscar had circled the *P* and made a little note—*email encrypted. strong suspicion informant Pronto, from email tracked two years ago—still believes he's anonymous? Return emails get bounced back.*

Well, it got weirder. All sounded like spy stuff to me. Tonio looked at me and asked, "Do you know his com-puter password?" And I told him no, and also that, if he had a moment, could he explain why he was breaking into my stepdad's computer maybe? And he said, "Later. Sorry. Any guesses?" and I said, "Chicken?" Because I saw a key on his desk connected to a keychain from that SizzlePop place he was always ordering from.

And then—*we really should have gotten out of there faster*—Oscar was there, grabbing me and then Tonio. He basically threw me out of the room but kept ahold of Tonio. "Thought so," he said, but with, like, a growl. He was *mad.*

I yelled, "What are you doing?! MOM!" and he turned a look on me even worse than the looks he gives me every day. Tonio was totally frozen, the back of his shirt all knotted up around Oscar's fist, and he looked *bad*, like freaked out, face all red—and then my mom came out, but it didn't help anything. He was yelling—"They *broke into my office!*" And Mom was yelling at him to calm down, and eventually he did, but then he said he was going to drive Tonio home *right away*, if he was going to disrespect household rules. My mom tried to talk him down, but of course, she was looking at me the whole time like what did *I* do wrong, why did *I* ruin everyone's night, and I *told* Tonio that's what would happen, but I couldn't talk to him about it because he was already crying anyway, so I guess he knew.

Mom attempted to be the one to take him home, but Oscar insisted, and then I was alone in the house. I tried to tell Mom about what I'd seen in his office, but she didn't really give me a chance to talk, just sent me to my room. And then when Oscar got back, he was just stomping around and slamming doors—he burst into my room just for a second to say, "We'll talk about this tomorrow. I don't know what you saw—" and I said, "I saw that you're, like, obsessed with dogs for some reason?" and he—well, actually, he looked kind of scared.

"I don't know what you're talking about." That was all, just "I don't know what you're talking about." But, uh, I know what I saw. I went back to my bed, and I was really freaked out, but eventually I fell asleep.

And then the speaker in my backpack turned on, and—well, Tonio spoke through it, and he told me to come talk to you. And since that wasn't even the weirdest thing to happen tonight, I snuck out my window. And now, uh, here I am.

So, that's what happened. I hope that all meant something to you, because from *my* perspective, you're a dog, and even though I've seen a lot more dogs in the last twenty-four hours than in the entire rest of my life, uh, I'm pretty sure I know what a dog is.

C'mon, give me something. Did you understand any of that?

Please?

Yeah, I should have figured. This is ridiculous.

— 25 —

Well, Lasagna, this report is just for you now.

I knew Tonio had given me a choice. Parker saw a lot in Agent Sykes's office, and he definitely had enough information to know *something* was weird, but . . . believing in smart dogs was a whole other step for him to take. By sending him to me without all the information, Tonio had let me decide: tell another kid the truth and risk our relationship with Dog Court forever, or let Parker go home thinking it was all some kind of prank.

I tried to think through my decision while he talked. When he got to the office, none of that was surprising—if anything, it was a little gentler than what I'd imagined—but then he said something that perked my ears. *Pronto?* The *informant*? If Parker's stepdad was right, it would mean that a lawyer of the court—the exact same lawyer that fought so hard to get me sent away forever—had tipped off the Department of Nonhuman Intelligence about Jpeg. *Why?*

"C'mon, give me something. Did you understand any of that?"

Someone trapped you. I felt my body heating up with

anger. There was even more to this that I didn't know. Pronto, a member of the Court, set up Jpeg so Tonio and I would get involved—but then *another* court agent, Shadow, had pushed me into giving up on Tonio.

"Please?"

But *why*? I still felt like I was missing something.

"Yeah, I should have figured. This is ridiculous."

Parker was standing up and getting ready to leave Tonio's room—if I was going to say something, it was now or never. My computer was still out and open, off to the side—Parker showed up right as I finished my report, so I hadn't sent it out yet. I was already unsure about sending it anyway.

There could be another use for my report, though. If I was willing to risk it.

"STOP!" I barked, which to Parker just sounded like "ARF!" but the message came across. I scooted my laptop along the carpet to bump into Parker's foot. Once I had his attention, I swiped the wheel in the middle to go to the bottom of the document and typed in a flurry: *IF YOU WANT TO KNOW WHAT'S GOING ON, READ THIS.*

Parker watched me, eyes wide and frozen. I really thought he might just run away—but then he found that same cool pose he always wore, and his face calmed down. He lowered himself to the ground and nodded.

"I see." A smile started to creep up on his face. "This is it. It's my hero moment."

Hm. I tilted my head in a question. Parker explained: "I mean, I always knew I was special. And now—I know I was right. I'm learning a secret thing nobody else knows." He looked very proud of himself. "This is when my story starts. I'm a main character."

As far as reactions to life-changing news went, I figured that one was fine. But— *Maybe I should edit a little,* I typed, nervous. He giggled as I typed, a nervous laugh I'd never heard from him before. *I can cut out all the less important parts.*

"No, no." Parker shook his head. "I'll read fast. I need to know everything if I'm going to live up to this responsibility."

Reluctantly, I stepped away from the laptop. Parker swiped up to the top of this report and began reading.

"I'm the bad guy," Parker moaned miserably from the floor. "I'm not the hero at all!"

I knew I should have edited, I thought. But I typed: *That's just because of the way I told it. You can still be a hero!*

Parker pushed himself up on his elbows. "I guess. Oscar's *even worse* than I thought! I can't believe that's possible!" He paused for a moment, stunned again by all the new information, but shook his head to refocus on the problem in front of them. "What do we *do*? Tonio and Jpeg didn't know where they were, either. And we didn't find anything in his office."

I had time to think about this while he was reading. *I think we have two leads: Jpeg's folder and the computer. If we get Jpeg's folder, I can go over it in more detail, and if we can figure out the password, we could have access to everything the DNI knows. That would be amazing.*

"My mom might know!" Parker realized. But his face fell. "My mom . . ."

Careful, I warned. *If we tell an adult, and they tell the police about this—*

"I know. They could be working with him. Or the truth gets out, and y'all are in trouble."

Not just us. You too, now.

"Mm." Parker crossed his arms. "I agree with Tonio. Dog Court is the worst. Everyone should know about this."

Yeah, I thought. *I'm starting to feel that way, too.* We couldn't ask humans for help without putting ourselves in danger—and Dog Court couldn't help us unless we figured out where Tonio was being kept. But I said: *Even if we save Tonio and Jpeg, Dog Court has more power than we do right now. We need to be careful how we move forward.*

"I get it, I get it." Parker frowned thoughtfully. "Trust me, I don't want to get in a fight with any dogs."

The sun was starting to rise. Parker had gotten my attention without waking the Pulaskis, but if they woke up and found him here, there'd be plenty of questions we couldn't answer.

"We need to go," Parker said. "But how do I talk to you while we're out there?"

I grabbed the tablet off Tonio's desk and held it up to Parker, who tucked it under his arm. We snuck downstairs quietly—Parker put on my harness, and we headed out into the chilly morning. He stopped at the bottom of the stairs, and we realized our first mistake.

"Oh, right." Parker's bike was chained to the railing, and it definitely didn't have a dog seat. I mimed running as a suggestion, but Parker shook his head. "It's too far." I must have looked disappointed because Parker laughed. "Sorry! You're small!"

I'm medium, I wanted to clarify. *But fine.* A few minutes later, we were speeding down the road, Parker standing on the pedals and me on the seat with my front paws holding on to his shoulders. It made the Pulaskis' truck feel like a smooth ride, but Parker was a good cyclist. (And I focused really hard on staying balanced, even as my paw pads slid on the seat.)

When we arrived at Chime Hollow, Parker punched a code into the gate, and it opened easily. As soon as his house was in sight, though, he turned behind a different house and peered around the corner. "Oscar's car is gone. Weird, but it means we're okay. You can come with me."

I walked alongside the bike, listening to the clicking

as Parker pushed it on the sidewalk. I closed my eyes and tried to focus on the sounds, the smells—were there any dogs around? Was Shadow hovering in the . . . uh, shadows, somewhere, watching me working with another human? I couldn't sense anything, but I knew better than to trust my nose completely. Especially where Shadow was concerned.

When Parker opened the front door, I *did* hear something—crying. Parker could hear it, too, muffled, in the back of the house. He immediately started walking faster, and I took that to mean he recognized the sound. *Mrs. Feldman*, I guessed.

The house was a lot like Parker described it—all the walls were bare, and everything was clean and beige. The house was technically fancy—it was *big*, at least—but there was no personality inside—barely anything memorable at all. The crying was coming from the first floor, past the kitchen and deeper into the house. Parker rushed toward the sound but stopped short at the island that separated the kitchen from the living area. He picked up a note.

At this point, I was more interested in information than being careful. Now was the time for *action*! So I jumped onto the counter and snooped over his shoulder. The note was written in small, precise handwriting—like Tonio's, I thought, but with less beauty. All function.

Josephine,

I am leaving. I am sorry to tell you this way, but I knew there would be nothing gained from further conversation.

When we met, I believed we could make it work. But you and your son's repeated disrespect for my needs make it clear we have grown too far apart for repair. Tonight, when he broke into my office, was the last straw of many. I cannot risk my career to your lenience as well as my health.

All the best. I hope one day you can reclaim your life from that selfish boy. I'll be in touch about the paperwork.

Oscar

By the time I reached the end, Parker's hand was shaking. He crumpled the note up and threw it, hard, against the kitchen wall, yelling another word Tonio couldn't say as it landed in the sink.

This is a lie, I underspoke. *He's trying to manipulate you! Don't listen!*

But Parker didn't know Underspeak. He just saw a dog standing on his kitchen island and twitching his paws. His face was burning red, furious . . . and he was *right* to be mad, I thought. This letter, for all its simple, straightforward language, was nasty. It was rude, to

Parker *and* to his mom—and, if I understood right, it was a declaration of divorce. All in a few short paragraphs. I licked at the back of his hand, but I didn't expect to change his mood.

If this was true, Oscar was leaving, which meant he was going to take Jpeg and Tonio with him, and we didn't have any more time. Parker must have realized that, too: Instead of going toward his mom's bedroom, he marched down the hall and threw open the door to Oscar's office. It wasn't locked, so the doorknob turned easily.

Everything was gone. The room looked a lot more like what Parker had imagined Oscar's office would look like—except now, there weren't even papers. Nothing in the closet, nothing on the walls, and nothing on the desk.

No folder, and no computer. There was no evidence left.

26

"Parker? Is that you?" Mrs. Feldman must have heard the door slam. She came out of her room and soon was in the office doorway, watching as Parker flung open empty drawers and pushed at the walls of the closet. "And . . . Buster?"

At the sound of my name, I wagged my tail and sat like a dog who *wasn't* panicking over the fate of his two best friends in the world, now that all the ways to find them were completely gone. Parker turned to look at her, and when he saw her red eyes and disheveled hair, his anger melted away into sadness.

"I'm so sorry, Mom. I'm sorry." He kept his back straight and his eyes on her. "I know I'm a bad kid, but I didn't think—I didn't mean for—"

"Oh no, Parker. You didn't read that note, did you?"

Parker nodded, but he kept his chin up.

"Well, put it out of your mind." Mrs. Feldman stepped forward and pulled him in for a hug. "I don't believe a word of it, and neither should you."

"But it's my fault." Parker didn't lift his arms up to hug her back. "You can't have your own life because of me."

"You *are* my life. And I like it that way." She kissed the top of his head, her brown-and-blond hair falling to mingle with his—exactly the same shades. "I would trade a hundred boring jerks to keep you the person that you are."

Parker didn't answer. "Do you believe me?"

Still no answer. She leaned back a little. "Look at me. I love you more than anything else in the world. Tell me if I'm lying. Am I lying?"

"No." And finally, Parker hugged her back and cried. Just a little bit, and not for very long. She gave him another squeeze, then let go after he'd calmed down. With a glance around the office, she sighed. "I used to wonder why he never bought anything. Why he kept this house so . . . empty?" She shook her head. "And now I guess I know. Easier to pack up and go."

Parker struggled to think of something to say—I think he wanted something he could give back to cheer up his mom. He was uncomfortable being comforted when she had just had her husband disappear. But all he could think of, ultimately, was a joke. "At least we won't have to eat fried chicken anymore."

Mrs. Feldman's mouth fell open in pure, sudden joy. "Oh god, you're right. No more SizzlePop! I hated that stuff."

"It wasn't even good."

"And the stick didn't add anything! They just put chicken tenders on skewers!"

Where had I heard that name before? *Oh, right. SizzlePop: Fried Chicken on a Stick was the food Agent Sykes kept bringing to rehearsal.* Apparently he really liked it, because that was Parker's first guess at his computer password, too. But . . . before rehearsal, I'd never heard of it. The kids never talked about it.

"Arf!!!" I barked, urgently. I didn't want to invade their conversation—really, I wished I could leave them in that moment forever—but we didn't have a lot of time.

"Oh yeah." Mrs. Feldman looked down at him again. "Why do you have Buster?"

"Uh, Tonio asked me to watch him until rehearsal. He had to go . . . somewhere." *Way to sell it.*

"It's really nice you two are friends again." She leaned down to pet me, but I couldn't accept the scritches of her pleasantly long nails. I stared at Parker and danced my feet on the ground. "What's he doing?"

I wove around her legs and tugged at Parker's pants with my teeth. "Uh, I think he needs to use the bathroom. I'll be right back."

Parker followed me to the front door, grabbing the tablet on his way out. We ran around the back of the house—I patted my paws into the dirt impatiently as Parker turned on the tablet and opened the keyboard for me to type.

Where is SizzlePop? I asked finally.

"The fried chicken place? No clue. Oscar always

went without us. Uh . . ." He pulled his phone out of his pocket and tapped around with his thumb. "Here." He showed me a map—SizzlePop only had one store, and it was twenty miles away from here.

That didn't make sense. *Why would he drive* twenty miles *when Wing, Wing is right here in Bellville?*

"I guess because he liked it? There's—" Parker froze. It dawned on him, too. He checked his phone again. "They don't even have a website. How would he have found it in the first place?"

Unless there's something else there.

"The key on his desk!" Parker's eyes narrowed with a sudden focus. "SizzlePop isn't real."

There wasn't any time to waste. If Agent Sykes was ready to leave his family, he might commit all the way to kidnapping my friends. How were we going to get there, though, without a car? Last time Tonio needed to travel secretly, he'd asked Skyler—but Skyler didn't know Parker, and the explanations would *really* make her panic. Biking there would take too long. And suddenly asking Mrs. Feldman to take them *to* SizzlePop seemed suspicious, and with a high chance of having to break in . . . not ideal.

And, honestly, I didn't feel safe going with just the two of us. I'm not the strongest dog around, and Parker was still just one kid. "We need to call everybody," Parker said. "All your friends."

But if we tell them—

"Forget Dog Court." Parker gave me a serious look. "Tonio tried to tell you, and he's right. Something's wrong, and they're not gonna fix it. We need to talk to the people who will."

He was right. Shadow, and Pronto, and who knew who else—were up to something. We couldn't trust Dog Court to handle this quickly. I gave Parker a number to call.

"Uh, hello?"

Danny, one of Mia's dads, answered the phone. "Yes, who's this?"

"This is Parker. Can I talk to Mia?"

"One second." Muffled sounds of talking. "She says she's not here."

"Tell her it's important!!" More muffled noises. The phone was passed between hands.

"Did I do something to make you think we're friends?"

Parker groaned. "I would love to fight with you, but we don't have time. Buster and I are on our way to your house."

"What? Why? Where's Tonio?"

"That's the problem. He—" Parker panted. He was worn out from all the pedaling. "Tonio's in trouble. But you can't tell anyone."

"What did you do?"

"I didn't do anything! But—*hoo*—Buster says—*hahh*—Jpeg's in trouble, too. He said you'd care about that."

Mia was quiet on the other side of the line for a long time. "*Buster* says that?"

"Yes. He says—*oh gosh, this hill*—to ask why you called Tonio's parents last summer. Why you said he was—*almost there*—staying at your house that night, when he wasn't."

Silence again. Then, "He said he was doing something important, so I helped."

"And he says—*FINALLY, made it*—to ask, do you remember when Tonio said he was keeping a secret? A big one he couldn't tell anybody?"

"How do you know all this? Really?"

"I told you! Buster told me!" Mia made an irritated sound in her throat. Parker let the bike roll down the hill on its own and kept talking. "*This* is that secret. Tonio is involved in some big stuff—scary stuff—and he's in trouble. We need a ride to SizzlePop: Fried Chicken on a Stick."

"I've never heard of it."

"It's out of town. Buster also says we need Leila. And we *really* don't have a lot of time."

"If any part of this is a trick, I will actually murder you."

"I accept these terms!"

After a moment: "One second." The phone beeped, and then rang . . . and then a familiar voice answered.

"Hi, Mia!" Devon chirped. "What's up?"

"Hey, Devon. Are you hungry?"

"Not . . . really."

"Well, I am. Parker's here."

"Uh, hey."

"How cool!"

"We need a ride to a fried chicken place out of town."

Devon didn't even pause. "Oh, sure, I can call a car. Are you at home?"

"We'll meet you by the gate."

"Awesome. Wait, um . . ."

"Yeah?"

". . . Is this a utility-belt situation?"

Parker wheezed a laugh.

"Devon. It is *absolutely* a utility-belt situation."

"YES! See you soon!" And Devon hung up.

"He can *call a car*?"

"I expect an explanation about all this," Mia said.

"It'll be easier when we're together. I promise." He hung up and curved past Bellville Square down the road toward the Lin Shelter, lights still sparkling in the trees.

⟞ 27 ⟝

"I wasn't supposed to tell you, because it's a secret that I'm an agent. But that's what's been going on." I tucked my tail apologetically and bowed my head toward Leila. "I wish we'd found her earlier. I told you as soon as we figured it out."

"That's all right." Leila looked out the window of the car and let the breeze run over her face for a moment. "I'm here now, when it matters. Thank you for letting me save her."

"Of course."

Devon leaned over to Mia and whispered, "What do you think they're saying?"

Each kid was scrunched up in the back seat of a car, summoned from an app, with the dogs in their laps. Mia had some trouble answering under Leila's huge bulk. "I—dunno." She looked, for the first time in a long time, a little bit scared. "I'm still not sure they're really talking."

"They are." Parker gave them both a serious look. "I've seen him type, too."

The man in the front of the car peered at us in the rearview mirror. "What are you kids talking about?"

"Uh, we're—rehearsing." Parker smiled at him. "For a play. The dogs speak on command."

"How neat!"

"Yeah." Parker nudged me to be quiet, and everyone else followed suit. Before long, we were driving up into the parking lot of a little shack in the middle of nowhere. It looked like a whole strip mall had been here at some point, but it was demolished except for our destination—SizzlePop: Chicken on a Stick, marked by an ugly orange-and-red sign. A teeny-tiny building on a wide ocean of flat concrete. The windows were all tinted dark, and it didn't look open.

"You kids sure this is the right place?"

"Absolutely!" Parker pushed open the door, and all the kids and dogs spilled out.

"Thank you!" Devon said. Mia seemed mostly thankful she could breathe again. "Can you wait for us over on Finley Street? Awesome."

We stood in the middle of the parking lot, sun high overhead, staring down the old building. Mia clutched a tennis racket, Parker had a prop sword strapped to his back, and Devon eyed both of them with his hands in his pockets, clearly feeling underdressed. Parker pointed at a gray van parked beside the building. "That's Oscar's car."

Mia clutched her tennis racket. "So he's really here."

Devon took a dog whistle from his utility belt (which turned out to be a fanny pack with the *Sun Squadron* logo on it) and blew a few quick bursts, *ee ee ee*, so at least Jpeg might know they were there. Mia walked forward and tried the door—a sign said they were closed on Sundays.

"It's locked."

*WHAM. WHAM. **CRUNCH.***

"Not anymore," Leila growled.

"Good girl." Mia grinned. The lock of the door was totally snapped, and it swung open on its own, sending a wave of chicken and grease smell out into the parking lot. No sound, though—and at first glance, no sign of Agent Sykes.

I slipped past Mia and took the lead. The chicken smell overwhelmed my nose, and I realized how brilliant the location was—even hunting dogs wouldn't be able to pick out any other smells underneath all this food. The inside of SizzlePop was just as small as it looked on the outside—a few seats by the windows for dining in, a long counter with a menu above it, and a kitchen beyond the counter.

The humans checked the front room while we leaped over the counter and spread through the kitchen. In just a few seconds, we'd seen everything—none of the machinery was on, and no one else was here. I went back to the front to signal the kids that it was safe, and they followed behind.

A tiny chirp from Devon's whistle got our

attention—he'd found something. We all moved toward where he was pointing at a hatch in the floor that said *EMPLOYEES ONLY*. Mia pulled it open—and revealed a staircase heading underground.

Leila took the lead, followed by Mia and her racket. I was behind her, with Devon behind me and Parker, plastic sword held up dramatically, descending last.

At the bottom of the staircase was a storeroom with supplies for SizzlePop's kitchen. A big freezer door was on one side, and on the other side was a hallway that continued down much farther than the building above, with one door on either side before a final door, on the end.

Now, here, I began to smell a familiar smell—*Tonio! And Jpeg!* We were absolutely in the right place. My farsmelled nose confirmed that they were definitely somewhere in the hallway, but that was the best I could do. Leila pushed her nose to the ground and sniffed repeatedly, moving past the bread crumbs and ketchup bottles, past both of the doors on either side of the hallway, and stopped in front of the last door.

This one, she underspoke. *They're in here. But I think the agent is behind there.* She pointed with her nose at the door on the right. No sounds, though—we'd come down there quietly. It could be that he didn't know we'd arrived.

Leila set up in front of the door. It swung outward, so if Agent Sykes tried to escape, he'd have to push her out of the way—not an easy task. It would at least buy a few seconds.

Parker opened the last door. Fluorescent lights lit an uncomfortable room *filled* with wire crates, mostly empty.

Except for two.

"Buster!!" Tonio whispered. He pushed up to the edge of his crate, and I rushed to his side. We pressed foreheads together on either side of the bars. "You found me!"

We *found you*, I posed. I turned and looked back. Tonio followed my nose and gasped.

"You did it. You told them."

I couldn't have done this without them. Including Parker.

Tonio's eyes widened when he noticed Parker, too.

"Sup," Parker grunted. They couldn't quite look each other in the eyes.

Mia crouched in front of Jpeg's cage. "I'm sorry, girl. I didn't know. But we're here now."

Jpeg smirked. *well, this is interesting*, she underspoke. *you've really made a mess, buster.*

I didn't have a choice!

i like it.

Devon knelt next to us and inspected the locks on the cages. They were simple padlocks, like the kind you'd use on a locker. He rummaged around in his utility belt and came out with several long pieces of metal.

"Lockpicks?!" Parker whispered in surprise.

"I got this set for my birthday," Devon offered. "I could do the practice one when I followed along with the video?"

And so, Parker pulled out his phone and found a video he could mute, on double speed, for Devon to watch while he looked at all the tools.

I really need a phone, Tonio underspoke.

"Oh, okay," Devon whispered. "I think I only need these two? This one to turn the key, and this one to wiggle in the—"

Pop. He got Tonio's cage, and then a minute later he had Jpeg's. "Got it!"

"Who's there?" A voice—Oscar's voice—from behind the door. "This is private property! I *will* call the police!" Scrabbling sounds—Leila was pushing against the door as it tried to open. Jpeg bolted out of the cage and ran to Leila—they nuzzled noses as the bigger dog strained against the door.

"I saved you," Leila grumbled.

"Really I sent the message," Jpeg pointed out. "So, technically, I saved myself."

"You're the worst." *Thump.* Oscar was slamming his shoulder into the door now, and it moved a good two inches out before Leila forced it back closed.

"Dogs," Oscar growled from behind the wall. Jpeg yanked Parker's phone out of his hand and started

swiping frantically. The kids all looked to each other for a signal—no one knew what to do next. Jpeg underspoke for Tonio to translate.

"She says we need to get out of here. It's about to get dangerous, and she's calling Mozart to bring in the locals. The humans need to leave, before everyone in Bellville knows they know."

WHAM. Leila lost ground again. She pushed back, but Oscar wedged something into the door. "We will stop you, dogs!" Oscar yelled. "You can't hide forever!"

Stop us? I wondered.

Parker already had a stubborn look on his face. "I'm not leaving."

I started to whine in protest, but Tonio placed a hand on my head. "We have to stall him. Can you do that?"

Parker grinned. "Oh, for sure." He cracked his knuckles. "And I can get some answers, too."

"Who's there?" Oscar barked, voice terrifyingly clear with the door wedged open. "Show yourself!"

Parker raised his voice. "It's me, *Dad.*" Agent Sykes froze. In that instant of calm, Mia reached out and jabbed the handle of her tennis racket into the box he'd wedged into the door, knocking it away. Leila slammed the door closed again. Jpeg, Mia, and Devon crouched low and ran across to the stairs.

Tonio, go on, I underspoke. But he shook his head, eyes on Parker.

"Parker?" Agent Sykes's voice was sharp, angry. "What is this? What stupid trick are you pulling this time?"

"I—" Parker's voice came out choked, suddenly squeaky under Sykes's aggressive tone, even through the door. Tonio's hands twitched—he wanted to Underspeak, but Parker wouldn't understand.

You know what he needs? I asked. Tonio nodded, but he looked unsure. I nudged his hand with a cold nose. *Then help him!*

He stepped right in front of Parker. Silently, he pushed Parker's chin up with one hand and pressed another hand into his back, adjusting his posture. Just like Parker had done for him at auditions. Parker searched Tonio's face. Tonio grabbed his hand and closed it into a fist. *You have all the power here.*

When he spoke again, Parker's voice was full of confidence.

"Oh, Oscar. You fell right into my trap."

And all of a sudden, he was performing again. His expressions, his movements, his words . . . everything sounded believable. Real. I felt a chill as Parker fell into a brand-new role. "And here *I* thought you would have figured it out by now."

A rustle on the other side of the door. "Stop playing games, Parker. You don't know what you're messing with."

Parker laughed. "Really? *Me?* I'd think harder about who's on which side of that door."

Agent Sykes was silent for a long time. "Parker," the agent finally said, "how about you come in here so we can talk?"

Parker looked at us. Tonio shook his head. I bared my teeth *no*. Leila looked exasperated. "Okay," Parker said, to the immediate frustration of literally everyone else. "But you need to move away from the door, or I can't promise your safety against my friends." He pointed at Leila, who rolled her eyes but growled with a deep, loud rumble.

"Friends?" Another moment of silence. "You're working with *the dogs*?"

"Move *back*, Oscar."

"I—I am. I will." I pressed my ear to the door and listened to his footsteps retreat farther into the room. He was far enough away he couldn't block the door again. I looked at Leila, who did *not* look happy about this, but Parker crouched down to her.

"He used my mom," Parker whispered. "And me. I don't know everything about what's going on, but . . . I have to know why. Please." At our dubious poses, he smiled a big, confident grin. "I got this. I promise." Reluctantly, Leila moved away from the door.

Parker stood, grabbed the doorknob, and pulled the door open.

28

Agent Sykes looked like someone who'd recently fled with all their belongings into the basement of a fried chicken restaurant. His hair was disheveled, his clothes clearly thrown on without thought—and he looked tired. He'd been up all night, too, getting out of that house.

Parker, on the other hand, stepped forward with confident poise—his hands clasped behind his back, his eyebrows arched critically as he swept his gaze around the room. "So this is where you've been hiding, Oscar."

The room around him was deeper than I expected, but it was completely packed with stuff. Files, computers—all the notes Parker had described were hastily dumped in a pile on a desk under a series of small screens that appeared to show not only SizzlePop, but other places—a quick glance and I recognized Bellville Middle School, the community theater, and Parker's house.

We'd been filmed all over town, and we hadn't even realized. And not just us—*all* dogs. If they knew how to read Underspeak—if they knew how Underspeak worked at all—they'd have a mountain of evidence about what we were doing . . .

I could smell Parker's fear, but still, he laughed. "How do you think people will react when they find out 'IRS agents' have gotten into kidnapping?"

Sykes tried to lift his shoulders and meet Parker's energy. "Who's going to tell them?"

"Please. We have this place surrounded," Parker lied smoothly, but Sykes obviously believed it. His shoulders sagged again. "Dogs everywhere. Not that we need it. I'm sure Leila here could handle you."

"How did you find me?"

"A good guess."

"And *you* brought them here?" Sykes's eyes grew wide, like he'd just put the pieces together. "You spoke to them?"

Parker didn't answer.

"Parker, you *cannot* trust these creatures! They are not what you think they are!"

"What do I think they are?"

"Pets. Friends. *Cute.* That's all part of the trick. They're using you."

"Like you used my mom?" Parker's real anger poked through his mask. "She used to say *you* were cute. But it was all your job, wasn't it. Your *mission*."

"Your mother—"

"Lived in the right town? Didn't ask too many questions about you?"

"She's a perfectly nice woman. I never meant . . ." He

grunted. "My work is too important. I can't worry about hurt feelings when there are lives on the line."

Tonio was struggling to stay quiet—his right hand was squeezing the bicep of his other arm, nails digging into the skin as his chest moved. He was having a panic attack. I moved to the side to press against his leg.

Tonio stared down at me in fear—he couldn't see what was happening and must be imagining the worst. *Bad timing, anxiety*, I thought. But it always had bad timing. And, in a sense, I guess it was the *best* timing. There was a lot to be scared of in the basement of a bad guy's lair. But as I watched—Tonio changed. He stared at me, then looked over at Parker. His breathing slowed as he clearly focused hard—he was working to keep it down. Gradually, his panic attack was subsiding.

Parker smoothly continued the conversation. "What do you mean, 'lives'?"

"I've been watching these dogs. They act like everything's normal, like they're just animals . . . but they're plotting. Planning." Sykes wiped sweat off his face with his sleeve. "They're going to take over everything if we let them."

"You sound ridiculous."

"I'm *not*. That boy can talk to them. I've been watching him. He was talking to that dog the whole time he was here." He pointed to a monitor. Tonio winced.

"But if *you* can talk to them, Parker . . ." He looked

at Parker with excitement for the first time I'd ever seen. Genuine kindness. "If that boy showed you how to understand them . . . we don't need him. You can do it."

"Do what?"

"Save the world, son."

"From the *dogs*?"

"Yes! Yes. If they've shown you—if you know about their plans, or their government, or the way they speak . . . my bosses are very powerful people, Parker. They could give you whatever you want. Whatever Josephine wants."

Parker's calm mask dropped again. "My mom wanted someone who loved her," he spat.

Sykes's face changed, too—he tried to look gentler. Genuine. "Parker, when they went public . . . you'd be famous. You would be the single most important person on *earth*."

"Oh, wow." Parker's fists clenched and unclenched behind his back. "What an easy choice, seeing as I'm *selfish* and *obnoxious* and you're so *nice* and *honest*."

"I shouldn't have said that. You're right." Sykes shook his head. "I wasn't happy, either, living a fake life. Marrying your mother, becoming your father—I didn't get to choose any of that. *Of course* I wasn't in the best mood all the time. It's hard, keeping secrets." He swallowed. "But if you come with me—if you help me get away from these dogs—I can be the *real* me."

I wanted to bark in his face. This man didn't care about anything but the mission. But then I saw Tonio staring at the ground, and a knot formed in my throat. I realized what he was thinking: Oscar Sykes was doing what he thought was right, too, for his mission. And he'd been using Parker just like us. Sykes was exactly what Dog Court wanted *me* to be. Perfectly obedient to the person holding my leash.

But he wasn't like us. He was *so* committed that he was willing to do whatever it took. Hurt anyone. Lie to anyone. Kidnap dogs and threaten kids. All for a cause he didn't really understand. We weren't taking over the world—we were just being people. We were protecting ourselves from humans like him.

I watched Parker consider what Sykes had said—so many promises. The life his mom wanted, a chance for fame, a dad who cared about him—all things that sounded good to me. And . . . I hated to admit it, but Parker *could* help him.

Parker had only known Tonio and me—*really* known us—for a day, and in that day he'd found out we were lying to him for weeks and worked for an organization he didn't trust or understand. I'd made him the villain in our story. He'd known Oscar as his stepdad for *two years*, and now he knew he represented the government—represented humans, which Parker was one of. He could try and stop us, if he wanted. He could tell the world about our secrets. He could choose to be the hero for humans everywhere.

Parker was quiet for a long time.

And then he chose to be the villain.

"You're right. It is hard keeping secrets. I should know." Parker smiled a small, smug smile. "I can't believe you fell for it."

Sykes looked confused. "Fell for what?"

"Everything." Parker laughed again, a cackle. "You really think you're *that* good? I've known who you were from the beginning. My mom, too." The lies flowed with such confidence they completely erased all hope from Sykes's eyes. "And now, finally, you've done exactly what we wanted you to do: lead us here." He gestured to the room. "All of your information. Everything DNI knows."

Sykes swallowed nervously. "I've been watching you for years. There's no way."

Parker spread his hands, palms up. "I think the results speak for themselves, don't they?" As if on Parker's cue, dog whistles sounded from above—and I could hear footsteps moving in the restaurant.

Mozart was here.

In moments, dogs were pouring into the basement. Samoyeds and collies, malamutes and terriers, hounds and all kinds of mutts growled as they filled in the space around us. Fur sprang from every inch of the hallway, and Sykes was surrounded before he even had a chance to move. The Dogs of the Lin Family Shelter had arrived—not trained officers. Normal dogs. To Sykes, though, it might as well have been a pack of wolves.

"Now then," Parker cheerfully asked, stepping forward and clicking a mouse on the desk, "would you mind writing down your computer password?"

29

"I'm going to clip these three leashes to your collars, okay? And then we're going to go for a nice walk." Cerberus tilted his head back—one real head and two puppet ones. As he reared up on his hind legs, smoke poured from the edge of the River Styx. Heracles held up three golden leashes. "Get you some sun—bet it's been a while since you've seen the sun, huh? Maybe we can catch something from the surface to eat? Yeah, that's right! Just a few quick clicks—"

KRAKOW. Lightning struck in the Underworld. When it dissipated, Hades was there, glaring from the top of a great stone. "*What* is the meaning of this?!"

"Oh, uh—"

"You were taking . . . MY DOG?" Thunder rumbled again. Children just offstage wiggled the cloth of the River Styx to give the illusion of movement.

"The LABR app says I'm supposed to take him for a walk. Totally free, don't worry about it."

"*My* dog?" Hades stepped from stone to stone, cloak billowing behind him. "The guardian of the gates to the Underworld?" He leaned down into Heracles's face, putting his skull face paint right up next to the hero. "The last line of defense keeping the spirit world from overrunning the land of the living?"

Heracles winced. "I see now why that's a problem."

"What miserable creature put you up to this?"

"It's just an app. If you complete twelve tasks you get a prize, and—" Hades slammed the phone out of his hand. "Ah! My phone!"

"There!" Hades shrugged. "Your master is defeated."

Heracles lifted up his phone by the corner, distraught. "Do you have any rice?"

"Nothing grows in the land of the dead."

"You don't understand! If I do all the tasks, I'm supposed to get a special prize!"

"Oh, really?" Hades chuckled and rubbed Cerberus's real head. Cerberus wagged his tail. "And what is this *prize*?"

"I don't know!"

"So you—" His laugh grew bigger, louder. "Mindlessly follow the commands of a being that promises an *undefined reward*."

"I—"

"YOU ARE A FOOL!" Hades yelled. His microphone added a reverb effect to his voice, and *FOOL* was vibrating through the audience long after he'd finished. "I have seen many driven to my realm by such thinking."

"Everyone is using LABR! Hera told me so! But I was doing the best of all of them until *you*—" Heracles jabbed his finger at Hades's chest. All the gods watching from above exchanged glances. Hera improvised, "That boy is *doomed*." And the whole audience laughed.

"*You* threw my phone into the River Styx! That'll wipe *all* of its memory."

"Maybe you should talk to Zeus, then," Hades spat. "See if the god of thunder saved it to his *CLOUD!*"

But Heracles did not back down, and they held each other's gaze for a long time. Gradually, the river settled and the lights brightened. The Underworld had just gotten a little less dark.

"You are brave," Hades admitted. "And you may borrow my dog, if you wish. But heed my warning well: That device is a tool, and you are not the only one using it. Hera, and Hermes—even that king—*they* are using it, too, to control you."

"It's just a game," Heracles argued. But he didn't sound so sure. "And I'm winning!"

Suddenly, Hades pointed his finger and yelled: *"TO LIFE!"* Lightning cracked, and Heracles's phone lit up. He ascended his stones again. "Heed my words or not, mortal. It matters not to me. From where I sit, however? *You* are the one being played."

Darkness fell, and Hades fell into it. At his exit, the audience applauded. (A few people even cheered.) Heracles looked at the smoke, and then at his phone, and then at Cerberus. "Let's go, boy. This place gives me the creeps." He led Cerberus offstage as the curtain fell for the scene to change.

Parker and I did a five (Parker low, me high), and I went around the back to find Tonio, still lying on the mattress that caught him when he fell off the stage.

I'm going to die, Tonio underspoke.

You were amazing, I posed. *But c'mon, we gotta go!* I grabbed the sleeve of Tonio's robe in my teeth and tugged him up. Tonio grabbed his black laurels and placed them back on his head as we ran farther backstage and deeper, down below.

"What do we tell Sweetie?" he whispered. We'd received a letter—just like the letter that got us into this mess—to meet the Judge down below again, between Tonio's last scene and curtain call.

The truth. Just like we talked about. We want to help dogs, but we want to actually help dogs. *Not just help* some *dogs keep our world a secret. She'll listen to us. I know she will.*

Tonio nodded. He opened the last door and moved into that strange storage space—old props, instruments, and set pieces made it hard to move around. The only light was from the show above, but with the final confrontation of Heracles, Megara, and Hippolyta against Hera, Eurystheus, and Hermes, the lights were more than bright enough to see. They flickered and changed rapidly as the gods showed their power.

As we walked around the bow of a shipwreck, I saw the cushion Sweetie had been sitting on before—but this time, Sweetie wasn't there. Sitting on her cushion, with Shadow on one side, was Pronto. *That* Pronto. A Siberian husky with his nose in the air and a folder on the floor in front of him.

Ah, you're here. Perfect. I assume Underspeaking is fine for all present?

Tonio and I exchanged a look. Pronto was bad news. *What's going on?* I posed. *Where's Sweetie?*

The Court agreed with me that her little experiment— Pronto gestured to me and Tonio—*has gotten out of paw. She's been taken to a higher court to answer for her decisions, and I have been put in charge as Judge of this region. And what a time to be a Judge! With the DNI's records, we now know* hundreds *of dogs have failed their duty to keep our secrets.*

My mouth fell open. *What?* They were going to use the records we'd saved . . . to send *more dogs* to court? And . . . what did he mean *out of paw?* Parker had put on a big show of confusion as soon as the dogs had grabbed

Sykes, and Tonio had insisted the other boy didn't *really* know what was going on.

I looked to Shadow, who hadn't moved a fraction of an inch since we'd entered. She stared me down with no expression at all.

Pronto gave a little cough to refocus attention on him. *Shadow, of course, provided testimony as to your conduct and the level of professionalism, or lack thereof, your human partner displayed. And in the end, you put several other dogs at risk to fix your mess. Plus that child you roped into your scheme.*

So this was it, I realized. This was the whole plan, Lasagna: Pronto set up Jpeg, Shadow set me up, Sweetie was taken down. And now Pronto is in charge.

There will be no further missions, pending my review of the current situation. You are to remain silent and secret—to a far *greater extent than I've seen so far. Agent Shadow will be keeping an eye on you, and she has been instructed to remove Buster immediately should she notice anything inappropriate. Understand?*

I looked at Shadow again. She revealed nothing—or, I realized, not quite nothing. Her tail was tilted toward distaste. As I watched her, her lip curled *juuuust* slightly.

She hates me, I realized. *She always has.*

Pronto closed the folder in front of him and rolled his neck side to side. *Shadow told me about her time here in detail! I thought the bit where she pretended to know your parents was especially interesting. She really is the best agent we have.*

I felt like I was falling right into the trap from my dream. But then, right as I thought I might disappear into the darkness, Tonio was there pushing me out of the way. "Who cares?" he whispered. "We're family. And you're not going to make us feel bad for saving our friend."

At that, Pronto shrugged. *I care—and I mean this—not at all about your feelings. However . . .* He looked up at the floor of the stage. Faint music was building—Heracles was dialing all the friends from his many adventures to help him save the day. *I believe our time is up.*

"DNI knows more than you thought, don't they?" Tonio wasn't ready to leave. "Dogs can't stay secret forever, and you know it!"

I suppose we'll see. That's all. Shadow stepped forward, and the threat was clear—get out, or she'll make us. Tonio stared her down, every bit of him channeling the god of death he looked like—until I tugged on his robe again.

Don't worry, Buster, Tonio underspoke in front of his body so the other dogs couldn't see. *This isn't over.*

Tonio's right. Lasagna, this is the end of my report. Whatever happens after this . . . I don't think it's safe for me to write it down. I have a feeling Dog Court is about to get a lot harder to deal with under Pronto's control.

I hope you'll help us. You, and any other dogs ready to change the world.

Beamblade Club

Sykes had taken his files from Parker's house, but he'd left his security system. The tech that kept Shadow out before could do the same now—better, even, now that Jpeg had her paws on it. "How's it looking out there?" she asked.

Leila, in the back of the house, responded into her collar mic. "We're clear."

"Clear here, too," Lasagna confirmed at the front, voice squeaking seriously.

"Perfect. Come back inside." After both of them were across the threshold, Jpeg hit the big red button to turn everything on—alarms at every window and door and cameras outside every wall. Parker set up his closet for Jpeg when she and Leila moved in—and now it was amazing. She had four different computers, two on the floor and two on a higher level that she could manipulate all at once. A dog's dream. Feeds from the cameras lit up all around her—and they each confirmed no one was nearby. "Okay, everybody!" she barked. "We're safe!"

Buster translated for Tonio, who repeated the message. Everyone in the upstairs playroom relaxed: Parker and Devon stopped pretending to play video games, Mia quit brushing Mozart, Tonio put his markers down, and Buster stopped losing practice fights with Leila. The group gathered around the center table and found a seat.

"Welcome," Tonio began with a little smile, "to the first official meeting of Beamblade Club. I'll translate for the dogs."

"FIRST ORDER OF BUSINESS!" Mia immediately interrupted, holding up a printed piece of paper. "The shelter is doing great. We got so many adoptions this year my parents got me a present." She held up a printed-out plane ticket and a brochure. "I'm going to visit Sloan! At ski camp!"

Sorry, LOSERS! Mozart posed from his spot on top of the table. *Collared Rat-o, here we come!!!*

She laughed at Tonio's blushing translation. "Don't think this gets you out of streaming Dogblade. Though I have a feeling adoptions are going to be a *lot* easier to organize these days."

Devon grinned. "My business is that I finished the Lovesword story. I'm currently looking for an agent."

I can recommend somebody, Lasagna underspoke.

"Well, I didn't bring anything for show-and-tell." Parker leaned his chair back, feet against the table to hold it on its back legs. "Does this mean I have to learn how to play y'all's nerd game?"

Buster growled. *It is a serious strategy exercise!!!*

Tonio nodded. "Actually, yes, if we're going to keep up the cover. We're going to see if we can find a teacher sponsor for the club, too, so we can hold meetings at school—another place dogs can't really monitor us. We don't want Court interference until we know what we're doing."

What about humans? Leila asked. *Could the DNI be at your school?*

"It's possible," Tonio agreed. "But Jpeg is working on finding their list of agents."

if i can. Jpeg gave a wiggly, unsure motion with her paw. *it'll be tough.*

Leila patted her on the head with a giant paw. *You can.*

Buster's heart was warm. Tonio was standing up and leading these kids and dogs—people who cared enough to save him and trusted him to teach them. Kids who were creative, and kind, and driven—dogs who were hackers, and wrestlers, and maybe even heroes.

And he was nervous—oh, Tonio's heart was pounding—but he was doing it. He had one eye on the security cameras and one eye on the faces of his friends, but none of that was going to stop him. Buster was, more than anything else, proud.

"I don't have a plan. I don't know what we should do next." Tonio looked at the table: Devon grinned back.

Lasagna adjusted his little tie. Mia popped her bubble gum. Mozart posed to give his best angle. Parker rolled his eyes. Jpeg and Leila pressed their fur together and watched. Buster, as always, was looking at his face.

One by one, Tonio made eye contact with each of them. "But I know we can figure it out together."

◗━◗ Acknowledgments ◗━◗

First, those this book is dedicated to: strange names for a strange land, where adventurers battle vampires, werewolves, and witches. Thank you, Andy Carter, Austin Jenkins, Faith Jones, Lucy Ralston, and Peter Reitz, for telling tabletop stories with me throughout the pandemic. Hopefully by the time this book is out we will have finally defeated Strahd!

They weren't the only ones who kept me going during this time, though, and I want to make sure to thank the young Heroes of Castle Rosethorn, Floretton, Nazrul 2, and Aquatia for inspiring me every week. Y'all are already incredible storytellers yourselves. Critical successes for everyone!

This book would never have been written without Michael Shillingburg, whose constant support and encouragement are all I could ask for. You heard every line of this book before anyone else, patiently listening to my silly voices for hours at a time. Thank you, I love you, thank you!!!

Before it existed, the Buster series was championed by one person more than anyone else: David Levithan, my editor. I trust you completely, and none of my books would be the same (or even exist!) without your faith in me. You are a dear friend and an unparalleled creative ally.

Thank you, Charlie Olsen, and the entire team at InkWell for keeping me functioning and saying yes to all my silliest ideas. There are so many more to come!

The whole team at Scholastic gives such care and love to each of my projects, and I am *so* grateful for the work Maeve Norton and Betsy Luk have done in designing the books and creating their gorgeous covers. Buster is so real, and more importantly, he's *so cute*. (Also, I saw a style guide for the first time this year and . . . thank you, copy editors. How do you do it????)

Speaking of art, *thank you thank you THANK YOU* to Olivia When, whose work on the Buster preorder bonus art breathed so much life into the world and made the whole cast feel real and beautiful and fun. Also to Pei of Pei Reads, whose dog inspired Mozart, and Juliana Chen, who I mention here with Pei because they are all part of our undefeatable Splatoon Squad!

(Also a shout-out to Scout Underhill for their amazing Combuster fan art and even more amazing comics, also featuring game-playing dogs.)

In a book with so much theater, it would be silly not to mention my biggest inspirations and patient supporters from my theater days. Thank you to Mrs. Campbell,

Mrs. Holcombe, Dina Canup, George Contini, Kristin Kundert, Kayla Sklar, Ellie Engquist, Kathy Waldrop, Amber Bradshaw, T. Anthony Marotta, Will Murdock, John Patrick Bray, and everyone else who directed, advised, or performed alongside me. You helped me become the person I am today.

Finally, I've already received so many sweet messages from readers who loved Buster, and I read and love every single one of them. It means a lot that you take time out of your day to let me know my books meant something to you. (And that you read all the way to the end of the acknowledgments!) Thank you. I hope to meet you soon!

━● About the Author ●━

Caleb Zane Huett is a tabletop gamemaster, a former bookseller, and has not been replaced by two cats in a sweater. He's performed in many plays and even written a few. His favorite myth is Theseus and the Minotaur, but he thinks they should have been friends. His other books are *Top Elf* and *Buster*. You can find him at calebzanehuett.com.